Hope

KERRY BOOK SERIES BOOK 4

CAROL CANNON

"May the God of hope
fill you with all
joy and peace
as you trust in him,
so that you may
overflow with hope
by the power of the Holy Spirit."

Romans 15:13 (NI

This book is a work of fiction. Names, characters, places, and incidents either are products of the author's imagination or are used factiously, any resemblance to actual events or locales or persons, living or dead, is entirely coincidental.

Second Edition

Editing Services by Janet Bessey at Dragonfly Editing
http://dragonflyediting.blogspot.com/
Cover by Perry Elisabeth Design | perryelisabethdesign.com
Layout by Penoaks Publishing | penoaks.com

For My Father

I dedicate this book to the first man I ever loved
And who loved me unconditionally, my father.
He had great hopes that I would write a book one day.

This one is for you, Daddy!

Chapter One

Nona walked out onto her back deck sipping her first cup of coffee from her favorite mug, which she'd bought as a souvenir last summer at the Braves game. It was 6:30 AM on a Tuesday morning—her favorite time and favorite day. Since she'd handed over a portion of her workload from her law practice to her partner, Nathan, she'd taken off every Tuesday. She called it "Nonaday." She sat down on the swing that hung on her back deck where she could easily look out at the trees that surrounded her backyard. She'd always enjoyed watching the various behaviors of the wildlife in their natural environment. As she swung back and forth, enjoying the rich taste of her coffee, she noticed a radiantly ruby-red cardinal land on the bird feeder that hung from the limb of an old chestnut oak tree. He was soon joined by two other brightly colored birds. Nona watched as a small gray squirrel crept slowly down the tree to the ground below, hoping to feast on the sunflower seeds the birds dropped from their feeder.

Nona had always found a deep peace sitting in her swing early in the morning, but this morning, the troubles of the past few days were robbing her of that peace. She had been served with divorce papers from her husband, Bill. It'd shaken her to her very core when Deputy Snyder walked into her office last Friday to serve her with the papers. She had known that divorce was the most likely outcome of Bill's affair with his much younger personal trainer, Amy, but she hadn't expected Bill to serve her. As the injured party, it was only right that she should have been the one serving Bill with divorce papers.

After forty-two years of marriage, divorce was not how she'd imagined the end would come. Until a year ago, she had assumed their marriage would end when one of them passed away. She was ashamed to admit it, but sometimes during this past year the thought had crossed her mind that it would be nice if Bill would just go ahead and pass on now. She knew she should feel guilty for thinking such a horrible thought, but she couldn't deny that it would make the whole process so much easier, at least for her. She'd never admitted such a wicked thought out loud to anyone—not even to her best friend in all the world, Layne.

As Nona continued to swing, she thought about the life she and Bill had shared before his affair. She'd been questioning whether she'd ever truly been in love with Bill. Had she loved him when they married, or was it a matter of convenience? Her mother and father had been persistent about her finding someone with whom she could share her life. After all, marriage was the accepted, as well as expected, path for a woman to take during the sixties and seventies—marriage followed by children. Nona had fallen right in with those expectations. Lately, she'd been wondering if it was love that had taken her to the altar to marry Bill or if it was the pressure put upon her to fulfill her projected role.

Nona went back into the kitchen to pour a second cup of coffee. She knew she should be getting ready for her weekly weight-loss group meeting with the *Skinny Dippers*, but couldn't resist heading back outside. As she fell back into the rhythm of the swing, her mind was once again occupied with the events of the past year. It'd been a tough year all the way around.

When Bill left her for a younger woman, it had wrecked her whole world. First of all, the ending of her marriage made her feel like she had failed. Nona had known very few failures in her life. Failing at anything made her feel weak, and she despised any form of weakness. Also, without Bill in her life, she was feeling lonely—a sensation she'd never experienced before.

She shook her head as she recalled that a year ago she'd even contemplated moving away from Kerry to Atlanta, to live near her daughter, Grace. The idea had come to her in one of her more vulnerable moments. She'd convinced herself that if she moved away from Kerry, where she was known, to a place where no one knew her, she might escape the sense of inadequacy that was clinging to her. She had made herself believe that living near Grace would make her feel less lonely and less like a failure.

Nona had recognized the error of her belief through a series of near tragic events. First, her best friend's husband, Mark Weaver, had been in an accident that nearly cost him his life. Second, another of Nona's friends was charged with Driving Under the Influence, which had caused the accident that left Mark in a coma, hovering between life and death. Third, Nona had to trust her instincts and her skills as a lawyer to save her friend from prison, and help to bring the healing of forgiveness to two families that were important to her.

She smiled now as she thought about Mark. He had recovered much faster than the doctors had predicted and was almost back to his normal self. She was thankful she had decided to stay where she was in her beautiful home, and continue practicing law. It would have been one of the biggest mistakes of her life if she had left Kerry. Through the events of the past year, she had come to recognize how precious her friendship with Layne, Dixie, and Betty Jo were to her. They were her family now, and with their love and support she would never feel lonely again.

She looked at her phone to check the time. If she didn't get off the swing and head upstairs to get ready for *Skinny Dippers* right now, she would never make it on time. She carried her half empty mug of cold coffee into the kitchen and set it down in the sink on top of the other dirty dishes from the week. She rushed up the stairs to her bedroom to shower and dress.

Even though Nona had hurried through two yellow caution lights, and only paused slightly at two intersections where she was supposed to come to a full stop while trying to make it to the *Skinny Dippers* meeting on time, she was late. Everyone had already weighed in and the leader was giving another one of her motivating talks when Nona came rushing into the room. When she accidentally let the door slam behind her, every eye turned her way. The leader paused. Nona gave an apologetic smile as she maneuvered through the maze of chairs to take the seat Layne had saved for her. She sat down as quietly as she could.

"Where have you been? I was beginning to get worried," Layne whispered.

Nona sighed, "It's just one of those days when I couldn't make myself leave my back deck."

Layne gave her an understanding smile as she turned to listen to the last of the talk.

When the meeting was over, Nona was allowed to step up on the scales so that her weight for the week could be recorded. She had lost one whole pound. She couldn't imagine how, when the only activity she had done all week was worry. She hurried down the back stairs to join her friends in the *Dream Bean Coffee Shop*.

"Well, if it isn't the late Nona Foxx!" Dixie teased.

"What can I say? I just couldn't pull myself away from being outside on this beautiful day," Nona said, as she sat down with her friends.

Dixie, Layne, and Betty Jo were Nona's best friends. Together, they had joined the *Skinny Dippers* over five years ago, when they had all decided they were going to get in shape. They had let their gym membership expire years ago, but they had stuck with the *Skinny Dippers.* The main attraction for the four was where the meetings were held—above the *Dream Bean Coffee Shop,* which had the best homemade blueberry muffins and chocolate donuts in the South. They would weigh-in and then head downstairs for a sweet treat. If they ever changed the location for the *Skinny Dippers* meetings, the four of them could not say for sure that they would continue with the group.

After they gave their standard order to the waitress, Dixie looked over at Layne. "I saw Mark yesterday at the hardware store. He looks like he's getting around pretty good without that leg brace."

"He is!" Layne said excitedly. It had been almost a year since Mark had nearly died in a wreck that had almost destroyed their lives. He had spent days in a coma and months in rehab after coming out of the coma. He was a walking and talking miracle. "I'll tell you the truth, we are all glad that he is rid of that heavy, bulky thing. He complained about that brace every day. It was just so uncomfortable."

Betty Jo reached across the table to take Layne's hand. "I'm just so sorry he had to go through all of that." It had been Betty Jo's husband, Don, who had hit Mark's truck on that awful day.

Layne put her hand on top of Betty Jo's as she smiled at her. "I know you are, Betty Jo. It's all behind us now and everything is looking up. The doctor told Mark that he can start back to work next Monday, and let me assure y'all, that's not a day too soon for both of us."

They all laughed as the waitress placed their order on the table. They quietly settled into enjoying their food.

Nona hadn't told anyone about Bill serving her with divorce papers. She'd needed to come to terms with it before she could talk to anyone else. She wasn't exactly heartbroken that he wanted out of the marriage, but it wasn't happiness she felt either. She had grown up in an era when society didn't accept divorce. She knew things had changed, but she couldn't get rid of that feeling of being a disappointment to her friends and family.

Nona cleared her throat. All eyes looked at her expectantly.

"Well, y'all, he really did it. Bill served me with divorce papers at my office on Friday," Nona blurted out, as she took a drink of her coffee.

"Oh, Nona," Layne said sympathetically. Although they all knew it was coming sometime, she thought it was callous of him to serve the papers at her office. "I'm so sorry." She took Nona's hand and squeezed it.

"I don't know what to say, Nona," Dixie added. "That's not like the Bill Harris I thought I knew."

"Well, he's not, Dixie," Nona said in a voice dripping with sarcasm. "He's a 'changed man' since falling in love with Amy. He told me so himself."

"Changed, huh?" Betty Jo said. "Sounds more like damaged." They all laughed at her statement.

"I need to do more of that," Nona said, when she regained control of herself. "It seems like a long time since I've laughed out loud."

"I'm so sorry that you're going through such a rough time, Nona," Layne said. "You know we're here for you whenever you need us."

Nona looked at Layne, Dixie, and Betty Jo. "I know you are. I can't even begin to tell y'all how extremely grateful I am for your friendship and support. I thank God each and every day for y'all."

They were all silent for a moment as they each considered how important their friendship had become to each of them.

Nona was ready to get home. She wanted to put on her comfy yoga pants and her well-worn Merritt Atlantic College sweatshirt. She thought she might just spend the rest of her day in front of the TV, watching old movies. As she pulled into her pecan tree-lined driveway, she was thinking of what old movies she really wanted to watch again—happy or sad? She abruptly stopped her car when she noticed that two people were sitting on her porch, in her newly repaired rocking chairs. They seemed to be right at home there. Both were waving at her as if she were their long-lost friend who had come for a visit. As she got closer, she realized who they were, and Nona didn't want to see either one of them. She made note of the luxury car parked to the side of her carport—Bill's new graphite Mercedes Benz E350 Sport Sedan. She wished she could put her car in reverse to leave the scene. Bill had brought that woman, who had wrecked their marriage, to HER home!

She drove up under her carport, trying to give herself some time to compose her thoughts and feelings. The last thing she wanted was for either one of them to think that they had the power to upset her. She plastered a big smile on her face as she opened her car door. Both Bill and Amy left the porch, hurrying down to greet her.

"Hey, Nona," Bill said, in a rather pleasant voice. "We were just in the neighborhood and thought we'd stop by to take a look at the house."

Nona just stared at Bill. Had he dyed his distinguished gray hair blond, and did he suddenly have deep green eyes instead of the dull hazel eyes he had been born with? That's why she had trouble recognizing the people waving to her from the porch. They were strangers to her. After getting over the shock of his changed appearance, her mind registered what he had just said.

"Why?" she asked defiantly.

Bill let out a small, nervous laugh and looked over at Amy. "Well, because Amy has never seen the inside of the house."

"And, why does she need to see the inside of MY house?" Nona spoke each word slowly and precisely.

Bill gave that stupid little laugh again as he took Amy's hand. "Well, Amy would like to see the house where she'll be living."

Nona felt as if she had just been gut punched, as anger spread through her. Looking directly at Bill, she said, "What on God's green Earth are you talking about, William Robert Harris?"

Nona could see that Bill was the one who was getting upset now. His face was turning red. It always turned red when he was angry. "Amy wants to see the house, so she can see what changes need to be made when we move in, Nona."

The full meaning of what Bill had just announced hit Nona between the eyes. "Over my dead body will she EVER move into my house." With that said, Nona turned away from them and started walking to the door.

"This is my house, Bill. You're the one who chose to move out and leave it behind. I'm the one who chose to stay." She turned around to look at both Bill and Amy. "You can both get off my property right now.

Bill stepped forward. "This was my family's house, Nona. You're the one who needs to leave."

Nona stomped over to confront Bill. "This may have been your family's house when we moved in, but I'm the one who made it into our home. It's my home now, Bill, and I'm not leaving." Having said that, she quickly turned away; ready to make a dramatic exit. Instead, in her haste to leave, she lost her footing when she tripped over the uneven pavement of the driveway. She tried, but failed, to regain her balance. She began falling forward and ended up flat on her face.

Nona was mortified as both Bill and Amy came hurrying over to help her up. She stood as quickly as she could, despite the pain and embarrassment she was feeling. The last thing she wanted was help or pity from either of them. She continued up the side steps to her house. Unlocking the door, she turned to look at both of them as they stood there open-mouthed, staring after her, and said in a controlled voice, "This is my house." She slammed the door behind her as she walked into her house.

Nona limped into the kitchen where she pulled out a kitchen chair and collapsed on to it. A small stream of blood was trickling down from her skinned knees. She reached over to the counter to grab the paper towel holder, tore off a section, and pressed it against her bleeding knees, stopping the flow. Both knees were stinging from where she had landed on them. In fact, it seemed like every muscle in her body was crying out in agony. She pulled herself up to check her reflection in the double oven door. Her usually neat hair was anything but neat. She had a small scratch on her nose and a huge scrape across her forehead. She couldn't decide if she should laugh or cry. She sat back down and put her head in her hands.

Nona had never even considered the possibility that Bill would want their house. After telling her about his affair with Amy, he had promptly packed up his things and moved out. To her knowledge, he had never looked back. It seemed to Nona that those actions signaled a lack of interest in this house—the house he had shared with her. It was clear to Nona that Bill had made the decision to start a new life without taking along any baggage from his old life. She knew that this had been his family's home place, but Bill had never seemed to feel any sentimental connection to the property. He'd encouraged Nona to make any changes to the house, without seeming to have any emotional attachment—until now.

Nona wanted to cry, not just from the pain of the humiliating fall, but also from Bill's announcement, which had caught her off-guard. As she sat there, she tried to figure out what had made Bill become interested in living in the house he'd left behind almost a year ago. Suddenly, it all became clear to her. It wasn't Bill's idea to live in this house again. This was all Amy's idea. Amy wanted this house—Nona's house. She was the one pushing Bill to get it back from Nona. That's why they were here today nosing around, invading her territory. They wanted to take this house away from her.

Even though Nona had considered selling this house and moving to Atlanta only a few months ago, it was her decision to make as to keep it or sell it, not Bill's, and certainly not Amy's. Once she'd made up her mind to stay, she realized just how much comfort she found every day when she walked through the door to her home. She would fight with all her strength to keep Amy and Bill from ever living in her home.

Nona slowly trudged up the back stairs to her bedroom to nurse her wounds and change clothes. She treated the scrapes and the bruises that were now appearing on her face as best she could. She began to feel a little better after changing into her comfy clothes. It had been a rough day so far, and it was only two in the afternoon. Nona was beginning to feel sorry for herself. She hated that feeling of self-pity. She needed something to comfort her. She returned to the kitchen to make herself some green tea with lemon. Green tea was one of her comfort foods, if you consider tea a food. She then took her mug of tea into her sitting room, where she stretched out her long legs on her chase lounger. When she felt comfortable, she picked up the book she'd started last night.

After twenty minutes, she realized that she had been reading the same two pages without comprehending any of the words. This wasn't working. Her mind was consumed with angry, ugly thoughts toward Bill. She had to talk this out with those who knew her and loved her. She needed the support of her friends—Layne, Dixie, and Betty Jo.

Nona reached out for her cell phone, which she'd placed on the end table next to her chair. She used the quick dial to call Layne. Nona was about to end the call when Layne answered. "Hey, Nona, what's up?"

Nona could hear a child's voice in the background. "Oh, you must have the kids. I'll call back later. It's nothing that important."

"No, it's okay. I'm not really busy. I just took Madison to the dentist. I'm putting her in her car seat right now to take her back to day care," Layne said. "Sounds like you're upset about something." Madison was Layne's two-year-old granddaughter. Her daughter, Blair, was a busy school teacher, and found it difficult, if not impossible, to get away from school to take her children to their appointments. Layne was more than happy to help out. Her mother had done the same thing for her when she'd been teaching and her children were small.

Nona hadn't been aware that her voice was reflecting her emotions. She thought she had those under control. She blurted out, "Bill and Amy were here when I got home today."

"You're kidding me," Layne paused, giving Nona her full attention.

Nona sighed, "I wish I were kidding. They were waiting for me on my front porch! I need to talk."

Chapter Two

After Layne had dropped Madison off at her daycare, she sat in her car and called Mark to tell him about Bill and Amy's confrontation with Nona. Then she sent a text to both Betty Jo and Dixie, urging them to drop what they were doing and meet her at Nona's house, as soon as possible. She received a call back from both of them letting her know that they would be there as soon as they could.

Within the hour, the Fearsome Foursome—that's what Mark always called them—were sitting on Nona's back deck sipping some of Nona's best white wine. Nona had just finished giving a blow by blow account of Bill and Amy's surprise visit.

"You're telling me that they in fact had the audacity to make themselves at home on your front porch?" Dixie asked incredulously.

"Well, he's out of his mind if he thinks that you're just going to hand over this house to him, after all he's put you through," Layne said.

"It will be over my dead body!" Nona said.

Betty Jo reached out to take Nona's hand. "Watch what you say, Nona. Amy took your husband; she might just think she has a right to take your life!"

Looking over at her friends, Nona said in a serious tone, "Sometimes I feel that she already took my life!"

"Well, she did not take your life, Nona, and we're going to make sure that she doesn't take this house away from you," Dixie promised.

Nona was shaking her head. "I just didn't see this coming. He never seemed to give a rat's behind about this house when he lived here. He has to be doing this for Amy."

"I guarantee that Amy is the one behind this. She's a greedy little thing and wants it all." With a sly smile, Layne added, "I would even bet she won't give Bill any lovin' until he gets her what she wants."

"Layne!" Dixie and Betty Jo said together.

"Poor lil' ol' Bill. That might just mess up his whole world," Nona said in her best Southern accent dripping with sarcasm.

They all laughed, and kept laughing until tears were rolling down their faces.

When they had finally calmed down, Nona said, "Now, that felt good. I needed that."

"We all did," Dixie agreed.

"But, now we need to make plans as to what can be done to stop their little scheme," Betty Jo said bringing them all back to the situation at hand.

"I would think that the first thing you need to do, Nona, is secure a good divorce attorney. You surely know several, don't you?" Layne asked.

"I've been thinking about that since I was served with the divorce papers. I've put some feelers out to some of my colleagues who have gone through a divorce that involved a dispute over property. I let it be known that I only want to hear back from those who won their cases."

Nona leaned back in her chair shaking her head. "What really gets me is that the thought never entered my mind that I might one day be looking for a divorce lawyer. I never considered that I would ever be a divorced woman." She paused for a moment, reflecting, before continuing. "When I married Bill, I took the vows I made before my family, friends, God, and to Bill, seriously. 'Until death do us part.' I believed that's how we would part. I keep asking myself what I did or didn't do that sent him into Amy's arms." Tears began to fill her eyes.

Layne, Dixie, and Betty Jo just stared at Nona. It was a rare thing to see Nona cry, and it took all three of them a moment to react. Layne got up and walked over to hug Nona as she cried softly into her shoulder. Layne patted her on the back as she repeated over and over, "I'm so sorry."

Dixie and Betty Jo were filled with compassion for Nona as they quietly watched. It was several minutes before Nona pulled away from Layne. She wiped her tears away, and in as strong a voice as she could manage, said in typical Nona fashion, "Well, that's enough of that. Who's ready for another glass of wine!"

They all held up their glasses as Nona refilled them.

"Hey, you know what?" Dixie asked, slapping her knee as she sat up, putting her glass down on the table next to her. "I just might know of the perfect attorney to handle your divorce." Looking directly at her friends, she continued, "Y'all surely know who Miss Dessie Mae Doolittle is, right? She's that eccentric elderly lady who drives her vintage Cadillac Touring Sedan down the middle of the highway like it had been built just for her convenience."

"Holy Cow, I sure do. I have to pull over to get out of her way at least twice a week. That lady is crazy!" Betty Jo exclaimed.

Dixie could see that she had everyone's attention as she resumed her story. "Yep, crazy like a fox. Alex has done a ton of work for her in that antebellum house of hers way out on the other side of Kerry County, where she lives all by herself. She's always wanting to remodel some room, or rip out her kitchen cabinets to have new custom cabinets installed, even though she rarely walks into the kitchen to do anything but get a glass of water—a maid comes in every day to cook and clean for her. But, as a contractor always looking for work, Alex is always more than willing to do whatever she wants. He likes working for her because she always pays well and on time. Anyway, one day she got to talking to him about how she happened to get that big ol' house and a whole pile of money to go along with it."

"Well, don't keep us in suspense, Dixie!" Layne asked, "How?"

"She got it all in a divorce settlement from her 'lying, cheating, no good, blankety-blank' of a husband!"

"Really?" Nona said, "I had no idea she'd ever been married,"

"She said she married a much older man, days after she graduated from high school, who had been an acquaintance of her fathers. It sounded to Alex like it might have even been an arranged marriage. When they got married, they moved into that big house that was Mr. Doolittle's family's home place. After three weeks, he left her all alone there to go on what he called a business trip. She'd begged him to let her go along, but he said she'd be in the way. He didn't come back for six months, and when he did, he brought a woman with him he said he'd hired to serve as her live-in maid. She was a live-in something all right, but my Mama wouldn't have called her a maid. Anyway, Miss Dessie Mae was too young to know what to do about it, so she just let him carry on with that woman for years. Well, to make a long story short..."

"Too late!" Nona, Layne and Betty Jo said in chorus.

Dixie, ignoring their comment, continued, "After living there for years and years in that situation, almost as a recluse, Mr. Deforest Darnell Doolittle sued her for divorce and told her, in no uncertain terms, to get out. He told her that the house was his and she was no longer welcome."

Dixie stopped for a moment as she looked around to make sure everyone was still listening to her story. "Miss Dessie Mae was beside herself about what to do. The only thing she could think to do was to contact her sister, Bessie, for help. When Bessie heard the whole story, she drove Miss Dessie over to Bradford and hired an attorney who ended up getting her almost everything old Mr. Doolittle owned, including his home place." Dixie sat back satisfied with her story.

"Well, don't keep us in suspense. Who was the attorney?" Nona asked.

"Oh, right, I almost forgot where I was going with that story," Dixie laughed to herself. "The attorney she hired was someone named

Montgomery." Turning to Nona, she asked, "Have you ever heard of an attorney named Montgomery, Nona?"

Nona looked at Dixie with disbelief. "You're kidding me, Dixie, right? You can't be talking about Michael Tyler Montgomery—the most arrogant, obnoxious, heartless human being this side of the Mason Dixon Line?"

Dixie considered this for a minute, then said. "I'm pretty sure that was his name, but I'm not sure about the rest of the stuff you said."

"You don't expect me to even consider hiring a man like Michael Montgomery to represent my interests, do you?" Nona asked incredulously.

Looking at Nona with all sincerity, Dixie said, "Well, Nona, he just might be the one person you need to fight for what's rightfully yours."

"She may be right, Nona," Betty Jo agreed. "You need someone who's determined, and maybe even heartless, to be on your side."

Nona looked at Dixie and Betty Jo as if they were crazy people. She looked over at Layne hoping she would make Dixie and Betty Jo understand why it was out of the question to hire someone like Michael Montgomery.

"Don't look at me," Layne said looking back at Nona. "I don't know the man, but he sounds like someone I would want in my corner if I were getting ready for a fight."

"I can assure you that he's not anyone I would hire to fight for me," Nona said.

"Good to know! Now, how about some more wine?" Layne said, as she held out her glass.

That ended the discussion about Michael Montgomery. The four of them turned their attention back to what could be done to stop Bill and Amy from taking Nona's house. They all stayed on Nona's back deck talking and laughing into the late evening.

As Layne drove away from Nona's, she was glad that she'd called Dixie and Betty Jo to join her at Nona's. Nona needed their support tonight. She also needed their laughter. When Layne thought about it, she had needed the laughter as well. It seemed like ages since the four of them had taken the time to be together, to enjoy one another's company. During the nightmare when Mark was in a coma, it had been Layne's friends who had stood beside her, giving her comfort and support through those darkest hours.

The past few months had been busy ones for all of them for various reasons. Layne's life had revolved around Mark's recovery for most of the past year. She knew that Betty Jo's time was consumed with making sure that Don was eating the right foods and getting the exercise he needed, since his Type 1 diabetes diagnosis. Layne wasn't quite sure what was going on with Dixie, but there was something that'd been occupying most of her time. Maybe she'd been busy baby sitting with Hailey's children, or tending to her needy son, Jason. As always, Nona's time had been filled with her law practice, which Layne didn't think she would ever give up. Whatever the reasons, the four of them had not been together for a long time. Layne hated that it had been Nona's troubles that brought them together tonight, but she had to admit she had enjoyed being with her friends once again.

When Layne turned into her driveway, her car lights fell upon a car pulled up next to Mark's truck. She didn't recognize it and couldn't imagine who would be at their house at this late hour. She pulled her car on into the garage, got out, and walked into the kitchen. As she set her keys and purse on the kitchen island, she heard a familiar voice coming from the other room. It was Bill's voice. She froze. What in the world was Bill doing at her house? She prayed that the next voice she heard would not be Amy's. She held her breath. Her whole body tensed as she eavesdropped on the conversation coming from the other room.

"That's quite a story, Bill," Mark said. "You're really going to fight Nona for that house, even though you admit that you'd rather build a brand new one more to your liking?"

Bill paused before answering. "It's what Amy wants, Mark. How can I not fight for what Amy wants?"

"Just tell her 'no', Bill."

"I can't do it, Mark. I've tried everything to get her to change her mind. I even had an architect draw up plans for a new house that would be bigger and much better than that old home place, but she won't budge. She wants that house and nothing else will do."

"I think you're making one big mistake here, Bill. Nona's going to fight you tooth and nail to keep that house. It's going to get really ugly."

"No doubt, it's going to be ugly. You should have seen Nona today when we stopped by. I think if she'd had a gun, we'd both be dead," Bill said with a chuckle.

"I don't think I'd be laughing about that, Bill. Nona just might kill you if you try to take her house," Mark said. "You of all people know how much she loves that place, and how much of her body and soul she has poured into it."

Layne couldn't be silent any longer. She burst into the family room knocking over the table lamp. Mark jumped up catching it right before it would have crashed on the floor.

"How could you, Bill?" Layne spit out. "After all you've done to her, how could you even think about taking her home away?"

Mark set the lamp back on the table and grabbed Layne's hand as she charged toward Bill. "Calm down, Layne."

Mark's words set Layne off into a rage. "'Calm down', you say!" she shouted back at Mark. "Why would I calm down when someone I thought I knew is going to hurt someone I love?"

Staring directly into Mark's eyes with a look that made him release her hand, Layne said, "What I want to know is why is it that you're calm, Mark?"

Layne stomped over to where Bill was sitting. "You should be ashamed of yourself, William Robert Harris. What kind of a low-life have you become?"

Not waiting for a response, Layne turned away and walked out of the room. Stunned, Bill watched Layne as she walked out of the room. He looked over at Mark.

Mark shrugged his shoulders. "I think that it's pretty obvious that Layne's upset with you, Bill. I think it's time for you to go home," Mark said as he walked toward the front door.

Bill followed without saying a word.

Dixie was starving when she got home from Nona's house. She had skipped lunch, thinking that she would eat a big supper. The last thing she'd eaten was the blueberry muffin after the *Skinny Dippers* meeting. It was too late now to prepare the big meal she'd planned. She wondered if Alex, her husband, had eaten, or if he was waiting for her. She could hear the TV blaring from the family room and knew exactly where Alex was, and probably had been since he'd come home from work. His hearing was not what it used to be, but he would not admit that to anyone, especially himself. It got on Dixie's last nerve when she heard the roar of the TV.

"Turn that down, Alex," Dixie said, as she walked into the family room.

It was obvious that he'd been snoozing in his recliner, as usual. "What?" he mumbled straining to sit up.

"The TV is too loud."

"Sorry, Honey, I must have drifted off waiting for you to come home, and didn't notice," Alex said as he used the remote to lower the volume.

"Have you eaten?"

"No, I wanted to wait for you," he said as he got out of his chair.

Alex walked over to Dixie, kissed her, and wrapped her in his arms. It felt so good to Dixie, so comforting, so loving. Before Mark's accident, their marriage had gone through a rough time, when they were slowly drifting apart, barely connecting with one another. It was as if they had forgotten how to be in love. When Mark was in the coma, it made them both realize how much they did love one another and how fragile life can be. Since then, they'd each made a conscious effort to show their affection for one another. Even though Mark's accident was tragic, it had turned out to be a true blessing from God for their marriage.

"You shouldn't have waited for me, honey," Dixie said returning Alex's embrace. "I think it's too late to cook anything now. Let's see what we have in the kitchen that we could eat, before I starve to death."

They both laughed at this. With their robust figures, it would take a very long time for either one of them to "starve to death." They quickly pulled out the makings for sandwiches and a salad from the refrigerator. As Dixie made the sandwiches, Alex made the salad. They carried both to the breakfast nook in the corner of the kitchen.

"Well, what was going on with Nona?" Alex asked.

Over their meal, Dixie told Alex about Nona's unpleasant visit from Bill and Amy. "I told them that story about Miss Dessie Mae and the lawyer she hired to fight for her."

It took Alex a minute to recall that story. "I haven't thought about that story in years. What made you think of it?"

"I thought Nona might want to hire that same lawyer who helped Miss Dessie Mae, but Nona doesn't seem to care for him at all."

"I wouldn't have thought that Nona would know him."

"I'm not sure if she knows him personally, but she seems to know of him. From the way she talked about him, I don't think he's the guy she'd hire."

"Well, it's up to her who she hires," Alex said.

Alex put down his sandwich and turned to face Dixie. In a serious voice, he said, "Dixie, there's something that we need to talk about."

Dixie fought to swallow the bite that she had just taken, but her throat had gone completely dry. She could tell by Alex's tone that what he had to say wasn't going to be pleasant to hear. She prayed that nothing bad had happened to their children. They had two children—Hailey, a successful pediatrician who was happily married with three precious daughters, and Jason, their thirty-year-old son, who had never settled down to a career or family. With concern, she turned her full attention on Alex.

"Hailey came by to talk to me about Jason this afternoon," Alex began. "It looks like Jason's lost another job. He's moved out of his apartment and has been staying at Hailey's place ever since."

Dixie let out a long sigh. In her opinion, Jason never seemed to get a break. "Oh, poor Jason."

Alex could think of other words for Jason, but held his tongue. Jason was the apple of his mother's eye and nothing could dissuade her from the belief that nothing was his fault.

Dixie thought for a moment, then said, "Hailey doesn't have enough room for him to be staying with her. We need to call him to let him know that he can just move back into his room here."

Alex shook his head. "I'm not sure that's the best thing for Jason or for us. You do remember the last time he moved back in with us, right?"

How can I forget, she thought? He'd stayed in bed most of the day and then stayed up most of the night. He'd driven both of them nearly insane with his inconsiderate behavior.

Dixie looked at Alex pleading, "What can we do, Alex? We can't just leave him there with Hailey and the girls."

Alex considered the options for a long time before answering Dixie. Knowing he was probably going to regret his decision, he said, "I guess that's the only thing that makes sense, Dixie. Give him the call."

Betty Jo found it hard to be away from Don for very long these days. Since the accident last year, and finding out that he had Type 1 diabetes, she'd been watching him like a hawk. She knew if she didn't, he might eat some sugary treat or fill up on potato chips. A proper diet and exercise were crucial in maintaining the right balance with this disease. She wanted to avoid another episode like the one that had led to that near fatal accident. The thought of how different their lives might be right now if Mark had died, or if Layne and Mark had not forgiven them, sent shivers down her back. She called his name as she walked in the door. When there was no answer, she didn't have to think long to figure out where he was. She walked out the side door heading to his garage.

Don was in his garage working on his dark blue 1959 Chevy Apache step-side pick-up truck, again. It had been banged up in the wreck and had spent the past few months under the care of Scott's Body Shop. It was looking better than ever. The same could not be said about Mark's Silverado. With all the plastic parts that were on the newer trucks, it had been totaled out by the insurance company. Don's older truck had come out in much better shape. He was determined to restore it to its original beauty. Betty Jo would have been happy if they'd sold it for scrap metal. After all they'd been through with the accident and all, she loathed that truck.

"Don?" Betty Jo called out, as she walked in the door of the garage.

"Down here," Don called back, from under the jacked-up truck.

Betty Jo shook her head and sighed. "What are you doing under that truck, Don? You know how dangerous that is," she said, exasperated by his lack of concern for his safety.

Don ignored her remark and continued working. He had just about reached the limit of his patience with Betty Jo. She was driving him crazy with her obsessive fretting over everything he did or didn't do. He understood that she was doing it out of love, but enough was enough—

it'd almost reached too much. He softly hummed, trying to block out the sound of her sighing.

When Betty Jo heard his humming, she knew it to be a sign that he was trying to block her out. In a more pleasant voice, she asked, "Have you eaten?"

Don stuck his head out from under the truck and answered with sarcasm in his voice. "Yes, I ate at six o'clock, just like I'm supposed to." Then he went back under his truck.

Betty Jo really wanted to ask him if he'd taken his blood sugar level and if he'd given himself a shot of insulin, but she held herself in check. Betty Jo decided that the wise thing for her to do was to leave, and not ask any more questions.

"That's good. I just came in to let you know that I'm back from Nona's." She said as she walked out of the garage, softly closing the door behind her.

Thank God for my friends. Nona thought as she finished putting the last of the wine glasses in the dishwasher and getting everything from the back deck put away after Layne, Dixie, and Betty Jo left. She knew what a blessing they were to her life. Not everyone was as lucky as she was to have such true friends. She'd needed them, and they'd come.

As she started the dishwasher and was turning off the kitchen light, her house phone rang. She checked the caller ID before answering. It was Grace, her one and only child. Grace lived in Atlanta with her husband Adrian. They didn't have any children yet, but Nona hoped they would one day.

"Hey, Grace."

"Hi, Mom, how are you?"

"I'm doing okay. It's good to hear your voice. It's been way too long since we talked."

"I'm sorry about that. I've gotten your texts and voice messages, but I've just been so overloaded with work that I haven't found the time to get back to you. I decided tonight that I was going to make the time." Grace was Georgia's Senators Communications Director, and even though they weren't in session, her job was a demanding one.

"Oh, darling, I'm so glad you did. How's Adrian?"

"He's great. His job took him to DC for most of this month. I was so bummed out that I couldn't find the time to go with him, but he's back home now." Adrian was a gun-control lobbyist and his job often took him to Washington, DC.

"That's good. What else is going on?"

"Nothing much." Nona could hear the hesitation in Grace's voice. She knew Grace well enough to know that she hadn't called just to chat or to see how Nona was doing. She had something else on her mind. Nona waited.

"Hey, Mom, I talked to Dad earlier today."

"Did you?"

"I did, and he was telling me how he and Amy stopped by to take a look at the house."

Now, Nona was on the defensive. Grace had always been close to her father and seemed to have supported his decision to move out to be with Amy. She had never offered Nona any support for the heartache she was going through. She had heard that Grace even had Bill and Amy up to her house for a weekend. Nona had not received an invitation to visit in over a year. When Nona thought about it, she realized that Grace had not been down to Kerry to visit her in over six months. They had met a few times for lunch when Nona had business in Atlanta, or Grace had to go to Savannah for a meeting, but they hadn't been together in Kerry for a long time.

"Yes, they did," Nona said warily. She braced herself for what she feared was coming next.

"Mom, why do you want to keep Dad out of his own house," Grace blurted out. "That house means so much to Dad."

Nona was stunned beyond belief. She'd known deep down that Grace would be on her father's side in this battle, but the reality of it hit hard. It felt like a betrayal to Nona. "It means a great deal to me, too, Grace," Nona stammered. "Your father left this house when he left me. This is my home, Grace, and I'm going to fight for my home."

"I knew you'd be the selfish one, Mom. You think of yourself first, and you don't care about the feelings of others. That house was part of Dad's family. What makes you think you deserve to keep it?" Grace said angrily.

It took Nona a minute to process the words that were spoken with such bitterness by the daughter she loved. It was clear now that Grace wasn't going to go easy on her mother. She finally said, "This is my home, Grace. If I hadn't stepped in and poured my money into the renovations, this house would have fallen in around your father's ears. He has never liked this house. I'm the one who saved this house. It's mine."

Nona ended the call. She'd had more conflict than she could handle for one day. Why was it that the most selfish people are the first to put that label on others? She realized that she did have to take some responsibility for Grace's selfishness. She'd made her only child believe that she was extra special and the world was hers for the taking. Grace had been an exceptionally gifted child, both academically and musically. She played the piano beautifully and won competitions both locally and nationally. Her talents earned her a full scholarship to Curtis Institute of Music, where she graduated with honors. Her ambition was to travel the world over as a concert pianist, but her goals faded when she met Adrian Bannerman. He swept her off her feet. After they married, they settled down to life in Atlanta. Grace's love of music seemed to wither. Nona wondered if Grace ever sat down to play the exquisite Steinway Grand Piano Adrian had bought her as a wedding gift.

Dear Lord, please help me to forgive my daughter for her words, which hurt me tonight. I pray that you will repair our relationship. Bless Grace with a loving heart.

After saying her short prayer, Nona turned off the kitchen light and began making her way up the stairs. With each step, she realized just how exhausted she was. It had been an emotional day all the way around. All she wanted to do was crawl into bed and pull the covers up over her head. She wished she could just sleep for days and days. As she climbed into bed after brushing her teeth and washing her face, she closed her eyes, hoping that sleep would envelop her and take her away. Instead, her brain kicked into high gear. It was the curse of her busy brain that robbed her each night of the restful escape she so desperately wanted. She'd never been one of those people who fell asleep as soon as their head hit the pillow, but lately she was finding it even harder to shut off the thoughts that zoomed around in her head. Tonight, her mind was churning with memories of Bill and the life they'd shared BA—Before Amy.

Nona Jane Foxx had grown up in Kerry, but her parents had sent her to the private school in Dupree, Georgia, about twenty miles away. As a young child, Nona had known that she wanted to be a lawyer like her father, James Riley Foxx III. Her father had tried to discourage Nona from becoming a lawyer from the beginning, when she'd first made her intentions known. He had thought a woman was much "too delicate" to be a lawyer. He had considered law as a career meant only for men, strong men.

Mr. James, as everyone called him, had one son, James Riley Foxx IV. He had been called Riley from the beginning. Mr. James had such high hopes for his only son to join in his law firm as he had done, and as his father before him had done, but Riley was a huge disappointment to his father. Instead, he'd pursued a career in technology. He'd left for San Jose, California, right after college. Riley only returned to Kerry once a year, much to his mother's dismay and his father's joy. Riley was four years older than Nona. Nona adored Riley. She had tried to fill the empty place that Riley had left in her parent's heart, by being the perfect child. It'd never worked, but she'd kept trying.

Because Nona had gone to a private school, she and Layne had never met until fate brought them together as roommates at Merritt Atlantic College. They hit it off from the beginning and soon had become best friends. Nona had been determined from the very start to be in the top one percent in her college classes. She had rarely been seen outside of her classes, the library, or her dorm room.

Nona had been one of those girls everyone noticed right away. It could have been her naturally blond hair that hung in waves all the way down her back to her waist, or it could have been her long, shapely legs, which always seemed to be tan. Maybe it had been her forest green eyes, which seemed to reflect all the light around her. Most likely it had been Nona's figure that caught everyone's attention. It had been simply perfection. None of that mattered to Nona. She'd been so focused on her studies that she never seemed to notice how her presence affected those around her. When she'd first arrived on campus, she had been asked out almost every night. Her answer had always been a polite, but firm "No." Because she'd never accepted those countless invitations, she'd become known as "No No Nona." Her two best friends at Merritt had been her roommate, Layne and Layne's boyfriend, Mark. If, on the rare occasion she had done anything other than study, she'd done it with them.

Nona had graduated Suma Cum Laude from Merritt in only three years, by going summers and carrying as many hours as was allowed. From Merritt, she had gone on to Emory Law School in Atlanta, Georgia, where she'd received her Juris Doctor Degree. Nona had passed the BAR with ease. Her goal had been to practice law with her father, but he hadn't been ready to have a woman in his practice. So,

Nona had taken a position in the Atlanta Federal Court as a law clerk for Judge Wilbur Edward Dumont. It was during that time that Layne and Mark introduced her to Mark's best friend, William Robert Harris. He told her on their first date that his friends called him "Bill." She'd teased him by calling him "Billy Bob" since his name was William Robert. Nona was the only person in the world who had ever gotten away with calling him "Billy Bob."

Bill had been over six feet four inches tall, with an athlete's body. He'd played football in high school and Lacrosse in college. His dark brown hair had been a little long over his ears. Nona had always wanted to push it behind his ears, but resisted. He'd had perfect, straight teeth, the product of a good dentist and a fine set of braces. His nose had been just a smidgen out of proportion to the rest of his face. He had been handsome in a rugged sort of way, just the way Nona had liked a man to look. As a couple, they had been strikingly attractive.

Bill had seemed to know from their first date that he wanted to marry Nona. However, it'd taken him a while to convince Nona that they were right for one another. Nona had been physically attracted to him, but had felt she might be getting that attraction confused with love. It hadn't been long after their first date that Bill asked Nona to marry him. She had decided that Bill was about the closest she'd come to loving someone, so she'd answered "yes." They had been married that spring, and had moved to Kerry the summer after Nona finished clerking.

After moving to Kerry, they'd set out to build a good life. After much persuasion, Nona had been given a position in her father's firm. Bill had been hired by Citizens Fidelity Bank and Trust Company of Kerry as a loan officer. They'd settled into Bill's family home, which he'd inherited from his mother who had passed away shortly before they had moved to Kerry. Nona had loved the house with its long pecan tree-lined driveway from the very beginning, but it had needed a great deal of work; work that Bill hadn't been willing to pay for out of his meager salary. Nona had taken it upon herself to be the interior decorator and had hired Alex, Dixie's husband, to do the needed repairs and renovations. It had become one of the nicest houses in Kerry, and had always been on the Kerry Garden Club Tour of Homes.

When they had their daughter, Grace Ellen Foxx-Harris, Nona had thought their lives had reached perfection. Both Nona and Bill had poured themselves into their professions. After several years, Bill had become the president of Citizens Fidelity Bank and Trust Company of Kerry. Nona had worked hard to be the first female partner in her father's firm, Foxx, Foxx, and Foxx. The fact that the firm had originally been started by her great grandfather, handed down to his son, and eventually taken over by her father, made it even harder for Nona to make partner. It had definitely been a "Good Ol' Boy" firm. Through her hard work and determination she'd finally made partner. Those years had been good ones for both of them.

Things had changed after Grace went off to college. It had been as if they no longer knew what to talk about now that Grace was gone. They had built so much of their lives around the activities of their daughter. They'd muddled through their long evenings together until Bill announced that he was going to retire at the end of May. Once Bill had retired, he'd become a different man.

Bill had taken out a gym membership at Kerry Fitness and had begun power lifting. At first Nona had been glad that he was getting out of the house. It had been her fear that when he retired he might sit around the house all day. The exact opposite had happened. Bill went to the gym several times, both day and night. It had become an obsession with him. Some evenings Nona had come home after a long day in court, hoping that Bill might grill something for their supper, and found a note telling her that he would not be home for supper and would grab a bite at *The Grill*.

"Really, Billy Bob, really!" Nona would mutter to herself. Then she would fix some soup and sit in front of her computer, eating and working on some case. This was not the life she had thought they would have when he retired. She'd imagined it all much differently.

Then the blow, which literally knocked her off balance, had come. It had been a Wednesday night. Nona had been getting ready to go to choir practice at the Methodist Church. They were practicing for their Christmas Cantata and she had a solo. Bill had walked into their bedroom fifteen minutes before she had to leave. She remembered that he had been antsy and hadn't been able to stand still. Nona had been in the bedroom, sitting on the bench at the end of the bed, putting on her shoes, getting ready to walk out. Bill had sat down next to her. He'd gently taken her hand in his and turned her head toward him. When she had looked into his dark brown eyes, she'd known what he was going to say next would rip her world apart.

"Nona, I've fallen in love with someone else," Bill had said in a soft voice.

Nona hadn't made it to choir practice that night.

Nona shook her head, hoping to clear away the memory of that night. It still hurt to remember when the world she knew was changed forever. She gave up on sleep. She got out of bed, put on her robe, and headed down the hall to her office. If she couldn't sleep, at least she could get some work done.

Chapter Three

It was 3:30 AM before Nona shut down her laptop and headed to bed. She got a few hours of sleep before her alarm sounded at 6:00 AM. Wednesdays were always rough for Nona, but without the rest she needed, it was going to be even rougher on her. She got ready for the day and headed to work.

Lily, her assistant, met her at the door with a smile and a strong cup of coffee.

"You are a godsend, Lily," Nona said as she took the coffee.

"Mom told me that you might need some TLC today, after having a tough day yesterday." Lily's mother was Betty Jo, one of Nona's good friends who had come to her aide yesterday.

"Your mom was right about that!"

"At least you're not in court today. That's one good thing," Lily said with a smile.

"That's true. I worked on the Stubbin's brief last night. I uploaded it to your work folder. I need a hard copy of it ASAP." Turning toward her desk, she added. "Oh, one more thing, Lily, I need the number of an attorney in Bradford by the name of Michael Montgomery."

"I'll get right on it," Lily said as she turned to leave Nona's office. "I think I just heard Nathan come in. What time do you want to meet for the day's briefing?"

"Let's set the staff meeting for 9:00 this morning. Thanks."

Lily closed Nona's door as she left her office. Nona picked up her coffee and sat down at her desk. It was strong and hot, just the way she liked it. She began looking through some files. Her mind drifted back to last night. Sometime during those sleepless hours, the story Dixie told and the conversation that followed had entered her mind. The thought occurred to her that maybe her friends were right. She did need someone who was ruthless to be on her side. The least she could do was talk to him to get a feel for whether or not she could tolerate his unpleasant personality.

She needed to put the incident with Bill and Amy, as well as the thoughts of divorce out of her mind and get on with the day's business. There was a light tap at the door.

"Come in," Nona said expecting it to be Lily.

Instead, Nathan stuck his head inside the door. "Hey, Nona, do you have a minute?"

"Sure, come on in, Nathan." Nathan was Nona's law partner and the oldest son of Layne and Mark. "What can I help you with?"

"Well, it's a kinda weird thing. I got to my office this morning to find Mr. James sitting at my desk."

"What?" Nona said as she stood up from her desk. "Why would Dad be at your desk?" Nona's father had retired over ten years ago from the law firm. He was always welcome to stop by any time he wanted, but for him to be at Nathan's desk was more than unusual.

"Well, Nona, it seems that he's working," Nathan said hesitantly.

"Working? What's he working on?" Nona asked, as she walked out of her office heading for Nathan's.

Nathan followed close behind. "When I asked him what he was doing, he just said he was 'working'."

Nona opened the door to Nathan's office. Sure enough, there sat Mr. James at Nathan's desk bent over a yellow legal pad busily writing.

"Good morning, Dad," Nona said, as she went around the desk to give him a kiss on the cheek.

"Good morning, to you," Mr. James said in his deep Southern voice, as he looked up from the tablet.

"What are you doing here this morning, Dad?"

Looking up at Nona, he answered in the irritated voice that Nona knew all too well. "I came in early to work on the Conrad Case, but I keep getting interrupted."

It took Nona a minute to process what case her father was referring to. She looked over at Nathan to see if he knew anything about a Conrad Case. He gave her a blank look and shrugged his shoulders. Then it hit Nona what case her father was referencing. The Conrad Case had been one of the big money cases her father had won back in the '90s involving the death of two employees at the Conrad Processing Plant, due to unsafe working conditions.

Nona almost laughed out loud thinking her father must be playing a joke on them—which she realized would be totally out of character for him—but then she noticed the look on his determined face. He was serious. She wasn't quite sure what to do or say to her father.

What has made him think he needs to work on the Conrad Case?

He had been sick with a fever a few weeks ago. Maybe his fever had come back. She placed her hand on his forehead. It was warm to the touch, but not feverish.

"Dad, you won the Conrad Case years ago," Nona said softly. "Don't you remember?"

Mr. James looked up at her, and for a brief moment Nona saw the confusion in his eyes. Then his eyes cleared, and she could see he was back to the father she had always known.

"Of course, I remember. That was one of the cases that I was thinking that a young lawyer like Nathan might want to study. I came by to impart some of my expertise of the law to Nathan," Mr. James said with authority, as he looked at Nathan. "Come on over here, son, and let me show you what I've written down for you."

Nathan gave Nona a puzzled look before going to Mr. James. They were all aware that something was "off" about the whole situation, but not sure exactly what it was.

Nathan leaned over his desk to see what Mr. James had written down for him. It seemed that he had indeed been making notes about the case for Nathan. Nona walked out of the room, unsure what had just taken place, leaving the two of them in Nathan's office discussing the Conrad Case—a case that had been settled for decades.

Nona's father left the office shortly before the 9:00 AM staff meeting. Neither Nathan nor Nona mentioned the scene they had both witnessed earlier with Mr. James. The staff meeting was shorter than usual, but long enough to bring everyone up-to-date on their ongoing cases. When the meeting ended, Nona asked Lily if she had the files she'd asked her to print.

As an after-thought, Nona asked, "Have you gotten that phone number I asked you for?"

Lily handed Nona the printed files as well as Michael Montgomery's phone number. Nona knew what to do with the files, but still wasn't quite sure what she was going to do with the phone number. After the phone call last night and her conversation with Grace, she'd decided she needed to at least contact Michael Montgomery before making her final decision as to whom she wanted to hire. The truth of the matter was that Nona hadn't really taken the time to consider any lawyer. It was extremely unusual for her to put off something as important as this, but deep down she had hoped it wouldn't get to the point where she would need a lawyer. She'd hoped that she and Bill could come to an agreeable settlement without involving lawyers. It was clear that wouldn't be happening now that Bill wanted to take away her home and give it to Amy. Thinking about the scene yesterday made her angry all over again. It was time to move forward with finding someone to represent her interests.

The phone on Nona's desk buzzed, pulling her out of her reverie. She punched the intercom button on the phone. "Yes?"

Lily's voice came back to her. "Mr. Stubbin's here for his appointment."

The rest of Nona's day was filled with appointments and paperwork. She hadn't had another minute to think about her impending divorce. That was one of the things that Nona liked about working—there was no time to think about personal issues. The bad thing was that at the end of the day those issues often came crashing back on her.

At the end of the day, she still wasn't sure whether or not she should call Mr. Montgomery. Since Nona's practice didn't include divorce, she hadn't had the occasion to be in the same courtroom with him. She'd seen him in the court house on several occasions, but didn't know him personally. However, she knew a great deal about his reputation. She'd heard some of the clerks, and even judges, talk about him. He was a tall man you could tell worked out to keep in shape. He had a head full of white hair. Nona had heard some men referred to as a "Silver Fox" when they were reasonably attractive and with white hair like his. Most people referred to Michael Montgomery as the "Silver Wolf," because of his egotistical, calloused, cold-blooded actions in the courtroom. Maybe her friends were right. He was exactly the person she needed to have on her side. She closed her eyes and prayed.

Dear Lord, help me choose the best person as my lawyer.

Nona felt awkward saying this prayer. She was usually confident about the choices she made. Her prayers were said for other people; rarely did she pray for something for herself. She didn't need to put this off any longer. She would sit down and talk with Mr. Montgomery. How could she make a sound decision without even meeting with him?

It was just past five. She decided that now was as good a time as any to call Mr. Michael Montgomery's office to arrange for an appointment.

She pulled out the paper on which Lily had written his information, and punched in the numbers, hoping that someone would still be in his office to take her call.

"Michael Montgomery speaking."

Nona was taken aback. She hadn't considered that Mr. Montgomery would be the one to answer his own office phone. It took her a moment to regain her composure and her confidence.

"Hello, Mr. Montgomery. This is Nona Foxx."

"Well, well, Ms. Foxx, to what do I owe the honor of your call?" he said with a tone that dripped arrogance.

Nona came close to ending the call, but continued in a voice she hoped was filled with confidence. "Mr. Montgomery, I find that I am in need of a divorce attorney and would like to make an appointment to see if you are the one I should hire to represent my interests in this matter."

To Nona's surprise, she heard him give a slight chuckle. "Of course, you want the very best representation, Ms. Foxx. I can assure you that you've contacted the right person." He paused.

His blatant conceitedness was almost more than Nona could stomach. She rolled her eyes as she waited for him to continue.

"Looks like I can squeeze you in on Thursday afternoon at 5."

Squeeze me in? What does he think I am, a piece of cheese?

She purposely took her time as she checked her calendar. "I believe that will work with my schedule."

"Good." With that, he ended the call without saying another word.

It took Nona a minute before taking the phone away from her ear. *What a jerk!* Nona thought, still unsure if she would keep her appointment.

Nona didn't leave the office until well after 7:00. Instead of going straight home, she stopped off at *The Grill* to pick up supper for her father and her. Nona had never enjoyed cooking and now hated it even more when she was just cooking for herself. Most nights she either picked up something on her way home or stopped somewhere to eat. But every Wednesday, she and her father would share a meal at the family home after she got off work. She'd stop by *The Grill* to pick up her father's favorite meal—a loaded cheese burger cooked rare, served with deep fried pickles, and onion rings. She usually opted for a grilled chicken sandwich with a side salad. She wondered how her father could eat a hamburger that was almost bloody. It made her stomach turn, but that was his favorite meal. As long as he was the one eating it and not her, she was good with it. After placing her order, she took a seat at the diner's counter.

As she waited, she began to think back on her day. She realized that she had pushed her father's bizarre behavior this morning out of her mind. The whole incident distressed her. She found it hard to believe that he'd come to the office early in order to teach Nathan. He had never offered Nathan lessons before today, why now? With a shudder, she remembered that brief look in his eyes. She couldn't quite put her finger on what she'd seen, but it almost seemed like he was lost to himself for a moment. She could almost see fear in his eyes. In all her years, she'd never seen fear in any part of her father's whole being. He was the most confident man she'd ever known. She'd never thought of her father as arrogant, like Michael Montgomery had been on the phone, simply self-confident. She made a mental note to call Dr. Arnold to schedule a complete physical for her father.

"Hey, Nona."

Nona looked up to see Max Freeman staring down at her with a yellow-toothed grin on his unshaven face. Max was several years younger than Nona. She'd handled his case when he'd been arrested for assault, after a bar fight several years ago.

"Hello, Mr. Freeman. How are you?" She hoped she sounded polite without being encouraging.

"I can't complain. You sure are looking mighty fine tonight, Miss Nona," he offered, and just stood there, as if he was waiting for her to invite him to sit with her.

Nona gave him a courteous smile. "That's nice of you to say, Mr. Freeman," she said. "You have a good evening." She turned back to the counter, hoping that he would walk away. It took a minute, but finally he turned away from her to go back to his own table where his buddies were waiting for him. He said something to them and the whole table erupted in laughter. Nona hurriedly picked up her order, paid, and left; making sure that Max was still sitting at the table with his friends before walking out the door to get into her car.

Nona didn't knock as she walked in the back door of her father's old Victorian house, where she had spent her childhood. She loved this old house, but it no longer felt like a home to her. Her mother had made it into a home, but since her passing several years ago, it seemed empty. She walked through the kitchen to the formal dining room that held a gate-leg mahogany table with a captain's chairs at each end, and ten needle point straight chairs along each side. She walked over to the matching china cabinet, where she took down two of her mother's china plates. Taking the plates back into the kitchen, she arranged the contents of the Styrofoam containers on each plate. She then made a pot of decaf coffee, which they both would drink after their meal. She carried the two china plates into the formal dining room and placed one at the head of the table with the other to the right. She went back into the kitchen to pour two glasses of ice water. Once she placed the water glasses at each place and retrieved the silver utensils from the bow-front side board, the table was set just the way her mother had taught her, and the way her father liked.

She knew she'd find her father in his study, sitting in his well-worn leather recliner, reading. They usually spent most of their meal discussing the latest book her father was reading. On average, he would read four or five books a week, which Nona found phenomenal. She never seemed to find the time needed to complete even one book a week. She pushed open the half-closed door to his study to find the room empty.

"Daddy?" she called, looking around the room, finding it hard to believe he wasn't there. She walked to the back of the room to the black and white hexagon tiled bathroom with its pedestal sink, to find the door open with no sign of her father. She walked out of the study toward the living room calling, "Daddy?" There was no answer. She went back through the kitchen and out the back door, checking to see if his car was in the garage. It was there. Panic began to creep into her thoughts.

Where is he?

Nona retraced her steps as she continued to call out to him. As she passed by her father's bedroom, something caught her eye. She had not really searched his bedroom, knowing that at seven in the evening it was too early for him to be in bed. As she stepped closer to his bed she realized that her father was in his bed.

With a sense of alarm, she rushed to his side. "Daddy," she said softly, as she pulled back the covers to see his face. "Are you all right?"

Mr. James bolted straight upright as he heaved Nona away. "What's going on?" he roared.

Nona fell backwards as he pushed back the covers. With his eyes wild with rage, all of his six feet three inches and two hundred fifty pounds came barreling at her. With the realization that he didn't know what he was doing, Nona screamed out, "Daddy, stop! It's me, Nona!"

Just as he seemed to be preparing to attack, he stopped and looked around as if he wasn't aware of where he was or who she was. His fury left him as confusion came into his eyes. Finally, he looked down at Nona, who was cowering below him. "Nona?"

With shaky legs, Nona made her way to her father. "Daddy," she said in an unsteady voice. "Do you know where you are?"

"What are you doing here?" he said confused. "It's the middle of the night."

Nona took his arm, leading him back to his bed to sit down. "It's Wednesday, Daddy, and it's only seven o'clock."

Mr. James sat down heavily on the bed. "It is? Are you sure?" he asked with pleading eyes.

Sitting down next to her father, she answered, "Yes, Daddy, I'm sure."

It took several minutes and a great deal of persuasion before Mr. James was convinced of the day and the time. The closer he came to fully understanding that he had forgotten the day of the week, and had gone to bed over five hours earlier than normal, the more disheartened he became. Nona tried to get him to put the whole incident behind him, but it was clear to both that something frightening was happening to Mr. James.

With a calm encouraging tone in her voice, Nona said, "I picked up your favorite meal from *The Grill* and have it all ready for us in the dining room. Let's go eat, Dad."

Mr. James looked up at her with blood-shot eyes, from where he was sitting on the corner of his bed. He was wearing a white V-neck t-shirt and a pair of green and blue striped boxers—his typical bedtime attire. The little hair he did have on his head was standing straight up. If it were not for the seriousness of the situation, Nona would have been laughing. Instead, she held her composure as she handed her father his robe. He reluctantly took the robe, stood up, and walked out of the bedroom to the dining room, leaning on Nona.

As her father took his place at the head of the table, Nona said, "If your food is cold, Daddy, I can warm it up in the microwave."

"I'm sure it's fine," he said, not seeming to care. He sighed loudly as he stared down at his food, but made no move to begin eating.

Nona decided that she needed to get his mind off what was happening to him. He needed a distraction. She hoped she had the perfect one. She casually asked, "Guess who was waiting for me at my house, sitting on the front porch rockers, yesterday when I got home?"

Mr. James made no attempt to guess as he continued to stare down at his plate of food.

"Bill and Amy," she announced, as she took a bite of her salad.

Her father slowly turned away from his food as he looked at her. Nona watched in amazement as what had been a shell of a man transformed into her father. She saw a fire in his eyes as he spoke. "What did that reprobate and his harlot want?" he growled.

Nona knew that her father, James Riley Foxx III, had no use for the low-life who had once been her husband, William Robert Harris, and even less use for the other woman, Amelina May Patten—Amy's full name still made Nona want to laugh out loud. This news should get his blood pumping.

"They want my house, Daddy."

Nona was startled as her father's two fists came down on the table with such force that it almost knocked over their water glasses. "Over my dead body will that ever happen!"

Nona smiled as she recognized that she now had her father back. As they both ate their now cold meal, Nona replayed for her father the events of the previous day. She left off the conversation she'd had with Grace. To him, Grace was perfect, and Nona wanted him to keep believing that.

By the time she had finished with her story, she had cleared away the dishes, and they were sitting in his study enjoying their hot cups of coffee.

Mr. James had said little as he listened to Nona, but she could tell that he had been upset by the events. She ended with telling him of her appointment with Michael Montgomery tomorrow after work.

"I know of Mr. Montgomery, but I can't say that I know him," her father said. "His reputation is one of being rather ruthless on his opponents," Mr. James paused before adding, "Which should work in your favor."

"That's exactly why I made the appointment," Nona agreed. "I need someone who will nail Bill to the wall and leave him hanging there." They both smiled at the image.

Before Nona left her father, she made sure that he was settled in his study with his latest book, fully understanding that it was nine o'clock at night and in one hour it would be his normal bedtime. As she drove home, she began to think about her father's strange behaviors that started in the morning and continued throughout the day. He was on only two medications; one for blood pressure and one for cholesterol. She wondered if it could be that his blood pressure was out of whack and that was the reason for the strange behaviors. She'd get him in to see Dr. Arnold as soon as possible. She had confidence in Dr. Arnold. She'd be able to get her father back on track. Wouldn't she? She said a quick prayer before closing the door to her father's house.

Please, Lord, be with my father and bring him back to being the man I've always known and loved.

Chapter Four

At five o'clock on Thursday afternoon, Nona found herself in the less-than-welcoming waiting room of Michael Montgomery's law offices. With the exorbitant fees she knew he charged, the least he could do was spruce up the place where his clients got their first impressions of him. The uncomfortable, wobbling chair in which she was sitting was almost enough to make her walk out and never come back. But she didn't. She waited. And waited. And waited.

At five minutes until six, she watched a tall man with a full head of gray hair, deep green eyes, and clean shaved face walk into the waiting room. He was wearing a dark navy-blue bomber jacket over a white, long-sleeved shirt, and blue jeans. He came right over to her and sat down beside her as if they were long lost friends. With a white-toothed smile that made his green eyes seem to sparkle, he offered his hand as he said, "Hello to you, Mrs. Nona Foxx-Harris. I've been looking forward to this meeting all day."

Nona's breath caught in her throat. She'd forgotten just how strikingly handsome Michael Montgomery was. She'd seen him several times in the courthouse, at a distance, but she'd never been this close to him. His dark-brown complexion was set off by his distinguished gray hair. It took her a moment to take his outstretched hand. "Thanks." Then added, "It's just Foxx, leave off the Harris."

With a sincere smile he said, "Good to know."

He held onto her hand as he lifted her out of her chair. "Let's go into my office. Shall we?"

Before Nona could answer, he was on his way. Nona quickly followed. She noticed, as they walked down the long corridor past closed doors, that she didn't see another person. He stopped before a magnificent heart-pine door. He turned the antique brass door knob and pushed the heavy door open with his shoulder. Nona was stunned as she took in the scene before her. To say that the office was a mess would be a vast understatement. There were mounds of files, books, and filled yellow legal pads in stacks around the room, lining the walls, and covering every available surface.

Where in this disaster of an office am I supposed to find an empty place to walk, let alone sit? Nona thought to herself. Nona had always prided herself in keeping her office neat and clutter free. She was appalled by the chaos that she found surrounding her now. It was overwhelming.

Just as she was considering a plan of escape before something disgusting crawled out from one of the file folders scattered on the floor, Michael Montgomery spoke. "Let me get some of this stuff out of the way for you." He began moving files and books and legal pads from the two arm chairs in front of his desk.

He motioned for Nona to sit down. She cautiously made her way across the room to his desk and sat in the chair he indicated. She was pleased to find that the chair in which she sat was leather, actually high quality soft leather, and comfortable. Without waiting for him to sit, she began, "As I told you on the phone, I'm looking for a divorce attorney." She pulled the divorce papers she had been served out of her purse. "I was served with these divorce papers last Friday."

Without saying a word, Mr. Montgomery gestured for Nona to hand them over to him. He put the papers to one side, leaned up, folded his hands, and looked intently at Nona with those deep green eyes of his. "I want to hear from you why you want a divorce. Tell me in your own words what happened that brought you to this point, Nona. Is it okay if I call you 'Nona,' or would you rather I continued with 'Mrs. Foxx'?"

Trying to match his intense gaze, she answered, "Yes, please call me 'Nona.' Is it okay if I call you 'Michael'?"

"My friends call me 'Monty.'"

"Are we friends?" Nona asked.

"That's entirely up to you, Nona."

Nona considered this before continuing. "Truthfully, I'd feel more comfortable calling you Mr. Montgomery, I'm not in need of a friend right now. I'm in need of a good, no, make that great, lawyer. I'm here to find out if you might be that lawyer."

"Okay, Nona, you can call me 'Mr. Montgomery' for now," he said, as he leaned forward. "Why don't you tell me your story?"

"I'll tell you my story and then you can tell me what you'll do to get me what I want." Nona began with the night Bill told her about his affair with Amy, and ended with Amy and Bill showing up on the front porch of her house telling her that they wanted her house, and were willing to fight her for it.

Nona was proud of herself that she'd gotten through the telling of all the events that brought her to this point without shedding one tear. However, she found that she was emotionally drained. She sat back waiting for his response. He hadn't interrupted her one time. As she sat back, she realized that he hadn't taken any notes while she'd poured out the details of her failed marriage. He'd simply listened.

Monty remained as he'd been the whole time, with his elbows on his desk and his hands folded. Silence filled the office. Nona was beginning to feel uncomfortable as he continued to stare at her. It was several minutes, but seemed to Nona that it was much longer, before he moved. He pushed up from his desk and began to walk around the room, pacing.

Nona almost jumped out of her seat when he asked loudly, with a critical tone in his voice, "Why didn't you file for divorce after Bill left you for another woman?"

She had asked herself that same question many times. Looking up at him, she answered honestly, "I don't know."

Sitting back down, he turned to her and asked, with a hint of sarcasm in his voice, "Did you hope that the two of you would reconcile?"

Sitting up straight, she gathered her thoughts. "I think that maybe, on some level, I hoped we would get back together. I never thought I would fail at my marriage. If I filed for a divorce, I would be admitting that I had failed. When we married, I truly believed in the vows we took—that only death would separate us."

With all seriousness, he asked, "So, are you saying that you hoped Bill would die so you wouldn't have to file for a divorce?"

At first Nona was shocked by his accusation, but when she considered his question, the realization came of just how close he was to the truth—a truth that she'd buried deep in her thoughts. Nona answered, as she looked down at the floor. "I'm embarrassed to admit it, and I hope God will forgive me, but you're right. I think that I hoped, in the dark places of my heart, that he would die."

"Good to know," Monty said as he leaned back in his chair. "Now, I know how to proceed."

Nona gave him a questioning look.

"No, we're not going to kill Bill," Monty said as he shook his head. "However, we are going to fight Bill and Amy with all we have, to keep them out of your house."

"That's exactly what I wanted to hear you say." Nona added with a sly smile, "I just might be calling you Monty after all."

Nona had been on Layne's mind all day. She hoped her meeting with the lawyer Nona had described as "rude and arrogant" went well. She had considered telling Nona that she'd go to the meeting with her, but decided against it. Nona was not someone who needed to have her hand held. She was a competent, intelligent woman who could handle herself.

Layne was in her car on her way to visit her mother. Since her mother Louise had moved into Whitchurch Assisted Living five years ago, after her father passed away, Layne tried to stop by to see her once a day. If she didn't make it there in person, she would call her. Talking to her mother on the phone had become a bit of a challenge since her sense of hearing had declined. She found herself exhausted after spending her time yelling into the phone so her mother could understand what she was saying. She sometimes wondered if the problem was her mother's hearing or her mother's listening.

Louise had been a good mother to Layne. She'd always thought that her younger sister, Valerie, had been the one blessed with a great mother. Maybe that was because Valerie was the youngest and had watched the ways in which her two older sisters had made their mother unhappy. Either Valerie didn't do those things, or she was very good at hiding them. Whatever the reason, it was obvious to everyone that Valerie was their mother's favorite. Truth be told, if Layne had been in her mother's place, Valerie would have been her favorite as well.

Layne knew that her mother missed her other two daughters—Valerie and Shelby. Valerie had married a Yankee, and now lived in a small town in Pennsylvania, which was much too far away to visit more than a few times a year. The same was true with Layne's older sister, Shelby. She and her husband had retired to a condo on Sanibel Island in Florida. So, Louise was left with her middle child, Layne, as her daily visitor—the one who filled her prescriptions and took her to visit friends and attend church.

Her mother may have not been the greatest mother to Layne, but she had been an awesome grandmother to her children. Nathan, Blair, and Aaron adored their "Nana," as they called her. She had a sharp wit and was great at telling stories. While many at Whitchurch accused Miss Louise of hurting their feelings by saying what she honestly thought, that had never been the case when it came to her grandchildren. When she shared with her grandchildren what she thought about some of the things they did or didn't do, they found it humorous. While Layne often found her mother frustrating, she had always been grateful for the love she showered on her grandchildren. Layne hoped that her own grandchildren would love her the way her children loved her mother.

"Hey, Mama," Layne said as she walked into her mother's room and leaned over to kiss her cheek.

Her mother was sitting in her recliner, with the afghan her mother had knitted years ago wrapped around her; watching *Judge Judy*. "I was beginning to think that you might not be coming today, Layne," her mother said. "You know it's getting late for you to be out on the road."

"It's only a little after five o'clock, Mama," Layne said, as she sat down in the chair next to her mother. "Isn't it time to go to the dining room to eat?" She said hoping to change the subject.

"Oh, that Francis Tucker says I'm not welcome to sit at her table anymore," Miss Louise said in a sad voice. "So, I thought I might just take my supper in my room tonight."

"What did you say to her?" Layne asked, knowing that her mother must have said something ugly to Miss Francis, to get kicked out of their group.

Miss Louise looked over at her daughter. "I called her a 'mean old bitty.' She won't let that sweet great-granddaughter of hers wear her brooch to her high school dance. She's afraid she might lose it."

Layne went over to her mother and sat down in the empty chair next to her. "You're not going to let Miss Francis keep you out of the dining room are you, Mama?"

Miss Louise thought about this for a minute before answering. "Not sure I'm up to fighting her tonight. I'm pretty tired."

This wasn't the answer Layne expected. Her mother usually didn't give up that easily. Layne couldn't remember a time when her mother had said she was too tired to fight back. She looked over at her mother. She seemed so small and frail, wrapped in her afghan. She didn't like to think about her mother getting older, but she was almost ninety-two years old.

"How about if I go get us both a tray, and I'll eat supper with you right here in your room?" Layne said excitedly. "We can watch *Judge Judy* together."

Miss Louise sat up a little straighter, and with a grateful smile said, "Sounds perfect."

As Nona got into her car, she realized that she was actually considering the possibility of hiring Michael Montgomery, or Monty, as she would now call him. When she'd walked in the door to his waiting room, her hopes hadn't been high for a successful meeting. She had already convinced herself before she met with him that he wasn't the one to represent her interests. It'd been hard for her to imagine working with someone with such an undesirable reputation for showing no mercy to his opposition. However, after meeting with him she wasn't so sure that it would be a bad idea to have merciless on her side.

A big smile crept across Nona's face as she thought about Monty taking Bill apart in the courtroom. Even better would be if Amy was summoned to the stand, with Monty firing brutal questions at her. Nona shook her head as if trying to shake that ugly thought away. What had made her change into this woman who wanted to wreak havoc on Bill and Amy? She knew the answer to that almost immediately. Something snapped inside her when Bill told her that Amy wanted their house, her house.

She decided to give Dixie a call, to thank her for recommending Monty. She used her car's Blue-tooth connection to call Dixie's number.

Dixie cheerfully answered, "Hey, Nona."

"Hey, Dixie, I just had a meeting with Michael Montgomery."

"You did?" Dixie asked skeptically. "And...?"

"It wasn't what I'd expected at all," Nona said. "Oh, Dixie, he's so full of himself and you should see that office of his. It's a total disaster. I almost turned around and walked out when I saw it, but once we started talking, things changed."

"Well, that's good, right?"

"I liked him better than I thought I would," Nona said cautiously, "But I'm still not sure he's the one I want to handle my case."

"He may not be the right one for you, Nona, but at least you now know more about him and what he has to offer you."

"You're right about that," Nona agreed. "He's a hard one to figure out, but I'm glad you gave me his name. I now have choices."

By the time Nona ended her call with Dixie, she was at her driveway. She stopped at her mailbox at the beginning of the drive to get her mail. As she drove up to her house, she cast an annoyed glance at her front porch, scanning it to make sure that Bill and Amy weren't lurking there. She pulled her car under the carport and got out, heading toward her side door. She unlocked the door and walked into her kitchen. As she walked across the kitchen floor, looking through her mail, she looked around the room. She couldn't put her finger on it, but something felt different about the house.

She tried to shake it off as just being jumpy from having a stressful day. She put the mail on the table and started to sit down to go through it. It was then she heard a slight squeak coming from the floor above. It was a familiar sound that she'd heard most mornings when she'd been fixing breakfast while Bill was upstairs getting ready for work. Their bedroom was directly above the kitchen, and when Bill would cross their bedroom floor heading to the bathroom, the old floor would give off a loud creak. That squeak had been her signal that he was almost finished dressing and would be down for breakfast soon. She'd always found that sound comforting, but today it made the hairs on the back of her neck stand up.

She stopped, stood completely still, and listened. In just a few seconds she heard the creak, loud and clear, a second time. It was then she knew with certainty that something or someone was in her house this very minute. With her heart pounding, she slowly and silently retraced her steps and backed out of the door she had just entered. When she had made it to the outside, she turned and ran for the safety of her car.

With trembling hands, Nona took her cell phone out of her purse as she locked her car doors. She called the first person she always called when she was in trouble.

Layne answered on the third ring. "So, how did your meeting with Mr. Montgomery go?"

In an alarmed voice, Nona said, "Layne, where's Mark?"

"What?" Layne asked confused.

"Layne, I need Mark right now," with her voice rising in a panic, Nona said. "Someone's in my house!"

In a matter of minutes, Nona heard the distant sound of sirens. The sound soon became more intense as Mark and his deputies pulled onto her property. She watched as they slowly got out of their cars, pulled their guns from their holsters, and cautiously walked toward her house. She recognized one of the deputies, Aaron, Mark and Layne's youngest son who, after Mark's accident, had joined the Kerry County Sheriff Department.

She opened her car door when she saw Mark approaching. Silently, he motioned for her to stay in the car. Nona hadn't taken her eyes off the house since she'd ended her call with Layne. She hadn't seen anyone leave. Whoever was in her house still had to be there. She wanted to let Mark know this, but she did as instructed and closed her car door.

Nona counted two other deputies who had accompanied Mark and Aaron. They began walking cautiously around the house. In her haste to leave, she'd left the back-door open, but they should find the other doors to the house securely locked. Mark and one deputy walked through the open door from which she'd made her escape, with guns drawn. She watched Aaron along, with the other deputy, guardedly walk up on the front porch, checking the area around them as they went. When they got to the front door, her breath caught in her throat as they entered her house through a door that should have been locked. Since the front door was rarely used, it was always locked, Nona knew for certain that she hadn't unlocked it.

Nona felt totally helpless sitting there, as she anxiously waited in her car. Questions with frightening answers began to run through her head.

What's taking them so long?

Was there really someone in my house just waiting for me to come home?

What had they planned on doing to me?

Was someone there to rob me, or waiting to hurt me?

Why didn't I get a security system when Bill moved out, like Mark suggested?

Her heart was pounding in her ears. She couldn't remember when she'd ever felt this frightened. Her imagination began running wild as she thought about what Mark and Aaron might be finding in her house. She bowed her head and silently prayed for their safety.

When Nona looked back at her house, she saw Mark, followed by Aaron along with his two other deputies, coming out of the side door. Their guns were holstered, and they were alone. Mark and Aaron were walking toward her with a look of concern on their faces. Nona rolled down her window as they approached her car.

Aaron was the first to speak. "You were right to call for help. Someone has definitely been in your house."

Nona took in a deep breath trying not to panic. "How do you know, Aaron?"

Aaron looked at his father and stepped back from the car. He would let him deliver the bad news.

"It's your bedroom, Nona," Mark said with concern. "It's been pretty much trashed. I can't tell if anything has been stolen. You're going to have to go through the bedroom and the rest of the house to see what, if anything, has been taken."

"Now?" Nona asked incredulously.

"No, not now," Mark said in a calm voice. "We don't want anything to be disturbed before we get the detectives in there to take a look."

Mark added in a reassuring voice, as he reached into the car to put a comforting hand on her shoulder, "You're spending the night with us tonight, Nona."

Chapter Five

Layne was standing at the door waiting for Mark to bring Nona to their house. As soon as she saw Mark's car, she rushed out to open Nona's car door. She wrapped Nona up in her arms. "Oh, Nona, thank God you're all right."

Nona held onto Layne's embrace for a long time. The fact that Nona did not pull away from her, let Layne know just how upset she was. Nona was the one who needed everyone to think that she was in control. The realization of just how vulnerable she must be feeling brought tears to Layne's eyes. She held her tighter.

When they parted after a few minutes, Nona asked, "Why? Layne, why would anyone want to break into my house? Who would even want to do such a thing?"

Layne didn't have an answer for her right then, but she had her suspicions of who it might be. Instead of sharing her thoughts, she simply shook her head sympathetically and walked with Nona into her house. When Layne had gotten that frightening phone call from Nona, she had been in the middle of making a variation of her mother's celebrated vegetable soup. It was her mother's recipe, which Layne had enhanced by adding her own personality to the ingredients. It was a soup that Layne's mother would take to family and friends when they were "feeling poorly."

She was glad she'd decided to make it for this evening's meal. She hoped it would help to calm and comfort Nona.

"Why don't you go upstairs to the guest room to freshen up while I finish getting supper on the table? I put a pair of my pajamas and a robe on the bed that you can wear for tonight," Layne said. Nona was thinner than she, but she didn't think her pajamas would fall off her. They'd just be a little roomy on Nona.

Nona gave her a grateful look. "Layne, what in the world would I do without you and Mark." She quickly hugged her neck as she left the kitchen.

By the time Nona returned to the kitchen, Layne had served up the soup, along with homemade cornbread. The three of them sat down at the kitchen table to enjoy the meal.

Mark prayed, "Dear Lord, we thank you for keeping Nona safe today. We ask you to bless this food that Layne has so lovingly prepared for us. Amen."

"I still can't believe that someone broke into my house." Looking at Mark, she asked apprehensively, "Do you think they were there to rob me?" She took a deep breath before continuing, "Or were they there to hurt me or both?"

Putting his hand over Nona's, Mark said in a sympathetic voice, "Right now, all we know for sure is that someone was in your house. Until we finish with the investigation, I can't answer your questions."

"You can tell me what you think," Nona said, as she took her hand out from under his. "Don't treat me like I'm someone who needs to be handled with care, Mark. What does your gut tell you that he or she or it was doing there!"

Both she and Layne stared at him waiting for him to answer.

Mark put down his spoon and pushed back his chair from the table. He ran his hand through his hair in frustration before answering. "If you want my 'gut' feeling, I think that someone was there with the sole purpose of scaring you."

"Scaring me?" Nona asked skeptically.

Layne now said what she had wanted to say when Nona had gotten out of Mark's car. "Maybe there is someone you know who wants you out of your house. Maybe that someone thinks you can be scared away."

It took Nona a moment to realize what Layne was suggesting. "Are you saying that you think this could have been done by Bill?" she asked in a weak, disbelieving voice.

"Who else would want you out of that house?" Layne asked.

Nona looked from Layne to Mark. "Do you think it was Bill, Mark?"

"I'm not saying it's Bill, but it seems like more than a coincidence that this happened right after he demanded that you give him the house," Mark answered.

The thought of Bill planning and executing such a desperate act as breaking into her house to scare her into letting him have the house, robbed Nona of her appetite. "I don't even know who he is anymore," Nona said, more to herself than to Layne and Mark.

"Well, I don't either, Nona. I'm heading to his house right now, and I promise you that I'm going to find out just what kind of a man Bill has become," Mark said.

Mark left the table and after kissing Layne on the cheek, was out the door.

Layne looked at Nona. "I don't know when I've seen Mark that angry. I sure wouldn't want to be in Bill's shoes tonight!"

"Neither would I," Nona agreed.

The thought of Mark questioning Bill put knots in Layne's stomach. Mark and Bill had been friends since they were young boys playing baseball together. Mark had been the one who had introduced Bill and Nona all those years ago. He had been Bill's best man at their wedding. Bill had put a dent in their friendship when he'd left Nona for Amy, but if Mark accused him of breaking into Nona's house their friendship might be wrecked for good.

After cleaning up the kitchen, Layne and Nona took their iced tea out to the deck to enjoy the peaceful view of the setting sun. Neither one felt the need to talk. They simply sat, silently absorbed in their own thoughts. When they heard the door behind them open, they both jumped.

"Mark, you scared me half to death," Layne said. "That sure didn't take you long to find out."

"Sorry about that," Mark said putting his hand on Layne's shoulder. "Well, it wasn't Bill who broke into your house," Mark declared, joining them on the deck.

Nona asked, "Are you sure it wasn't him?"

Mark took the chair beside Layne's and pulled it around so he could face both Layne and Nona. "They were in Atlanta all day today. They left yesterday morning and spent the night there. They don't plan to be back until Saturday afternoon."

"How do you know for sure they were in Atlanta?" Layne asked skeptically. "Bill could have just made that up as his alibi."

Mark shook his head as he said, "No, he was there. He has a witness who will corroborate his whereabouts for today."

When Nona looked at Mark's face, she knew immediately who had been the one to corroborate. "It's Grace," she said with certainty. "Bill and Amy were at Grace's, weren't they?"

Mark looked away without answering.

"It's okay, Mark," Nona said. "I know that Grace has had Bill and Amy up at her house a couple of times."

Turning to Layne, she said, "I meant to tell you that Grace called the other night, after Bill and Amy's visit to the house." With a hint of sadness in her voice, she added, "Grace thinks that I'm being unreasonable by wanting to stay in the house. She thinks that the house is rightfully her father's, and I should hand it over to them."

"You've got to be kidding me!" Layne said.

"Nope, not kidding." Nona added, "Wish I were. I must admit that I was shocked by the way Grace spoke to me about this whole situation. It was almost like she," Nona swallowed hard, "hated me."

"And after all you've done for that girl," Layne said shaking her head. "She could at the least show you respect."

"Layne, I think that Grace is so wrapped up in 'Grace' that she doesn't even realize how deeply she's hurt me with her words and betrayal."

Layne reached over to take Nona's hand. "I hate that she's treating you like this." Then squeezing her hand added, "I'd like to just shake some sense into her."

"Me too, but think it will take more than just shaking to get any sense in her," Nona said with a smile.

All three laughed at the vision of Nona shaking Grace until she had some sense.

"Getting back to what happened today," Nona said, "with Bill cleared, who else had a reason to break into my house?" she asked as she looked from Layne to Mark.

"That's a good question, and one that I'm going to work to find out just who it was," Mark said.

"Until he does," Layne said as she looked over at Nona, "I think you should stay here with us."

Nona thought about this for a moment before answering. "I appreciate your generous invitation, Layne, but I'm not going to let anyone or anything scare me away from living in my own home." As she stood she added, "I'll spend the night here tonight, but tomorrow night I'll be sleeping in my own bed."

Mark stood up, towering over Nona. "I wish you would reconsider Layne's offer, Nona. I would feel much better if you were here with us until we find who it was that broke into your house."

"My mind's made up, Mark," Nona said. "I'll be going home tomorrow."

With that, Nona left the deck. Both Mark and Layne shook their heads as they watched her leave.

It could have been sleeping in an unfamiliar bed or being in a strange room, but sleep escaped Nona for most of that night. She couldn't get the visions out of her mind of a stranger breaking into her house and going through or even taking her things. Why was it that her bedroom seemed to be their target? What had they been after? Around five in the morning, she got out of bed and put on the clothes she'd worn the night before. Mark had told her to stay away from her house until they had a chance to thoroughly investigate, so she decided to head to her downtown office. She needed to get her mind on something other than thinking about what had happened at her house.

Nona made the bed and quietly crept down the stairs. It was only when she walked out of Layne's house that she remembered she had ridden with Mark the night before. She didn't have her car there. How could she get to work? Walk? She wasn't quite sure how far she was from her office, but it would be farther away than a short walk would take her. Nona had never been the athletic kind of person. Walking somewhere would be her last choice in any situation. She did have her cell phone, but who could she call at this hour.

Nona made her way back into the house, heading for the kitchen where, after fumbling around to find a coffee filter, she made pot of coffee. She poured herself a cup and carried it out to the back deck to wait for Layne or Mark to wake up. As she warmed her cold hands with the hot coffee mug, her thoughts drifted to her father. He'd been her rock throughout her life. Like most of the women of her era and station, Nona's mother had handed over most of her child-raising duties to their house keeper, Miss Nadeen. Her mother had been more of a model on how a proper Southern lady should behave. But, it was her father who gave her the love of reading and made her a seeker of knowledge.

When her father had returned home in the evenings from his law practice, it was Nona who was waiting for him; to listen to the tales he had to tell of his day. She knew her father wanted Riley, his son, to be the one who took an interest in what he did each day, not his daughter. She could feel her father's disappointment in his only son, and often wished she'd been his son instead of his daughter. It hadn't been her father's intention for his daughter to fall in love with his life's work, but that's what had happened.

Nona smiled as she remembered how determined she was to become a partner in her father's law practice, and how determined her father was that she would not. It had taken a great deal of hard work and determination on Nona's part before her father recognized her skills as a lawyer. The day he offered her a partnership in the Foxx and Foxx Law Firm had been one of her best days, ever. They had worked together as partners for over thirty years. Through those years, they had formed an unbreakable bond of trust and love.

Nona couldn't deny that her father's actions from the other day frightened her, and she was not one to be easily frightened. She'd made the appointment with Dr. Arnold, but her father insisted that he go alone. When she made the appointment, she'd informed the nurse about her father's strange behaviors. She wanted to express her concerns directly to the doctor, but was assured that they'd been noted on his chart. The only detail that her father had given her of his visit was that they were "running some tests." She knew that the best thing to do was to wait for the doctor's report before letting her mind run away with worry. She needed to trust that God had her father in his hands. She wasn't sure she could turn it all over to God, but she was going to try.

"Good morning, Miss Early Riser."

Nona was startled by Layne's words. She'd been so engrossed in her thoughts that she hadn't even heard Layne walk out onto the deck. "Good morning, Miss Late Sleeper," she countered with a smile.

Layne sat down next to Nona with her hot cup of English Breakfast tea—she'd never acquired the taste for coffee. "Couldn't sleep?"

"I got some sleep, but not much." Nona sat up on the edge of her seat to look over at Layne with a you're-not-going-to-believe-this look. "Are you ready for this? When I couldn't sleep, I got up, and decided I'd head over to the office to get some work done," Nona added with a chuckle, "It wasn't until I walked outside and began to look around that I realized I didn't have my car here!"

Layne spit out the tea that she'd just taken a sip of as she began to laugh and cough at the same time. She bent over double trying to get control, but the more she thought about Nona standing there searching for her car, the harder she laughed. The harder she laughed, the more she coughed.

Nona jumped up from her chair and rushed over to Layne pounding her on the back. "I didn't mean for you to choke to death on my story, Layne."

Watching Layne laugh made Nona begin to laugh uncontrollably. Tears were streaming down both Nona's and Layne's faces as they fought to regain their composure. Hearing the commotion, Mark walked out wondering what it was about. There was Nona hitting Layne on the back laughing the whole time while Layne seemed to be choking to death. "What in the world is going on?"

When the two women looked over at Mark's confused face, it sent them into another laughing fit. Mark simply shook his head, turned around, and walked back into the house.

Chapter Six

After Mark fixed his famous biscuits and sausage gravy for breakfast for all of them, he took Nona to her house. It had been cleared by the detectives, and he needed for her to go through the house to see if anything was missing. Layne had wanted to be there to support Nona, but had already made the commitment to keep their youngest grandchild, Madison, for the day. As Mark and Nona pulled into the driveway, Nona found herself tightly gripping the arm rest. She took in deep breathes, trying to calm herself down. Nona was determined that she would not let what happened yesterday make her afraid of her own home.

"You okay," Mark asked, looking over at Nona with concern.

"I'm fine." She added, "Let's do this." With that, she opened her car door and began to make her way to the side door of her house. It was closed now, with a sash of yellow tape warning to keep out. Mark walked past her to take the tape from the door. He reached out for the keys Nona was holding tightly in her hand. Instead of handing them to him to open the door, she went by him to place the key in the lock. She turned the door knob and walked into her kitchen.

She bent over to gather the mail she'd knocked off table when she'd heard that creak from the floor above. She found herself listening for that same noise now.

Mark touched her arm as he looked around the kitchen. "Do you notice anything out of place in the kitchen?"

Nona silently looked around. "I don't think so. I will tell you that when I walked in here yesterday, it felt like something was..." She stopped speaking in mid-sentence having that same feeling she'd had the day before, "off."

Mark gave her a curious look. "What exactly do you mean by 'off'?"

"It means that something wasn't right, something gave her the heebie-jeebies," Aaron said, as he walked up behind Nona. "Right?"

"Right," Nona said with a smile, as she reached out to give Aaron a hug. "That's a good way to put it."

"Well, okay then," Mark said. "Not sure exactly how I'm going to write that up in my report though."

They all laughed.

"Let's check out the rest of the downstairs before heading upstairs to the bedroom," Mark said.

Aaron and Mark walked with Nona as they went through all the downstairs rooms, including closets and bathroom.

"I don't see anything missing or out of place down here," Nona said with relief. "I noticed that you just walked right in the front door yesterday, Aaron. It should have been locked."

"It wasn't locked yesterday," Aaron replied.

All three headed to the front door to check it out. It seemed most likely that this was the door where the intruder or intruders entered, since they had found the other two outside doors locked. After careful inspection, they couldn't find evidence that the lock had been tampered with. Either the door had accidentally been left unlocked, or whoever entered through this door yesterday had used a key.

Nona shook her head. "This door is always locked, Mark. I can't imagine how it got unlocked."

"You don't think you could have unlocked it at some point and just forgot to lock it back," Aaron asked. "I sometimes do that—forget to lock my door back," Aaron said with a sheepish grin.

"Truthfully, son, I can see you doing that, but I don't see that happening with Nona," Mark said. "Does anyone else have a key to this door?"

Nona thought about this for a minute. "Bill has one, of course. I gave Dad one years ago, but I don't think he would have unlocked the door."

As they were walking away from the door, she remembered another key she'd given out. "I gave one to Lily at the office, so she could check on the house when I was away."

Aaron and Mark looked at one another, and then back at Nona with suspicion. "Do you know where that key is right now?" Aaron asked.

"I would guess it's in Lily's desk at work," Nona said.

Aaron asked, "Why don't you give Lily a call right now and ask her to check to make sure that the key is still there'?"

Nona quick-dialed her office number. She'd already talked to Lily this morning to let her know that she'd be late getting to the office. She hadn't told her why, at the time. Lily answered in her professional office voice on the second ring tone. "Lily Morton speaking, how may I help you?"

"Hi, Lily, it's me."

"Oh, hi, Nona. I didn't check caller ID before picking up the phone to see that it was you," Lily said apologetically. "Is everything all right?"

"It is, but I need for you to check on something for me."

"Sure, anything."

"Do you know where my house key is? The one I gave you a couple of years ago?"

"Sure, I do. It's right in the middle drawer of my desk under the box of paper clips," Lily answered confused by the question. "Why?"

"Do me a favor, and just check to make sure that key is where you think it is?"

Nona could hear Lily rummaging around in the desk. It was several minutes before Lily came back on the phone. Nona heard frustration in her voice. "This is weird, but that key is not where it always is. I remember seeing it just last week when I put a new box of paper clips in my desk. It was right there, but now it seems to be gone."

Chills ran down Nona's spine. She looked over at Mark and Aaron. "Lily can't find the key. It's not where she keeps it."

To Lily, she said, "Keep looking to see if you might have placed it somewhere else. Call me if you find it." Nona ended the call without allowing Lily to ask any questions.

Mark asked, "Who has access to Lily's desk?"

"Just about anyone who walks through the door. The desk isn't locked." Then, more to herself, she added, "Who'd have thought that we needed to lock the desk?"

Aaron could tell Nona was bothered that Lily hadn't found the key.

"I'll bet Lily just put that key in a different place," Aaron said, trying to reassure her. "Bet she calls in just a little while to say she's found it."

Nona's spirits lifted just a little. "I hope you're right, Aaron."

Mark said, "It's time to go upstairs now, Nona." In a comforting voice, he asked, "Are you okay to keep going or do you want to take a break?"

"Let's keep going. I'm fine."

The three of them walked out of the living room and up the stairs to the second floor, which held three bedrooms, Nona's home office, and two baths. They walked through the two guest rooms, the guest bathroom, and Nona's office. Nothing appeared to be missing or disturbed in any of these rooms.

Taking a deep breath, Nona walked down the hall to her bedroom, with Mark and Aaron following.

Before opening the door to her bedroom, Mark turned to Nona. "Now, Nona, I'm not sure how we could have ever fully prepared you for what you are about to see. Please, try to stay calm."

Nona looked at Mark and nodded her head. "I'm ready."

Mark cautiously opened the door.

Nona had always thought of this room as her sanctuary. After Bill had moved out, she'd redecorated it in calming colors of white and light gray with teal accents. She had made it into her place of peace. The scene before her was anything but peaceful. The first thing that hit her was the overpowering aroma of bleach. She stopped at the door of her once beautiful bedroom unable to move as she took in the destruction before her.

One of the first things she'd done after Bill had left her was to hire Dixie's husband, Alex, to build a walk-in closet with cedar lined walls. He'd customized it with shelving specifically made to hold her folded clothing, divided drawers for her lingerie, and a hidden drawer for her jewelry box. There were shelves made to store her designer bags and her shoes. She loved her closet. It had held everything she needed each morning to get ready for her day.

The doors to her beloved closet now stood wide open. The contents emptied. Her dresses, suits, blouses, pants, jackets, shoes, lingerie— everything—had been piled in the middle of the room. From the discoloration, it was clear that all had been doused with bleach. The straps of her designer bags had been cut and lay in a heap on the floor.

Nona's expensive pale teal and white designer comforter set was streaked with bleach. The lamps that she'd bought in Charleston that had perfectly matched her decor had been knocked off the night stands and lay broken on the floor. The contents from the night stands had been smashed and strewn across the floor. The two paintings Nona had commissioned of Grace when she was a child, which had hung over her bed, were lying against the far wall with holes punched through and their frames twisted. The toile wingback chair with its pastoral scene, which had once resided in her mother's bedroom, hadn't escaped the attack.

Nona's knees buckled beneath her as she stared disbelievingly at the chaos. Mark and Aaron reached out to hold her up. Silent tears were running down her cheeks. She couldn't breathe. She couldn't move. It was so obvious from the way her room had been destroyed that this carnage had been done by someone who sincerely loathed her.

Nona found herself sitting at the kitchen table, with a glass of water in her hand. She couldn't recall how she'd gotten from her bedroom to her kitchen table. She had no clue as to how long she'd stood at her bedroom door gazing at the annihilation before her. All she knew for sure was that her life would never be the same from this moment on.

"Who would do such a thing? Who?" She kept mumbling to herself, not even aware if anyone else was in the room.

A comforting hand touched her shoulder as a familiar gentle voice answered, "Darlin', I don't know."

Nona put her hand over Dixie's hand and squeezed it. She held on as she began to softly cry. Neither one spoke for several minutes.

Nona released her hand as Dixie came around to sit beside her. "Dixie, how in the world am I going to get through this?"

"God will see you through this, Nona," Dixie said in a comforting voice. "Plus, you have Betty Jo, Layne, and me to help you. With God and the three of us on your side, what more do you need!"

For the first time since she'd seen the destruction of her bedroom, Nona smiled. "Nothing! Nothing at all."

Dixie smiled back at Nona, and said sincerely, "I'm so sorry this has happened to you. I can only imagine how you feel."

"Right now, I feel grateful that you're here," Nona said looking over at her friend.

Glancing around, Nona asked, "Where are Mark and Aaron? I thought they were right here."

"They left as soon as I got here. I'm sure they're out looking for whoever did this."

Nona gave Dixie a curious look. "How did you happen by here, Dixie?"

"Layne called me. Mark called her because he was worried about the way you reacted when you saw, well, you know what you saw."

She patted Nona's hand. "I think you might have blacked out for a little while. Anyway, since Layne had Madison, she called me to get over here as fast as I could. And that's exactly what I did. She and Betty Jo will be here soon."

"Thanks so much for being here with me, Dixie," Nona said in a soft voice, as she took a sip from her water glass.

"Can I get you anything else, Nona?" Dixie asked. "Maybe a cup of hot tea with lemon?"

It was obvious to Nona that Dixie needed something to do. "Hot tea sounds perfect."

As Dixie busied herself with the tea, Nona closed her eyes. The horrible scene from her bedroom came rushing back to her. She quickly opened them, wondering if she'd ever be able to close them again. She needed to get her mind focused on something else.

"How are Hailey and Josh doing? I haven't seen them around much," Nona asked Dixie, trying to get her mind away from the devastation in her bedroom.

Dixie was standing by the stove waiting for the water in Nona's tea kettle to boil. She turned away to answer. "They're both fine, just busy. Hailey's practice is growing and with that growth comes more demands on her time, which can be tough on the rest of the family. I try to help with the kids as much as I can, but the responsibility of getting them to their events and practices falls on Josh for the most part. It's a good thing he works for Alex and can get off when he needs to pick up or deliver a child somewhere."

Dixie exhaled heavily with a loud sigh. "If you ask me, the kids are in just too many things. Kids should be allowed to be kids. They don't need to have everything organized for them every hour of every day."

Nona could tell she had hit a sore spot for Dixie. She needed to get Dixie off that subject before her blood pressure went sky high. "I agree with you. How's Jason liking his new job?"

"He lost that one," Dixie said with a bit of disgust in her tone. "We found out that he's been living with Hailey because he didn't want to bother us with his problems. You and I both know Hailey doesn't need him there sleeping on her couch."

She paused as she brought two cups of hot green tea with lemon over to the table and set one cup in front of Nona. She shook her head. "So, Jason's moved back into his old bedroom at our house."

To stop herself from saying what she really wanted to say about Jason, Nona picked up her cup to take a sip. It seemed to Nona that Dixie was always making excuses for Jason, and never saw that he was trying every trick in the book to get all he could out of his mother. Instead, she said, "I'm so sorry, Dixie. I know that has to be hard on you and Alex."

Before Dixie could reply, there was a knock on the side door.

"Hello?" Layne called out as she opened the door and walked into the kitchen.

Feeling a great sense of relief, Nona got up from the table to embrace her. All the emotions of the day that she'd tried to keep at bay came rushing back to her as she held onto her best friend. Layne enfolded Nona in her arms.

"I'm so sorry, Nona," Layne said, as she patted her on the back offering comfort and trying not to cry.

When Nona had regained control of her emotions, she stepped back from Layne, looking into her eyes. "Oh, Layne, you won't believe what someone did to my bedroom, to my clothes, to everything."

"Mark said it was bad," Layne said.

"Well, 'bad' doesn't even begin to describe it," Nona said pushing her sadness away. "What they did was an act of depravity," she said as her eyes flashed with anger.

Layne could see that a fire was building in Nona. "Mark and Aaron are going to do everything they can to find out who did this horrible thing to you, Nona."

Nona nodded her head as she said, "I have all the confidence in the world that they will, Layne."

Betty Jo arrived within minutes of Layne. Dixie made a cup of tea for each of them. As they drank their tea, Nona told them about the key to the front door missing from Lily's desk, and how it appeared that the person who'd wreaked havoc on her bedroom had entered through the front door using a key. Both Dixie and Betty Jo were sure that what happened had to be the work of Bill. They were disappointed that their theory fell apart when Layne explained to them how Mark found out that Bill and Amy had been in Atlanta visiting with Grace.

"Bummer," Betty Jo said. "It would just make sense if it was Bill or Amy trying to scare you off from this place, so you would just hand it over to them."

"That was my first thought," Layne admitted. "But, truthfully, it sounds like it would be more work than Bill would ever do by himself."

Nona smiled. "I've got to admit that Bill did come to my mind, but I just don't think he would do anything so..."

"Mean?" Dixie offered.

"Yes, but even more than that."

"Evil?" Betty Jo suggested.

"That's the word, 'evil'," Nona said with a shudder. Turning to look at her friends, she asked, "Do y'all want to go upstairs to see what was done?"

Layne reached for Nona's arm. "Are you sure you're ready to go back up there? We don't want our curiosity to push you into doing something you don't want to do."

"Only if you want to show us," Betty Jo agreed.

"With y'all beside me, I can handle it," Nona said, as she looked gratefully at each of her friends. "I know it's a lot to ask, but would y'all mind helping me look through the mess to inventory the damage and see if anything is missing? I know Mark needs to know if anything was stolen."

"You don't even need to ask, Nona," Dixie said, "that's why we're all here, to help you."

"Of course, we'll help," Betty Jo agreed. "Now, what do we need to take upstairs with us to get that mess cleaned up?"

Together they gathered the items they would need— rubber gloves, trash bags, paper, pen, paper towels, etc.

Nona led the way as her friends followed her up the stairs, down the hall, and to the door of her bedroom. After Nona's initial reaction, Mark had shut the door while Aaron took her away from the scene. Now, as she stood before the closed door she wasn't sure if she had the courage to open it. Layne stood beside her, took her hand, and squeezed it. Nona took a deep breath as she turned the knob and pushed open the door. All four gasped as they took in the dreadful scene before them. They stood there in total disbelief for several minutes, unable to speak.

"I guess it's time to start cleaning up this mess," Nona said, with a sigh of determination.

Silently, the three friends followed Nona into the room. After putting on their rubber gloves, they began picking up the pieces of what had once held importance in Nona's life. They gathered and placed the items that were beyond repair in trash bags. The few garments that could be salvaged were placed back in the closet. As the wife of the life-long law officer, Layne recognized the importance of documentation and took pictures of each item with her cell phone.

As the trash bags grew in number, it became evident that shopping was in Nona's immediate future if she wanted an outfit other than the one she'd been wearing when she left her house yesterday morning. Layne had always admired Nona's sense of style. Since she'd worn the same size since college, Nona had a vast wardrobe of clothes for every occasion. To be a witness to what this person had done to her wardrobe broke Layne's heart.

Dixie was holding a trash bag as Betty Jo placed the damaged designer bag that Nona had purchased as a reward when she'd won her first case, when she asked, "Nona, I haven't seen any of your jewelry. Was it stolen?"

Nona suddenly jumped up from where she'd been working and rushed into her walk-in closet. She went immediately to the hidden drawer that Alex had made to look like it was part of the wall, almost invisible to anyone who didn't know it was there. She came out of her walk-in closet holding her jewelry box in both hands. She hurried over to place it on her bed.

"I can't believe I'd forgotten about my jewelry. I only keep a few pieces at home, but they're my favorites," Nona said, and then paused as she looked pleadingly over at Layne. "I'm too scared to open it."

"I'll do it," Layne said, as she walked over and sat on the bed. Dixie and Betty Jo stopped what they were doing to join her. She carefully picked up Nona's jewelry box and placed it on her lap. She looked over at Nona who had covered her eyes with her hands, shook her head with disbelief, and opened it.

"Look, Nona, it's here!" Layne said with delight.

Nona took her hands away from her eyes and looked into the box to see her that all her jewelry was intact. Big tears began to fall onto her cheeks as relief spread through her whole body. As Layne, Dixie, and Betty Jo watched Nona, there were tears in their eyes as well. They were tears of joy to find something good among the ruins.

"Thank heavens Alex put that secret drawer in my closet. He said I would thank him one day for doing that." Nona looked over at the Dixie and smiled, "I guess today is the day!"

Dixie smiled back.

"You know what I can't believe?" Layne asked as she walked over to the master bathroom. "That whoever destroyed your bedroom didn't wreak havoc on your bathroom."

Nona began thinking back. "It was when I was standing in the kitchen yesterday that I heard the sound of someone walking from the bedroom into the bathroom. That's when I knew someone was in my house. Do you think he might have been scared off before he had a chance to destroy my bathroom?" Nona asked.

"That must be what happened, Nona," Betty Jo said excitedly.

"Well, I'm just thankful you didn't walk upstairs to check it out when you heard someone walking up here," Layne said.

"You know what's weird about that, don't you? That's not really what I would normally do," Nona said disbelievingly. "My gut instinct is to go check it out before calling for help, but something stopped me from doing that yesterday. I'm not sure what, though."

"It was God looking after you, that's what," Dixie said with authority.

"You may be right, Dixie," Nona said smiling. "You just may be right."

While they were still busy clearing the mess from Nona's bedroom, Mark and Aaron stopped by.

"How's it going?" Aaron asked, as he entered the room. All four women jumped at the sound of his voice, even though Mark had called Layne before coming to the house to let them know they were on their way over.

"You almost scared us to death, Aaron," Layne scolded.

"Mom, I told you we were coming."

"I know, but still," she said, with an embarrassed laugh.

"Y'all have done a lot of work here today," Mark said, as he surveyed the room. "Have you even stopped to eat lunch?"

All four looked at one another with wonder. They hadn't even thought about lunch. They'd had a one-track mind of getting things sorted out and cleaned up as quickly as possible.

"Well, lucky for you, we picked up club sandwiches, " Aaron said. "I put them downstairs on the kitchen table."

They gladly stopped working and headed downstairs. They took their sandwiches, along with a cold glass of iced tea, out to the deck to enjoy the warm weather. They talked about everything but what had taken place in Nona's bedroom the day before. Nona was glad they'd taken time to relax and enjoy this time of being together. There was time enough for the work that had to be done upstairs. It could wait for now.

Chapter Seven

Dixie called Alex to bring his truck to Nona's so they could haul away the trash bags. Mark and Aaron helped him load everything into the truck. By six o'clock that evening Nona's bedroom was clear, with only her bed and night stands remaining. Dixie had even made the bed with fresh sheets and topped it off with a quilt she'd found in the linen closet. Nona was amazed and thankful that they could get so much accomplished in only one day. She wondered, for the hundredth time that day, how people made it through life without good friends. She thanked God for hers.

Nona had been persuaded to stay with Layne and Mark one more night, but was determined to return to her own home tomorrow. She felt that if she didn't resume living in her own home soon, then the person who had broken into her house would think he or she was the winner. She would not be defeated so easily.

Earlier in the day, she'd sent Lily on an errand to purchase essentials for her, and outfits to get her through the rest of the week. Nona would go shopping over the weekend in Savannah to get what she needed to replenish her wardrobe. Normally, she would have been looking forward to a day of shopping, but it didn't hold much excitement for her this time.

Nona had made the decision that she wouldn't tell her father about the break-in, just yet. She didn't want to add any worries to his life. Even though he didn't say it, she knew he was worried about the results of what the test Dr. Arnold was running would show. She knew she'd have to tell him soon. News traveled fast through Kerry, but she hoped the news wouldn't reach him before tomorrow.

She desperately wanted to call Grace to talk to her about the events of the past few days, but couldn't bring herself to make the call. After the last conversation she'd had with her, it was evident that her daughter held bad feelings toward her. Nona didn't quite understand why she would be angry with her and not Bill, the one who'd betrayed Nona and ended their marriage. With all she'd been through these past few days, she didn't think she could handle another rejection from Grace. That would just hurt too much right now.

Nona did what she usually did when things got tough— she threw herself into her work. She went in early the next morning, and said little to Nathan and Lily about the break-in when they asked her questions. It was obvious to them that Nona didn't want to talk about it. They knew it was best to give her space. She'd talk about it when she was ready.

Neither Layne nor Mark had said anything to Nathan about the break-in. It was still under investigation, so that subject was off limits, not that Nathan had asked. So, Nathan remained in the dark about what had happened at Nona's house.

However, Lily already knew about the break-in and what had been done to her bedroom. Unlike the others, Betty Jo had filled Lily and Don in on every detail that she knew. She even threw in a couple that she didn't know for sure. She just couldn't get it off her mind that Bill and Amy had something to do with what happened. It was just too much of a coincidence that they showed up one day, wanting Nona out of the house, and a few days later it was vandalized. She knew that Bill had the alibi of being with Grace, but Betty Jo wasn't convinced. She shared her suspicions with her family.

"Mom, don't tell anyone else that you think Bill had something to do with what happened, when you don't know for sure," Lily warned her. "That could come back as gossip to Nona, and that would not be good for my job or for your friendship."

"She's right, Betty Jo," Don agreed. "Be careful telling things that aren't facts."

Betty Jo looked at both of them as if they were crazy. "I'm not going to tell anyone else about this. I just wanted to share with my family."

Don and Lily weren't convinced.

After a long day at work, Nona knew she couldn't put it off any longer. She needed to tell her father about the break-in. She didn't want to do it over the phone. For the second time that week, she stopped off at *The Grill* to get a meal for her father. She hoped that she would not find him in bed this time.

She didn't knock as she opened the door to her father's house, but called out, "Daddy, it's me. I've brought you supper."

"Again?" her father's gruff voice answered.

She went through the door to his study, thankful to find him seated behind his large mahogany desk. He took off his glasses and stared at her. "To what do I owe this pleasure?"

"Can't a daughter surprise her father every once in a while?" she said, as she went around to give him a kiss on the cheek.

With a smile, he answered, "Yes, she can."

Instead of setting up to eat in the dining room with china and silver, Nona thought that it would be just as nice to eat from the Styrofoam containers with plastic forks. From the way her father attacked the food, it worked for him as well. As they ate, they talked about politics and events that had taken place in the world. Nona enjoyed listening to her father's intelligent, unique perspective on things. He was much better informed than she, since he read at least two newspapers a day—*The New York Times* and the *Atlanta Constitution*. She felt lucky if she read *The Kerry News and Dispatch*.

"Dad, while we're talking about the news," Nona began, "I have some news that I need to share with you."

Mr. James leaned across the desk toward Nona and with a stern look on his face asked, "So, you've finally decided to tell me about your break-in?"

"You knew about it, this whole time we've been sitting here talking, and said nothing?" Nona acted as if she was shocked he knew. Deep down, she knew he'd find out. There were too many people in this town who liked to be the ones who told the latest gossip—especially if it was bad news.

"I figured if you didn't want to talk about it, then I would respect that and stay silent on the subject."

As Nona looked over at her father's face, which was full of concern, she felt like she was seven years old again, wanting her Daddy to make everything better. "Oh, Daddy," was all she could say before the emotions of the past few days overwhelmed her. All she could do was cry, which she had rarely done in front of her father.

Her father came out from his desk and slowly walked over to his only daughter. He took the clean handkerchief from his pocket and handed it to her as he put his hand on her shoulder, gently squeezing it. This unexpected display of tenderness from her father was so unlike him. It touched Nona's heart. For the first time in a long time she recognized just how blessed she was to be the daughter of this amazing man.

Father and daughter remained as they were for several minutes before Nona regained control.

Through her tears, she looked up at her father. "Thanks, Daddy."

He gave her shoulder one last squeeze before taking the chair beside hers. "Now, tell me; what have they learned about this vile transgressor?"

"Not much," Nona began. "They do know that he used a key to gain entrance through the front door."

"A key?"

"Yes, sir, it looks like it might have been a key I gave Lily to use when I went out of town. It's missing from her desk drawer."

Mr. James considered this information for a minute. "That key could have been taken by any number of people who walked through your office."

"I know," Nona said.

"Has Mark given any consideration to the possibility that this could have been the vicious act perpetrated by your soon-to-be former husband, in hopes of getting you to leave your house behind?"

"Bill has an alibi," Nona said with a sigh. "He and his girlfriend were in Atlanta with Grace."

"With our Grace?" he asked disbelievingly.

"The very one."

They talked for a few more minutes, speculating on who might want to break into her house. It was after eight-thirty when Nona looked at the clock on her father's desk. She could tell that her father was getting tired, and she wanted to get home before it got too late.

"Dad, it's been a long day. I think I'll head home," Nona said, as she stood up.

"I think you should stay here with me until they find the perpetrator who vandalized your home," her father insisted.

Nona had thought that he might want her to stay with him, but she was determined to go back to her house. She couldn't live in fear. "Thanks, Daddy, but I need to be in my own home. I had all the locks changed, and a security system installed today, so the missing key is no longer an issue. I'll be fine."

Mr. James knew that if the same had happened to him, he would have wanted to get back to his home, too. "Well, you're a grown woman who knows her capabilities and limitations. I trust that you know what you're doing, Nona."

"Thanks, Daddy," she said, as she gave him a hug and quick kiss on his cheek. "I'll wash this and bring it back," indicating the handkerchief he'd given her.

"No hurry." He cleared his throat before saying, "By the way, I go back to Dr. Arnold tomorrow at one in the afternoon to get my test results. You're welcome to accompany me, if you have the desire."

"I'd really like to be there with you to get those results," Nona said, with a slight catch in her voice. "See you at one."

As Nona drove into the driveway leading to the house she loved, which had just been violated, she fought back the apprehension that was building inside her. She wouldn't give in to fear. Whoever had destroyed her bedroom must have hoped to destroy the feeling she had of her home as a safe haven and as protection from the world. She would not give in to that. This was her home, her shelter, her refuge.

She pulled under her carport and turned off the engine. The quiet surrounded her. She had always loved that sound of silence. It gave her a calm feeling after a long day of listening to others—here was peace. She breathed that peace in until it filled her. She kept telling herself that she had nothing to fear.

As a child, she'd learned Bible verses in Sunday School. The preacher at that time, Brother Richard, had called them "Heart Verses." These were verses that you knew by heart, and could recall them when you needed them to hold you up or move you forward. She'd depended on them many times throughout her life. One verse came to her mind now that she repeated over and over to herself as she opened her car door, walked up to her side door, and opened it with her new key.

The Lord is the strength of my life; of whom shall I be afraid? /Psalm 27:1

As she walked into her kitchen, a soft chirp sounded from the new security system that Lily had pulled some strings to have installed without waiting to be worked into a schedule. She used the code she'd chosen to disarm it. She locked the door and rearmed it. She turned on the lights and looked around. She shook off the feeling that something didn't feel right about the kitchen. It had to be her nerves giving her this uneasy feeling.

She turned on the light in each room as she walked from room to room. She checked the front door to make sure it was locked and armed. Then she walked back through the house turning off the lights as she went. She was back in her own home, and she felt safe. She sighed with a sense of relief. She was just getting ready to walk upstairs when her phone rang out with the tune she'd assigned to Layne. She knew that Layne had been worried about her coming back to the house. She'd begged her to stay on with her and Mark.

"Hey, Layne," she answered, forcing herself to sound cheerful. "I'm home and every thing's fine. You don't have to worry about me."

"I wasn't worried."

"Liar," Nona said with a chuckle.

"Okay, I may have been a little worried," Layne said. "I just called to wish you a good night and hope you sleep tight."

"Thanks, Layne," Nona said. "I'm just now heading upstairs to bed."

"I love you, Nona."

"Love you too, Layne," Nona said, as she ended the call.

She smiled. She was blessed to have a good friend like Layne. They'd been best friends since their college days. She could always count on Layne to be there for her no matter what. Of course, they'd gone through some rough patches together, but they'd always come out of those times even closer.

She turned on the light above the stairs and took a deep breath as she climbed the steps that led to her bedroom. She'd purposefully left the door open when she'd left the room the other day. She could see the moon shining through the window beside her bed. She found it comforting that the moon was full tonight. She always seemed to sleep better when the moon was full.

She turned on the light and looked around. It was so bare. Maybe it'd be better if she slept in one of the guest rooms. She turned to walk out of her bedroom, but stopped. If she didn't sleep in her room, in her bed tonight, that would mean she'd fallen into the trap someone had set. She turned around, determined this would be where she slept tonight.

Chapter Eight

The night passed much quicker than Nona had expected. Since she didn't have a clock in the room, she wasn't sure exactly what time she'd fallen asleep. She thought it was soon after midnight. It wasn't fear that'd kept her awake, but worry about her father's upcoming doctor's appointment. She imagined all kinds of illnesses that could be at the root of his symptoms.

Nona dressed in the outfit Lily had picked out for her. It was a pale shade of pink, really more of a salmon color, that made her skin take on a yellowish glow. She realized it was an outfit that would look great on Lily. That must have been why she picked this one out. She wished she had something else to wear, but her wardrobe was extremely limited for now. She'd just have to live with this outfit for the day. She'd go shopping tomorrow, for sure.

After working in her office all morning, Nona met her father at Dr. Arnold's office at one o'clock, as planned. They had to wait only a few minutes in the outer waiting room before they were taken back. The nurse led them to Dr. Arnold's office instead of an examining room. This made Nona nervous, but she tried her best to act nonchalant. On the other hand, her father seemed as "cool as a cucumber"—a favorite phrase of her mother's when she described someone who was calm.

"How did you fare the night?" Mr. James asked Nona.

She smiled. "Even better than I'd hoped."

"You know, you shouldn't be so nervous about this appointment, Nona," Mr. James said. "It's going to be okay, whatever the diagnosis is."

"I'm not nervous," Nona declared, as she tried to look him in the eye.

Before Mr. James could dispute her claim, Dr. Arnold hurriedly entered the room. To Nona, it seemed like she was always in a rush. She sat down and opened her iPad. It seemed to Nona that no longer were patient files in file folders, but were now kept electronically.

"Nona, it's always good to see you, but I'm especially glad to see that you came with your father today," Dr. Arnold said.

Nona smiled and nodded, willing her to continue. "As you know I've been concerned about some of his behaviors lately," Nona said, as she patted her father's leg.

"How have you been feeling lately, Mr. James? Any more headaches?" Dr. Arnold asked.

He hadn't said anything to Nona about headaches. She looked anxiously at her father as he answered.

"Several in the past few days," Mr. James said.

Dr. Arnold entered this information into her tablet. "Still feeling confused at times?"

Mr. James simply answered, "Yes."

Her father hadn't said a word to Nona about his latest incident. She'd learned about it through a call from Judge Baxter. Her father had gone to the courthouse believing he was there to defend a client. Judge Baxter had to come out from his courtroom to calm him down when he was told that he was mistaken. As far as Mr. James knew, the last incident Nona was aware of was when he'd been confused about the time when she'd brought him his supper. Nona glanced over at her father wondering what he'd not told her.

Once again, Dr. Arnold made an entry. Looking at her screen, she said, "Your blood work came back without showing any vitamin B-12 deficiency or thyroid disorder, which sometimes can lead to headaches and feelings of confusion."

"Well, that's good," Nona said hopefully, looking over at her father.

Dr. Arnold continued to scroll through the information on her tablet. "Yes, it is. Blood pressure and EKG were both good, but your MRI, along with your episodes of confusion give me some serious concerns."

"What do you mean by 'serious,' Dr. Arnold?" Nona asked.

Dr. Arnold set her iPad to the side of the desk and leaned forward looking directly at Mr. James. With a grave look on her face, she said, "I believe that we've come to the point where you need to see a neurologist, a specialist in the field."

Nona asked, "What 'field' are you referring to?"

Dr. Arnold said the one word that Nona had hoped she'd never have to hear when it concerned her father. Fear and panic began to fill her mind.

"Alzheimer's."

When Nona looked over at her father, it was obvious by his lack of any reaction that he was not surprised. He was looking straight ahead, waiting for Dr. Arnold to continue.

"I am referring you to Dr. Ledbetter at Savannah Memorial. He's one of the leaders in the field of Alzheimer's. I'll have Kelly set up the appointment. Since it may take a few weeks to get an appointment, I am suggesting that some precautions be taken in the meantime."

This had Mr. James' attention. With interest he asked, "What precautions?"

"I recommend that your main mode of transportation at this point should be walking or riding in a car with someone else driving."

"Are you saying no driving!" Mr. James almost shouted. "I've been driving since I was fourteen years old. I assure you that I have not forgotten the fundamentals of driving an automobile."

Nona put her hand on her father's arm as a comfort and to stop him from exploding at the doctor. "Daddy, let's hear what the good doctor has to say." She turned her attention back to Dr. Arnold.

"I would also recommend that someone stay with you. I don't think you need to be in that big house all alone for now."

"A baby sitter!" Now, her father was shouting. "You want me to hire a baby sitter so they can watch my every move?"

"She's not saying you need a baby sitter, Daddy," Nona said, trying to calm her father. "I've been telling you for years that you need to hire someone full time to fix your meals, keep the house straight, run errands, and things like that."

Looking at Dr. Arnold, she asked, "Isn't that what you're recommending, Doctor?"

"Most certainly," she said. Then with a smile, she added, "You're way too old for a 'baby sitter'."

Mr. James did not smile back. He was distressed and saw nothing humorous in her comments. Nona couldn't remember the last time she'd seen her father this upset. She needed to get him out of this office.

Nona stood and reached across the desk to shake Dr. Arnold's hand. "Thank you, Dr. Arnold. We appreciate your time and help. When do you think we can expect a call from Kelly, concerning our appointment with Dr. Ledbetter?"

"Within the week," Dr. Arnold said, standing to return Nona's handshake. She reached out for Mr. James' hand, but he ignored her gesture and made his way to the door.

Nona gave the doctor an apologetic shrug, and followed her father out of the office.

Nona's father insisted on driving himself home. Nona could tell he didn't want to talk about the bombshell Dr. Arnold had just dropped on them. Truth be told, Nona didn't know what she could say that might offer him comfort, not that her father had asked for it. She could tell that he just wanted to go home and not think about what further testing could show, and how that would determine the quality of the rest of his life. He wasn't the type of man who would dwell on what might happen. He'd wait to get the results before reacting.

As Nona watched her father drive away, she prayed. *Dear Lord, please be with my father and keep him safe.*

She got in her own car and drove to her office. She was glad that Lily wasn't at her desk. Lily would ask questions about her visit to the doctor's office, and Nona wasn't ready to talk about it. Lily had been concerned about Mr. James' behavior since she'd been a witness to the other day.

Lily cared about Mr. James. He'd been the one who'd hired her after her divorce from Matt. She'd needed a job, and he needed a legal secretary. It'd worked out well for both of them. When Nona's secretary, Pamela, went on maternity leave, Lily had filled in. When Pamela made the decision to stay home with her baby, Lily took the job full time, since Mr. James was spending fewer and fewer hours at the office. Nona didn't know what she'd do without Lily.

Nona walked into her office and closed the door. She looked at the files that were on her desk where she'd left them. She sighed, powered up her laptop, and began searching the Internet for information about Alzheimer's. She lost track of time as she looked through different sites about the diagnosis and treatment of the disease. Nothing she read eased her mind.

There was a soft knock at her office door. Lily stuck her head in. "Your three o'clock appointment is here. I printed everything out that you'll need. It's on the table behind you."

Nona had totally forgotten that her clients Jake and Rhonda Cormack were coming in today to finalize their wills. She closed her laptop as she said to Lily, "Give me a minute and then send them in."

It took her a minute to change from concerned daughter mode to her lawyer mode. She reached for the papers, put them in front of her, put a smile on her face, and then rose to greet her clients.

The rest of her day flew by and before she knew it, it was after five. It was time to pack it up for the day. As she was making some notes for tomorrow's meetings, her cell phone rang. She looked down at the number displayed, but didn't recognize it. Normally, at this late hour she'd let it go to voicemail, but she decided to answer it. "Nona Foxx speaking."

A deep baritone voice answered back. "I thought I'd have heard from you by now."

Nona could not place the voice. It sounded familiar, but she couldn't place it. "I'm sorry, but I'm not sure who you are."

"I must not have made an impression on you the other day," the caller said. "This is Monty."

Nona had totally forgotten about Monty. "Ah, Mr. Montgomery," she said, "it's not that I'd forgotten you, it's just that I've been busy dealing with some issues."

"Oh, yes, the break-in," he said. "I'm sure that has consumed much of your time."

Nona was astonished that he knew about the break in. It hadn't been in the papers yet. She wondered how he'd found out about it. She asked, "How in the world did you know about that?"

"I have my ways," he said. "Right now, you have more important things to deal with."

"Like what?" she asked a bit offended.

"Your divorce," he said with a serious tone. "I need to know if you're going to make a stupid mistake and pass up the opportunity to hire the best lawyer, in favor of some chump who'll lose that beautiful house of yours to the other woman?"

What arrogance! Nona could tell he wasn't making a joke. He honestly believed he was the best lawyer. She wasn't quite sure how to respond to his question. Of course, she wanted the 'best lawyer,' but she wasn't convinced that lawyer was him. She wasn't ready to make that decision right now. It'd been a long day for her, and she was in no mood to talk to Mr. Montgomery right now.

"Do you always call up possible clients to harass them and pressure them into hiring you?" she asked sarcastically. "Are you that desperate for business?"

There was a long pause before he answered. "On the contrary, Ms. Foxx," he began, "my business is quite good. I was under the impression that you were most anxious to get this divorce behind you. I figured, with the break-in, you would be even more eager to have things settled. I was simply following up with you." Nona sensed from his tone that her question had offended him.

"I didn't mean to offend you, Monty," Nona said, "but I haven't had time to even think about who I might hire to represent me in my divorce."

With a stern voice, he said, "I find your failure to hire someone to represent your interests foolish. Good day." With his sharp words, he ended the call.

Nona stared at the phone finding it hard to believe he'd just spoken to her like that. He'd just called her "foolish"—a word she was confident that no one had ever called her. What was wrong with this man?

Nona, Dixie, Betty Jo, and Layne left for Savannah bright and early on Saturday morning. Layne drove, since she was the most familiar with the town. Nona wasn't in the mood to shop, but today's shopping trip couldn't be put off any longer. Dixie was the expert shopper of the group. She knew where to go to get the "best bang for your buck"—Dixie's words. Since the insurance claim had yet to be fully processed, Nona was looking for bargains. When she received her insurance settlement for her ruined clothes, she'd take a weekend shopping trip to Atlanta, or maybe even Charleston, to replenish her wardrobe.

Nona had forgotten just how much fun she could have with her friends. The four of them laughed more than they had in a good long time. It felt wonderful to be away from Kerry and the troubles it'd held for her this past week. With the help of her friends, especially Dixie, she'd gotten some great outfits that were stylish and not out-of-fashion, like most of her wardrobe had been. At the end of the day, Nona felt light-hearted and optimistic.

They didn't get back to Kerry until around ten o'clock that night. As Layne pulled up to Dixie's house to let her out, they all noticed that it looked as if every light in the house was on.

"It looks like Alex might be having a party," Betty Jo commented.

Dixie frowned. "Well, if he is, he forgot to tell me."

As she opened her car door, a cacophony of music engulfed her. "What in the world?"

"Do you want me to go in with you, Dixie, to see what's going on in there?" Nona asked.

"No, thanks," Dixie said, with irritation building in her as she got out of the car. "I'm sure this is Jason's deal."

"Well, call us if you decide you need us," Betty Jo called after her. Then turning to Layne and Nona asked, "'Jason's deal'?"

Nona shook her head as she spoke, showing her disapproval. "Yes, she told me all about it the other day, when she came over after the break-in. Jason lost another job and had to move back home."

"Poor Dixie," Betty Jo said, shaking her head. "It was a disaster for her the last time he moved home. You know it can't be much better this time."

"This is going to be hard on both Dixie and Alex," Layne added. "We need to keep that whole family in our prayers."

Layne drove on to Betty Jo's house to drop her off next. As they drove up they could see that her house seemed to be a complete contrast to Dixie's. The only light they could see was the one shining from the front porch.

"Don's gotten into the habit of going to bed around nine-thirty," Betty Jo explained, as she gathered her package and purse from the floor of the back seat. "I was hoping he'd wait up tonight, but guess he was worn out. It seems that he's tired all of the time."

"Is that one of the side-effects of his diabetes?" Nona asked with concern.

"I think it's more of a side-effect of old age," Betty Jo said with a laugh.

Both Nona and Layne laughed at her remark.

"Well, I can relate to that," Layne said.

"Thanks for driving, Layne," Betty Jo said, as she got out of the car. "It was great to spend the whole day with y'all."

Nona and Layne talked the whole way over to Nona's house. Layne got out of the car to help Nona carry her purchases into the house.

As she carried in the last bag from her car, Layne looked around. "Whew! Look at all this stuff! Are you sure you don't want me to help you take these things upstairs?"

Nona looked at the kitchen table where they'd piled the packages. "I'm fine. I can take it up there a little at a time," she said smiling. "I know you want to get home to Mark. Thanks for driving today, Layne," Nona said, giving Layne a hug. "I don't know what I would've done without y'all today. I am truly blessed to have such awesome friends."

Layne returned her hug. "We feel equally blessed, Nona. It was a fun day for all of us,"

When Layne was out the door, Nona reset the alarm, kicked off her shoes, and began gathering packages to carry upstairs to her bedroom. She looked up at the clock on the wall above the stove and saw that it was already eleven-thirty, way past her normal bedtime. As she was deciding if she could handle one more package, she had that creepy feeling that someone was watching her. She stopped and looked around the kitchen. What was it about this kitchen that was making her feel uneasy? Nothing appeared to be out of place. It had to be her imagination working overtime. She shook off the feeling as she grabbed up her bags and made her way upstairs under the weight of her new purchases. She'd unpack the bags tomorrow morning. Right now, all she wanted to do was wash her face, put on her new comfy pajamas, and get into bed. Her last thought before falling asleep was of how nice it was to be sleeping in her own bed.

Chapter Nine

Nona was ready to get back to some resemblance to what had been her normal life. She liked things to be in order. Throughout this past week it seemed that things had gone from bad to worse. It'd begun its decline when Bill served her with divorce papers at her office and continued its downward spiral until it'd hit rock bottom with the worrisome news about her father.

Nona appreciated that she had been one of the fortunate ones who had been blessed with good luck throughout most of her life. She realized that there were people who were lucky and then there were those who seemed to be plagued with bad luck. She'd never shared her thoughts about being lucky with anyone because she was afraid if she acknowledged it out loud, then it might be taken away from her. It was when she was in the fourth grade that she first understood that she had luck on her side. She'd won a contest for creating the best health poster. She'd recognized, even at that young age, that while her poster was good, it was not the best. She believed it'd been her good luck that had brought her the prize.

Nona was aware that she'd worked hard for what she had achieved, but she'd never really had to go through a difficult time filled with struggles. Her hard work always seemed to bring her recognition and rewards, while she watched as others who had worked equally as hard as she never got the recognition they deserved. She was wondering if the good luck she'd enjoyed up until this week was now a thing of the past. This past week had been close to the unluckiest week of her life. She hoped it had been a fluke. She was ready for her life to get back on track.

Nona wanted to put the past week out of her mind. Even though she'd cut back on her work and given Nathan more responsibilities, she still had clients who were depending on her, and a law office to oversee. She decided that the best thing to do was to throw herself into her work.

"Good morning, Lily," Nona said, as she walked into the law office of Foxx and Foxx.

Lily looked up from her computer. "Good morning to you," she said, with a big smile across her face. "It's so good to see you looking so happy this morning."

"Thanks, I decided on my way to work this morning, that I'm going to have a good day," Nona said cheerfully.

Nathan came out of his office when he heard Nona's voice. "Am I glad to see you today," Nathan said as he reached over to give her a quick hug. "Mr. Abbott has been calling to see where we are with his workmans comp lawsuit. Since you were the lead in that case, I didn't have the answers for his questions."

"That's totally my fault, Nathan," Nona said. "With all that's been going on," she'd started to give Nathan a list of excuses, then decided against it.

She simply said, "I'm sorry, but if you can meet with me in my office in about ten minutes, I'll get you up to speed on his case, as well as the other cases we have pending."

Nathan said with relief, "See you in ten."

Nona walked into her office, closing the door behind her. As she looked around, she noticed that her law books were lined up neatly in order on the handcrafted walnut bookshelf, and the floor of her office was clear of debris. The deep brown leather chairs facing her desk were free of clutter, waiting for her clients to take a seat, while her desk was neat and organized. She believed that this was the way a professional law office was supposed to present itself to clients, not the way Michael Montgomery's office looked. She shook her head in disbelief as she realized that she was considering becoming a new client of his, and would have to overlook the chaos of his office. What was it about him—certainly not his office—that had instilled in her the confidence that it would be the correct decision to hire him to represent her interests in her divorce? She hoped she imparted that same confidence in her clients with her well-organized office.

She had just sat down behind her desk and set up her computer when Nathan knocked on her door as he entered. She smiled at him as he sat down in the chair across from her desk with his legal pad in hand.

"Let's get to work," Nona said.

Nona, Nathan, and Lily worked nonstop throughout the day. Nona was almost beginning to feel like herself again. Lily had lunch from *The Grill* delivered to the office so they wouldn't break their rhythm. They each had the sense that a great deal had been accomplished, when they decided to quit work a little after six o'clock. Nona would have continued to work, but she made herself stop, realizing that Nathan and Lily needed to get home to their families. Another factor to her quitting earlier than she normally would was that she needed to check on her father. She hadn't really seen him since the doctor's visit.

Nona made the decision to go home to change clothes before going to her father's house. As she drove down the driveway, she was alarmed by the sight of a white van in her driveway. As she pulled up next to the van, she recognized the slogan on the side of the van that announced *Come Home to Quality* and under that **Pate and Tate Construction**, which was a rival construction company of Dixie's husband, Alex. According to Alex, they would under-bid him on jobs, and their work was often shoddy. She had one question that was immediately on her mind: *What are they doing parked in my driveway?*

As she was getting out of her car to ask that question of either Mr. Pate or Mr. Tate, a car she knew all too well came down the driveway toward her—a graphite Mercedes Benz E350 Sport Sedan. As Nona stood there in disbelief, Bill and Amy emerged from the car. "Hey, Nona," Bill said, as he walked toward her, with Amy following close behind him. "Guess I should have called you to let you know we were coming."

With irritation bordering on anger, Nona said, "Yes, you should have, and why are you here?"

Amy was the one who answered, stepping around Bill to get closer to Nona. In her low-country, sickeningly sweet Southern drawl, she answered, "Well, I asked Mr. Tate to come over here to look things over so he can give us an estimate on a few improvements we want to make to Bill's house."

Anger flooded through Nona as curse words came to her mind as to just what names she'd like to call Miss Amelina May Patten at that moment, but instead, she took several deep breaths to calm down before replying. "I would like you both to leave now," she said in a firm, steady voice, looking directly at Bill, "and take Pate and Tate with you."

"Come on, Nona, you need to be reasonable about this. This was my family's home place," Bill said, as he took a step forward reaching out to her.

"That's right, Bill. This WAS your family's home place." Nona took two steps closer to Bill looking him in the eye, and with all the confidence she could muster, said in a cool voice, "Now, this IS my family home."

Bill said a few words under his breath that Nona couldn't quite hear, but did understand their meaning. Nona did not move away, but stood her ground. It took a few minutes as Bill contemplated what his next move should be. Finally, he walked over to the white van to talk to Pate or Tate or whoever was in the van.

Amy stayed where she was staring at Nona with hatred written on her face. "You're a piece of work, Nona."

"No, Amy, you're wrong," Nona said, as she looked right at her, "I'm the real thing."

It took all of Nona's strength to turn her back on Amy. With shaky legs, she walked to her car, got in, and drove away. She fought back tears as she turned her thoughts away from the scene she'd just left to focus on her father's needs.

Chapter Ten

After her confrontation with Amy and Bill, Nona was more than ready to proceed with the divorce. It was time to choose a lawyer—one who would fight for her. Deep down, she'd known all along that she was going to choose Mr. Michael Montgomery. Even though she despised his arrogance, his complete confidence in his abilities would work in her favor.

Nona decided to tell him in person that she wanted to hire him to represent her in this divorce. She thought it'd be a good idea to have Lily call his office to schedule her appointment. If she called, he might answer, and she wanted to get her thoughts in order before talking to him.

Lily had secured an appointment for her for tomorrow at four-thirty in the afternoon. That would work out well for her. She did have a busy day tomorrow, but could work it in. Before she knew it, she was on her way to his office. She walked in the door and was once again greeted by the same unwelcoming waiting room, with the same wobbly chair beckoning her. She marveled once again how he kept clients coming back when this was their first impression. She almost laughed out loud at the irony of that thought, since she was a returning client.

Nona was alone in the room, but she didn't have to wait for long before a young, tall, blond, strikingly attractive girl walked into the room. She smiled at Nona and in a shockingly high pitched, heavily Southern accented voice said, "Hello, Ms. Nona, I'm Crystal Jean, one of Monty's assistants."

Nona stood and looked in amazement at Crystal Jean who couldn't be much older than sixteen, and wondered if Mr. Montgomery hired high-school students as assistants. She managed to return Crystal's smile as she replied, "Nice to meet you, Crystal Jean."

"Monty's held up in Court today, but should be here in a sec," Crystal Jean said in her grating voice. "Can I get you anything while you wait? Maybe a Coca-Cola?"

"No, thank you. I'm fine." Nona couldn't seem to stop herself from staring at Crystal Jean, who was smacking down hard on her wad of chewing gum.

Just as she was opening her mouth to ask Crystal Jean the obvious question, Monty hurried through the door making apologies. "Please excuse my tardiness, Nona. I hope Crystal Jean explained to you why I was late." To Nona's astonishment, he walked up beside Crystal Jean, put his arm around her waist, and gave her a kiss on the cheek.

The stunned look on Nona's face made Monty laugh out loud. "I guess, by the look on your face, that Crystal didn't tell you she's my daughter."

With surprise and relief, Nona almost shouted, "Your daughter? This is your daughter?"

Looking directly at his daughter, Monty asked firmly, "Did you tell her that you were my assistant?"

Crystal Jean nodded her head, and then looked down at the floor, trying to give the impression that she was ashamed of her actions.

Looking over at Nona, Monty said, "She likes to shock people by telling them that she's my assistant. In truth, she's my seventeen-year-old daughter who's in big trouble right now," he said teasingly.

"Come on, Daddy, you have to admit it's a little funny," she said in a sweet, pleasant voice—one totally different from the one she'd first used with Nona.

She shyly looked over at Nona and asked, "Right?"

"Right!" she agreed, with an embarrassed laugh. "I have to admit that you really took me in. I was about to report your father to the Bar Association."

"I can only imagine what opinion you began to form about me," Monty said shaking his head. "I just hope Crystal's little prank didn't scare you off.

"By the way, she's only called Crystal Jean when she's in trouble," he said as he looked sternly at his daughter. "Isn't that right Crystal Jean?"

"Yes, sir," Crystal said.

To Nona she added, "I'm sorry. I hope you're not angry about my little joke."

"No, I'm in fact relieved," Nona said "to know that your father has a daughter with a sense of humor. Sometimes it's hard to see through his armor of arrogance that he's even human."

Crystal burst out laughing. "I think you found the chink in that armor of his."

To her father she added, "Watch out for this one, Daddy, I think she's got your number."

Crystal kissed her father on the cheek and walked out of the room leaving her father speechlessly looking after her.

"Are we going to conduct business here or in your office?" Nona asked Monty, bringing his attention back to her.

"My office," he said as he led the way down the hall.

Monty opened the door to his office, allowing Nona to go in first. She maneuvered her way through the clutter of books and folders littering the floor to the same leather chair she'd sat in on their first meeting. She moved the pile of papers from the chair and sat down.

Monty made his way to his cluttered desk, sat down and leaned back in his chair. "Tell me, Nona, what brings you back here today. I thought after I called you the other day, it might be the last time we talked."

"I wasn't ready to commit when we talked the other day," Nona said. "But, today I'm ready to hire you as my lawyer."

"Was it my charm that convinced you?" Monty asked smiling.

When he smiled at her with his white teeth and those green eyes shining, Nona was aware once again of just how attractive he was.

"No, closer to your lack of charm," Nona said flatly "It was definitely your arrogant attitude of complete confidence in your abilities."

Deflated, his smile left his face. "I am completely confident that I will get the best settlement for you, and Bill and Amy will never live in your house."

Pleased, Nona said, "That's what won me over, Monty."

Nona didn't leave Monty's office until after seven that evening. She felt good about all they'd accomplished. They got the business part of his fee taken care of, which she found most reasonable. They also decided that Monty would file a counterclaim with the court. They would counterclaim with two statutes—the marriage is irretrievably broken and adultery. That meant that Bill would most likely be served by the end of the week. She wanted Mark, in his official capacity as sheriff, to serve Bill the papers and hoped that Amy was standing right there next to him.

On her way home, Nona called Layne to give her all the details about her meeting with Monty. Layne thought the story about Monty's daughter playing such a trick on Nona was hilarious. It had been a long time since Layne had heard Nona sound so upbeat. She hoped that things were on the upswing for Nona.

When Nona ended her call with Layne, she realized she had told her what was happening with her divorce, but hadn't told her anything about what was happening with her father. In fact, she hadn't told anyone about what Dr. Arnold suspected, or that he was scheduled for further tests in Savannah next week. She didn't know if Nathan had mentioned anything to Layne or Mark about her father's bizarre behavior the other day in the office, but didn't think he had, since Layne had not asked about it. She'd asked Lily not to say anything to her mother since Betty Jo tended to "share" with others when she worked at the hospital. She knew that she needed to tell Layne and Betty Jo as well as Dixie about her father's possible Alzheimer's, but wasn't ready just yet.

Nona had called her father earlier in the day to let him know that she'd be stopping by that evening to discuss the issues that Dr. Arnold had brought up with driving and having help around the house. He'd genuinely seemed receptive to her coming over to talk, which she took as a good sign. As she drove into his driveway and shut off her car engine, it suddenly occurred her that the one person she should be talking to about what was going on with her father was her brother, Riley. She'd totally put Riley's right to know out of her mind. She was ashamed that it'd been weeks since she'd last spoken to him.

I'm a terrible sister!

As she took her cell phone out of her purse, she calculated the time difference between Kerry, Georgia, and San Jose, California. It would be four thirty there, which would be a good time to catch her brother. She pressed Riley's cell number from her contacts.

He answered on the second ring. "Hello, baby sister!" he said sounding excited.

"Hey, Riley," Nona said trying to sound as it this was a casual call.

"What's wrong?" His tone changed immediately to serious. She could never fool her brother.

"It's Dad." Nona didn't understand exactly why, but when she'd heard her big brother's voice, the emotions she'd been holding back overtook her. She began to cry.

Riley was silent, allowing her this time to calm down.

When Nona had regained her composure and could talk coherently, she informed him about their father's strange behaviors, their meeting with Dr. Arnold, and the possible diagnosis of Alzheimer's. She went on to explain the need for further testing, which they were going to have in Savannah next week.

"I'm sitting outside his house right now," Nona said. "I'm here to discuss hiring someone to sit with him, and that he needs to turn over his car keys to me. Riley, you know how well he's going to take this, don't you?"

"I do know, Nona," Riley said sympathetically. "Bless your heart."

They both laughed at Riley's words. Their Great Aunt Alma had always said, "Bless your heart" when she really meant "You're as dumb as a doornail, but you're mighty pretty."

Acting offended, Nona asked, "Why are you saying that?"

"Because it's a dumb thing for you to think that our father is going to just hand over his keys to you, or let you hire someone to watch him," Riley said. "That's why."

"So, Mr. Smart Aleck, what do you suggest I do?"

"You go in there and inform him that his son is on his way to Georgia for a long overdue visit," Riley said.

Nona screamed into the phone, "Really, you'll come home to help him?"

"Well, don't tell him that I'm coming home to 'help him'! He'd resist that."

Riley thought for a moment. "Tell him his wayward son is coming home, but play if off casually."

"How exactly am I going to 'play it off casually', big brother, when you haven't been home in almost three years?"

"Good question, sis, but if anyone can do it, it's you."

"You do know that you're always leaving me holding the bag, don't you?" Nona said, trying not to be irritated with her brother.

"I do know that," Riley said, sounding sincere. "I am sorry for that, but you know my history with Dad has always been complicated."

Unpleasant memories of the arguments between her father and Riley came flooding back to Nona. Their father had always been hard on Riley for not living up to his high expectations. She knew that was why Riley had moved clear across the country, and rarely came home. But now he was coming home. Nona thought she might start crying again, with the relief she felt that Riley was coming home to help.

"Don't worry about it, I'll think of something to tell him so he won't think that you're just coming home because he's sick."

"You do know that I'm coming home for you, to help you, because that's what big brothers do for their little sisters."

"I do know that, Riley," Nona said, as she swallowed the lump in her throat. "Thanks, big brother."

Riley ended the call saying he would text his flight information.

Nona got out of her car and walked into her father's house, searching her brain for ideas on how to put a positive spin on the news that Riley was coming home.

Dear Lord, I could sure use your help with a few ideas about now.

"Hey, Daddy, it's me," Nona called out, as she walked in the back door of her father's house.

Silence greeted her.

"Daddy, where are you?" she called out, as she opened the door to his study. Her father was not behind his desk. She continued to call out as she searched the house. She tried not to panic when she saw that he wasn't in his bedroom. She noticed that his bathroom door was closed. She tapped on the closed bathroom door.

"Daddy, are you in there?"

No answer came from the other side. She turned the knob and looked in. Her father was sprawled out on the bathroom floor with his face turned away from her.

"Daddy, are you all right?" Nona asked as she hurried to him. "Did you fall?"

Her father slowly turned his head toward her. Eyes that were empty of all understanding met hers. Fear gripped her heart as tears began to stream down her face.

This can't be happening!

Nona took several deep breaths, willing herself to be calm. She sat down next to her father and reached around him to lift him into a more comfortable position. She spoke softly as she kept repeating, "Daddy, it's okay. I'm here. It's all going to be okay."

With great effort, she could get him up into a sitting position with his back against the wall. He hadn't spoken a word or helped in any way. He just kept staring at her with his uncomprehending eyes. She sat on the bathroom floor in front of him with her hand on his chest holding him upright. She found that when she let go of him, he would begin to slide down the wall or topple over. It was as if his body could no longer remember how to sit. While holding onto her father with one hand, she used the other hand to fish her cell phone from her back pocket. It was a blessing from God that she had not put her phone back in her purse after talking to Riley.

She pressed 9-1-1.

A soothing female voice answered, "What is your emergency?"

"I need help. I found my father collapsed on the bathroom floor. He's awake, but unresponsive," Nona said into the phone, trying to keep her voice calm while hoping she was giving out enough information for the nice voice on the other end to immediately send help.

"What is your address?"

Nona carefully gave the dispatcher her father's address, and told them they needed to come in the back door since it was unlocked. All she heard was silence on the other end, and for a moment thought their call had been disconnected. Then she heard, "I've dispatched an ambulance, Ma'am. Do you want me to stay on the phone with you until they arrive?"

"No, thank you, but please tell them to hurry." She ended the call.

She looked at her father. She had never seen him look so helpless. His eyes were closed, but she could feel his steady breathing as she held him up. She pressed the speed dial number for the one person she knew she could count on to come running to help.

"Hey, how was..." Layne began before Nona cut her off.

"Layne, it's Daddy! Something is terribly wrong." She knew her voice was filled with the fear and panic that was overtaking her mind, but the instant she'd heard Layne's voice her emotions had come pouring out.

"Nona, you need to calm down. Tell me where you are."

Nona knew that Layne was right, but was finding it hard to breathe normally as she answered, "At his house... in his bathroom... come in the back door."

"I'm on my way," Layne said, as she grabbed her car keys from the hook by the garage door.

As Nona waited for help, she prayed out loud the first prayer that came to her mind as she held her father close.

Our Father, which are in heaven, hallowed be thy name...

Layne arrived about five minutes after the ambulance. She found Nona standing outside her father's master bath, anxiously trying to see what was happening inside with the paramedics tending to her father. Nona reached out to her when she saw her come around the corner. Layne wrapped her arms around Nona.

The two of them stood there holding hands as they silently watched the paramedics lift Mr. James onto a stretcher. They kept asking him questions, but he hadn't responded. Nona and Layne followed them out the back door and watched as they loaded his stretcher into the ambulance.

One of the paramedics stayed back to talk with Nona. "We're taking him to the Memorial General Hospital."

"I'll meet you there," Nona said, wondering how she would be able to drive.

"I'll drive," Layne said.

Nona gave her a grateful look as she opened the passenger door of Layne's car.

Layne started the car and pulled in behind the ambulance to follow it to the hospital.

"Oh, Layne," Nona said in a shaky voice, "I've never seen Daddy like this." Looking at Layne she added. "I never thought he'd go this fast."

Layne looked at Nona with concern. "Has he been ill?" Nona hadn't said a word to her about her father being sick.

"I'm so sorry, Layne, but I haven't told anyone except Riley about what's been going on with my Dad," Nona said as she looked out of the car's side window. "I just didn't want to talk about it with anyone. I felt that if I said it out loud then that would make it true."

Layne nodded her head, letting Nona know that she understood what she meant, but said nothing, not wanting to interrupt Nona.

"I've noticed little things that Daddy has done or forgotten to do that seemed odd, but not alarming," Nona began. "But then a few days ago, he came to the office and was acting just plain weird. He thought he had to prepare for a case that he won years ago. He tried to brush it off as a lesson for Nathan, but we all knew that wasn't the reason he'd come.

"That was when warning bells began to go off in my head. I got him an appointment with Dr. Arnold. We met with her last week. She's made him an appointment to go to Savannah for further testing," Nona swallowed deeply as she looked directly into Layne's eyes, "for Alzheimer's."

The words hung in the air between them. Layne's heart broke for Nona. She knew how much Nona's father meant to her, and she knew what a terrible disease Alzheimer's was. She didn't know of any words that would offer Nona the comfort she wanted to give her. She simply said sincerely, "I'm so sorry."

As they pulled into a parking place next to the emergency room entrance, they saw Mark and Aaron standing at the entrance.

"We thought it'd be better to meet you here rather than go to the house," Mark said, as Nona and Layne reached him.

"How's Mr. James?" Aaron asked Nona as they walked into the ER together.

"I wish I knew," she said worriedly, looking around for the stretcher that held her father.

A nurse came toward them to address the whole group. "Are y'all here for the patient they just brought in by ambulance?"

"Yes, that's my father," Nona said anxiously.

Giving Nona a dismissive smile, she said. "I need for you to wait out here. The doctor is evaluating the patient right now, and will be out to talk with you when he finishes." She turned around, leaving the group staring after her.

"I guess we wait," Aaron said.

Remembering the hours that turned into days waiting for Mark to wake up, Layne said, "I hate waiting."

"I think we all do, Layne, but sometimes that's all we can do," Mark said as he walked over to the chairs against the wall and sat down. All but Nona followed him, taking a seat to wait while they watched Nona pace back and forth.

Finally, a doctor walked out from the curtained room where he'd been tending to Mr. James. Nona hurried over to him as the others joined her. Layne recognized Dr. Berry right away. He'd been the doctor who'd taken care of Mark when he'd been brought to the ER after his accident.

"It would seem that Mr. Foxx hit his head pretty hard when he fell this afternoon. He has a pretty nasty bump on his temple. His confusion has me concerned. I'd like to keep him overnight for observation," Dr. Berry explained.

"I think you should be aware of the fact that my father's confusion may not be related to the fall," Nona began. "He's had several episodes of erratic behavior in the past few weeks. His doctor suspects Alzheimer's."

"That does help to explain a few things," Dr. Berry said, "but I still want to keep him overnight."

"If you think that's best," Nona said.

"He'll be taken up to the third floor as soon as a room becomes available," Dr. Berry said as he turned to leave.

"May I see him?" Nona asked.

"Of course," Dr. Berry said, as he indicated for Nona to follow him.

Nona reached out to take Layne's hand in hers. "Please come with me," Nona said.

Layne took her hand. "Right here with you," she said, as she squeezed Nona's hand.

The two of them followed the doctor to the curtained room. As Nona entered, she expected to find her father on a gurney looking frail and vulnerable, with tubes running in and out of his poor, defenseless body. Instead, she was met with the scene of her determined father sitting on the side of the bed arguing with a nurse who was trying to make him lie down.

"I'm walking out of here. I'll not be treated as if I'm an invalid," her father shouted at the young nurse who was only trying to carry out the doctor's orders.

"Sir, I need you to calm down and lie back," the nurse said, as she placed both hands on him trying to restrain him.

When Mr. James saw his daughter enter, he looked at her with the determined eyes that Nona recognized. "Get this young lady to release me immediately."

Nona rushed to him as she tried to make him understand. "Daddy, she's trying to help you."

"I don't need her help," he said with authority. "I'm perfectly capable of leaving this institution under my own power,"

In a calm quieting voice, Nona offered her father the facts. Her father always needed to know the facts in order to deal with a situation. "You're not leaving. You must spend the night so they can make an assessment as to whether or not you have a concussion, as well as making sure that there's not another consequence as a result of the fall you took this afternoon."

Mr. James stopped quarreling with the nurse as he listened to Nona's explanation. He thought for a minute about what she'd just told him. He turned to the nurse and asked, "Well, why didn't you tell me that?"

The nurse gave Mr. James a patient smile as she helped him back into his bed. "I'm sorry, Mr. Foxx. I should have told you."

"From now on, tell me before you do anything else to disturb me," Mr. James said in a gruff voice. "Do not simply assume that your patient knows your thoughts."

Nona shook her head in exasperation. "Daddy, be nice," she urged him.

Looking at Nona he protested, "I am being nice."

After Nona had settled her father in his room, and was satisfied that he was comfortable, she left him in the capable hands of the Memorial General staff. Layne and Mark had invited her to grab a bite to eat with them, but all she wanted to do was go home. As she walked out of the hospital into the crisp night air, she was thankful that Aaron had been kind enough to bring her car from her father's house to the hospital parking lot. She didn't have any problems finding her car. It was right where Aaron had said it would be. She got in and headed for home.

As she drove, she thought about all that had happened throughout this month and that it was only half over. She knew she'd have more to deal with in the upcoming weeks, but decided she would put those concerns to the side. She needed to put her mind on a positive spin. As she drove home, she mentally made a list of the things she was grateful for:

Her father hadn't been hurt badly in his fall.
Riley would be home tomorrow.
She had a new wardrobe of clothes.
She was going to sleep in her own bed tonight.
She had good friends who were there for support and help when she needed it.
She had a competent, although arrogant, lawyer who would fight for her.

Before she knew it, she was pulling into her driveway. As she looked at her house, the thought occurred to her that someone else might think of her house, standing there dark and silent, as eerie. However, to Nona, her house was a welcoming, peaceful harbor, protecting her from the stress and pressures that were working to wreck her life. Knowing she had hit total exhaustion about three hours ago, she couldn't wait to crawl into her bed. She got out of her car and took a deep calming breath. It was all going to be okay. She was home.

Chapter Eleven

After a restful night's sleep, Nona fixed herself a light breakfast of cinnamon raisin toast, apple juice, and coffee. She was anxious to get back to the hospital to see how her father was doing this morning. She hoped he had been able to get some sleep. She knew it was hard to get any rest in the hospital, what with nurses waking you up every few hours to check vital signs. She checked her email while she ate. She had several from people who had heard about her father being taken to the hospital by ambulance. She wasn't sure if they were inquiring about his health out of concern or curiosity. She replied to the few she felt were genuinely concerned and ignored the rest.

As Nona was preparing to close out her email and shut-down her laptop, one email caught her attention. There was no subject, but it was the sender that made alarm bells go off in her head. It was from "GOTYOURATTENTIONNOW." When she first noticed it, it had seemed like it was a collection of random letters, but when she looked closer she wondered if it might be a cryptic message of "Got Your Attention Now." She started to double click on it to open the message, but stopped herself. If she opened it, it might be one of those emails that were sent out to infect her computer. Nona decided that she needed to show this to someone who knew more about technology than she did. Both Nathan and Lily were good with technical things. She'd show it to them.

After putting her plate, glass, and cup into the dishwasher, and tidying up her kitchen, she took a good look around. What was it that had made her feel so uneasy the other night when she'd come into the kitchen after her shopping trip to Savannah? She didn't see anything out of place or missing. She chalked the feeling up, once again, to her stressful week—it had surely been one of her worst. She took her car keys from the bowl by the door, grabbed up her purse, and disarmed and reset the newly installed security system as she left.

When Nona got to her father's hospital room, he was sitting up on the side of his bed picking at his breakfast. She walked over to him to give him a kiss on his cheek and a hug. She looked at his tray of food and said enthusiastically, "That looks pretty good for hospital food."

"It's not terrible," her father said in a tired voice.

He did look tired. She asked with concern, "How are you feeling this morning, Daddy?"

Putting down his fork and looking directly at her, he said in a weary voice, "If they'd let me get some rest I might feel better, but someone was in my room all night long, either watching me or poking me or sticking me." In a loud voice he added, "How do you think I feel!"

"I'm sorry, Daddy," Nona said, as she pressed the call button. "Let me see if I can find out when they're going to release you."

"I can tell you that they're not releasing me soon enough," Mr. James said.

A nurse's voice came through the speaker. "Yes, Mr. Foxx, how may I help you?"

Nona answered, "This is his daughter. Can you tell me when my father will be released to go home?"

Nona and her father waited in silence for an answer.

A young doctor Nona had never seen before walked into her father's room. He held out his hand for Nona as he introduced himself. "I'm Dr. Davis."

Nona took his hand shaking it as she said, "Nice to meet you. I'm Nona Foxx."

Speaking to both Nona and her father, Dr. Davis got right to the point of his visit. "Dr. Arnold contacted me to ask me to check on your father. I specialize in Geriatrics. She told me of her concerns about your father's recent behavior and the possibility that he may be showing signs of Alzheimer's."

Hearing once again the pronouncement of the possibility that her father could have Alzheimer's gave Nona a sick feeling in the pit of her stomach.

Dr. Davis continued. "After your episode last night, Mr. Foxx, I would like to conduct further testing. I don't want to jump to any conclusions until we have the results of these tests."

Nona said hopefully, "Do you mean that there's a possibility his behavior may not be due to Alzheimer's?"

"I'm saying that we need to run more tests before making that assumption," Dr. Davis said.

Mr. James cleared his throat as he stood to announce in his authoritative voice, "Dr. Davis, I'm not sure what tests you intend to conduct, but I can assure you that I will not be spending another night in this hospital."

Looking at Mr. James with all seriousness, Dr. Davis said, "I can assure you that I will not be releasing you until the tests have been completed."

"Then I shall be leaving AMA," Mr. James said defiantly.

Nona knew her father meant what he said. He would leave AMA—Against Medical Advice. She also knew that he needed to have whatever tests Dr. Davis needed to run, in order to find the underlying cause of what had been causing his disconcerting behaviors. She needed to offer a compromise so each could be satisfied.

She asked Dr. Davis, "Do these tests require that my father be a hospitalized?"

Dr. Davis thought for a minute before reluctantly answering, "Not necessarily, I suppose."

Nona continued. "If he was released to his home with someone with him at all times, and that someone could make sure he was available for all tests and procedures that you deemed necessary, would you consider releasing my father?"

Once again, Dr. Davis took a minute to consider her proposal. "I would," he said, and then added, "but I won't, unless I have your assurance that he will have someone with him at all times."

Looking confidently at the doctor, Nona said, "I can assure you that someone will be with him at all times."

Nona's father gave her a curious look as he asked, "You're going to stay with me?"

"Not me," Nona said. "Riley." It was then she realized he didn't know about Riley. She'd intended to tell her father about Riley's promise to come help when she'd found him on the bathroom floor.

"Riley?" her father asked incredulously.

"Yes, Daddy, Riley," Nona confirmed. "I talked to him last night before I discovered you sprawled out on the bathroom floor. He told me he wanted to come home to check on me because he was concerned about how I was handling the situation with Bill leaving me." She knew she wasn't being completely truthful with her father, but hoped he'd accept the news that Riley was coming home, if he thought Riley had already decided to come home out of concern for her situation with Bill. He wouldn't like it if he thought Riley was coming home to take care of him.

"Either Riley can stay with you or you can stay in the hospital," Nona said sweetly. "Your choice." She knew which one he would choose, even if he did have to depend on Riley.

"Fine, Riley can stay with me," Mr. James said without enthusiasm.

"Then I'll sign the papers for you to be discharged as soon as Riley gets here to pick you up," Dr. Davis said with a smile.

Mr. James looked at the doctor and said with annoyance. "Excellent!"

Nona left her father at the hospital. She could tell that he was upset with her, but she also knew that he'd get over it. He always did. Riley had texted her that his plane had safely landed and he would be there in his rented car around three o'clock that afternoon. She'd told him to come straight to the hospital when he got into town. She needed to be there when Riley got there, to be the buffer between her father and brother. Their relationship had always been unpredictable, but since her mother passed away it could become explosive without the right influence. Nona intended to be the influence they both needed.

She had just enough time before Riley's arrival to stop by her office. As she was driving there, Nona couldn't get the strange email sender name out of her mind. She tried to focus on other things, but that sender name kept coming back to her. She'd wanted to believe that it was one of those malicious emails that were sent out globally to wreak havoc on the unsuspecting email subscriber, but it felt like something more sinister. Instead of heading to the office, she turned toward the Kerry County Sheriff Department. She needed to show this to Mark.

Nona was relieved that the first person she saw as she walked in the door of the Kerry County Sheriff Department, pulling her laptop bag behind her, was Aaron.

"Miss Nona," Aaron said, looking at her with surprise, "what are you doing here?"

"I just stopped by to see the best-looking deputy in Kerry, Georgia," she said as she reached over to give him a hug.

With a sly grin on his face, Aaron answered, "Well, give me a minute, and I'll see if I can find him."

Nona punched him playfully on his arm. "Well, if you can't locate him, I'll settle for you."

They both laughed.

When they'd finished laughing, Nona said with a serious tone, "Truthfully, Aaron, I'm here because I'm concerned about an email I found when I checked my email this morning."

Aaron looked at her with concern, and asked in a low voice, "Was it pornographic?"

"Well, the thing is, Aaron, I didn't even open it. It was the sender's name that caught my attention."

"That must be some weird name if it stopped you from opening it. What is it?" Aaron asked.

"I think it'd be best if I show you," Nona said. "Is there a place where I can plug in my laptop, preferably somewhere private?"

Aaron looked around the busy office. "If Dad's in his office, we can set up there. I'm sure he'll want to see it, too."

Nona followed Aaron to Mark's office. He knocked on the door and opened it when he heard his father say, "Come in."

Mark was sitting behind his desk with his reading glass perched on his nose intently studying a document from the file folder that was open on his desk. When he saw that Nona was walking in behind Aaron, he quickly closed the folder, took off his glasses, and stood up.

"Nona, what a surprise," he said, as he moved from behind his desk to greet her.

"Sorry to barge in on you, Mark, but something's come up that has me more than just concerned," Nona said. "I'd like for you and Aaron to take a look at it and, hopefully, tell me that I'm overreacting."

As Nona was talking, she removed her laptop from her bag and set it up on the conference table, to the left of Mark's desk by the window. Nona powered it on. When the home screen came up, she navigated to her email. Mark and Aaron stood next to her bending close to the computer as she began to scroll through her emails. Nona pointed out the strange grouping of letters, "GOTYOURATTENTIONNOW." As

Mark and Aaron stared at the letters, they saw the same four words that Nona had deciphered earlier—Got Your Attention Now.

"I didn't open it because I was worried that it might be a strange way someone was trying to infect my computer, but the more I think about it, the more it disturbs me."

"I think you were right to not open it, Nona," Mark agreed. "I think we need to have Nate, our tech guy, take a look at this."

"Are y'all thinking what I'm thinking," Nona asked, as she looked over at Mark and Aaron, "that this might have something to do with the person who broke into my house?"

"I'd rather not jump to any conclusions, Nona, let's see what we can find out," Mark said, hoping to reassure her. "Can you leave the computer here for Nate to check it out?"

"Sure," Nona said, "I won't need it today. I'm going to be busy refereeing my father and Riley for the rest of the day."

"Riley's here?" Aaron asked excitedly.

"Well, he's not here yet, but he'll be here soon," Nona said, as she gathered her things to leave.

"I have some great memories of Mr. Riley telling all of us kids stories of his adventures," Aaron said with a smile on his face. "Does he still travel all over the world?"

"How can you possibly remember those stories, Aaron? You were just a toddler when he was traveling for Boeing. Plus, I don't know if you should even believe those outrageous stories he told," Nona said. "I never did."

"Well, either way, he made me believe every word."

"I hope your father's going to be okay," Mark said, interrupting their reminiscing. "I know he's been going through a rough time lately. Tell him we're praying for him."

As Nona turned to leave Mark's office, she said, "Thanks, Mark. Let me know when I can get my computer back. I can't wait to hear what Nate finds out about that email."

Mark called Nate Billingham into his office and explained how the sender had used a cryptic user name to send Nona an email. Nate took the laptop with him to his office, promising to get to work on it right away. Mark was surprised twenty minutes later, when Nate appeared at his door with a piece of paper in his hand.

"You need to look at this, Sheriff," Nate said, as he set a computer print-out down in front of Mark.

Mark put on his glasses and picked up the paper. He read through the message, and then looked up at Nate with concern. "This is the message from that email?"

"Yes, Sir."

Mark read through it again, carefully noting the spelling and punctuation errors. Were these mistakes made by an illiterate or were they intentional, to give the illusion that an uneducated person had written this message?

You saw what I did to your bedroom. I nothing compaired to what Im going to do to you if you egnore me again.
DO I GOT YOUR ATTENTION NOW?????????

He took off his glasses, placed them on his desk, and leaned forward, rubbing his temples. There was no doubt about it; someone had sent this email as a threat to Nona. Mark was taking this warning seriously after seeing what this person had done to her bedroom.

"Were you able to find out anything else about this email?" Mark asked.

"Yes, sir, the email was sent from a fake email server. It's one of those email servers set up to give anonymity to the sender. The sender can make up any name they want as their user name. I'm sorry to say that there's no way to trace who essentially sent that email."

Nate handed Mark his notes as he explained," I made some notes about that company. I know it's not much help, but that's all I could find."

Mark studied the information Nate had just handed him. He was right about it not being of much help in learning the identity of who had sent the threatening email.

"By the way," Nate said, "I know you noticed the errors throughout the email. I think they were deliberate, to make us think that someone who's not very smart sent the email. In my opinion, it took an educated, informed person to set up that email account."

"If you're right about that, Nate, that's even more disturbing," Mark said. "Thanks for your help."

"Sorry I couldn't find out who sent it," Nate said, as he left Mark's office.

Mark sat back in his chair as he thought about what Nate had just told him about the email. It was now up to Mark to break the news to Nona about this latest development. He wished he could put off telling her. She was going through so much now with her father and her impending divorce. He hated to add to her burden with more distressing news, but knew he needed to tell her sooner rather than later.

Dixie finally had the house to herself, and was just sitting down to read when her cell phone rang. From the ring-tone, she knew it was Layne calling. "Hey, Layne," Dixie said into her cell phone.

"Hey, Dixie, I wanted to give you an update on Nona's father."

Layne had called both Dixie and Betty Jo the night before to let them know about Mr. James being taken by ambulance to the hospital. Both of them had wanted to go to the hospital to be there to support Nona, but Layne had convinced them that it would be better to wait until they found out exactly what was going on medically with Nona's father. Dixie listened as Layne filled her in on what had transpired since they'd talked last night.

The most surprising thing to Dixie was that Riley was coming back to Kerry to help Nona with their father. She couldn't recall the last time she'd seen Riley, but was sure it'd been well over five years. It would surely be a blessing for Nona to have Riley here to share in the challenge of caring for their father. Layne ended with telling Dixie that Mr. James would be going home today, but needed to have someone with him always.

As Dixie put her cell phone down on the end table next to her chair, she couldn't stop thinking about Nona and all she was going through right now. It troubled her that Grace seemed to be turning her back on Nona and defending her father's affair, which had broken her mother's heart.

How could a daughter do something like that to her own mother, who'd always supported and encouraged her to be the best she could be?

Dixie had often shaken her head in amazement as she'd watched throughout the years, at all that Nona had done for Grace—the expensive private piano lessons, the piano recitals, the private college, the extravagant wedding, etc. A few times, she'd even been upset with Nona for doing too much for Grace. It had made her feel that maybe she wasn't doing enough for her own children.

Now, she felt ashamed of those times when she'd been agitated with Nona. Her heart ached for her. She knew that Nona would always love Grace, no matter what. She couldn't imagine how she would feel if her children treated her the way Grace was treating Nona, but she knew she'd still love them and be proud of them, no matter what they did to her, just like Nona.

She smiled as she thought about her children now. She'd always been so proud of Hailey, who was able to handle a pediatric medical practice and keep up with three small children. Jason had always had her heart from the minute she'd held him in her arms. He was going through a rough time right now, after losing his job, but she was sure things would turn around for him soon. She loved them both so much that it brought tears to her eyes.

Every day, when she and Alex said their morning prayers, they prayed for their children and grandchildren, and those who were going through difficult times. Dixie realized that with all the troubles that Nona was going through while facing an uncertain future, they'd need to ask God for an extra blessing of perseverance for Nona.

Betty Jo had been called early that morning to fill in on the pediatrics floor for a nurse who'd called in sick. Even though she was retired, she found that most weeks she'd get called to work two or three days. With the nursing shortage at the hospital, she was glad she could help. However, she liked that it was ultimately her decision as to whether or not she'd work that day. Most days she'd take the job. She'd never admit it out loud, but she often got bored just being home all the time.

She loved working on the pediatrics floor, especially on the day shift, but today had been an especially rough shift. Two children had been severely injured in a car accident, due to the fact that neither one was properly placed in their car seats. The mother had simply placed the children down on the back seat and covered them with a blanket. She'd run head-on into a tree when she failed to follow the curve of the road. The result had left the children with massive internal injuries and motherless. They had both undergone major surgery and were still in critical condition. Betty Jo had been the primary care giver to the two-year-old boy. She wasn't sure that he would make it through to the next day.

She had just walked out of the hospital to get into her car when her cell phone rang. It was Dixie calling.

"Hey, Dixie," Betty Jo said in a weary voice.

Dixie could tell from her tone that something was wrong. "Are you okay, Betty Jo?"

"Rough day today." Betty Jo sighed as she explained, "I worked on the pediatric floor today with a little boy who was severely injured in a car accident, and it all could have been prevented if his mother had buckled him into his car seat."

"Oh, I'm so sorry," Dixie said. "You can call me back later if that would be better for you."

"No, that's okay," Betty Jo said, as she opened her car door. "Now's as good a time as ever." She felt her body begin to relax as she sat down behind the wheel.

"I just talked to Layne, and I wanted to fill you in on what's going on with Nona."

Dixie tried to remember everything that Layne had told her so Betty Jo could be fully informed, but worried that she may have left off something important. She should have made notes when she'd talked to Layne.

"I think that's everything," Dixie said in conclusion.

"I'm glad to hear that Mr. James is going home today. I thought for sure that they'd keep him a few days to run some tests and such."

Concerned, Betty Jo asked, "Is Nona going to stay with him?"

"Oh, my goodness, I knew I'd left out something important," Dixie almost screamed into the phone. "Riley is coming to stay with Mr. James. He's probably here already."

"Riley!" Betty Jo said excitedly. "That's great. He can be a big help to Nona."

"Well, let's hope so," Dixie said without enthusiasm. "You know he wasn't much help when Ms. Edith was sick."

Betty Jo had forgotten about that. Riley didn't come until the day of her funeral. "Well, the fact that he's here now shows he wants to help out," she said hopefully.

"You're right about that," Dixie agreed.

Betty Jo asked, "Do we need to do anything to help out?"

"Nothing I can think of right now, except keep Nona in your prayers," Dixie said.

"I will."

When they ended their call, Betty Jo started her car and drove straight home. She wanted to take a long hot shower and put on her baggy t-shirt and her comfy pants with the elastic waistband. Then she just wanted to "chill," as her granddaughter Kendall would put it.

Chapter Twelve

Nona was sitting in Memorial General's lobby waiting for Riley when she got the troubling phone call from Mark. She was surprisingly calm as Mark gave her the alarming details of the contents of that email. As she listened, it came to her that this was what she'd correctly expected when she first saw that foreboding username.

"Can you think of anyone who would want to hurt you in any way? Anyone you once paid attention to and now are not?" Mark asked. "It might be a former client that may have it in for you."

Nona thought about his question before answering. She knew that throughout her career she had clients who were not happy with the outcome of a legal problem, but she couldn't think of anyone who had ever been upset with the way she handled the case. This threat seemed more personal, not professional. She was well aware that not everyone liked her, but couldn't think of anyone who would want to do her harm for not paying attention to them. It made no sense to her.

"I can't think of anyone, Mark."

"Nona, I believe you should take this threat seriously," Mark warned. He waited for Nona's response. When she said nothing, he continued. "I would advise against staying at your house alone until we can find out who sent this email."

Nona was more determined than ever that whoever was threatening her was not going to scare her away from her own home. "I'm not leaving my home, Mark," Nona declared. "If whoever is doing this thinks they have scared me away, then they win and I lose."

With a stern tone, Mark said, "Nona, this isn't a matter of winning or losing. This could be a matter of life or death."

"I've made up my mind, Mark," Nona said with determination. "I'm not leaving."

Mark was so angry with Nona that he wanted to shake her. Maybe he could shake some sense into that thick skull of hers, but he'd known her a long time and knew that when she'd made up her mind you couldn't budge her. It was a waste of time and effort to even try.

Mark let out a long breath before responding. Defeated, he said, "You are one hard-headed woman, Nona Jane Foxx. You win this round, but I am sending a patrol car there to watch your house."

"Suit yourself," Nona snapped back. Then she added in a nicer voice, "I do appreciate you, Mark. I know you're worried, but don't be. Everything's going to be fine."

"Nona, don't take any chances. Be aware of what's going on around you," Mark warned.

"Thanks for the advice, Mark, and right now I'm aware that my big brother, whom I haven't seen in a very long time, is walking in the door." Nona said excitedly. "Bye, Mark!"

As she watched Riley walk through the door of the hospital, she noticed that his salt and pepper hairline had receded, and his girth had expanded since the last time she'd seen him. He was still wearing his thick glasses with old-fashioned horn-rimmed frames. He'd struggled with poor eyesight since he was a toddler. His glasses had gotten thicker with each visit to the eye doctor. When he'd been in high school someone had referred to the thickness of his glasses as "coke-bottles."

He was wearing a light blue, long-sleeved shirt, buttoned all the way up to his neck with one of his signature bow ties. This one was dark navy and red plaid. Nona loved Riley's bow ties, and always found them endearing. He'd worn them since he was a child and had hundreds of them stored in a special place in his closet.

Others might look at Riley and think "nerd," but Nona had always thought "extraordinary." She watched him as he glanced around the lobby, looking for her. When he spotted her, his face lit up with a big smile. She rushed into Riley's outstretched arms. They stood in the middle of the lobby for several minutes wrapped up in each other's arms. As Nona embraced her brother, she realized just how much she'd missed him, and how truly happy she was that he was here with her. Tears began to stream down her face.

"Oh, Riley," Nona cried into his shoulder, "I've missed you so very much."

Riley squeezed her a little tighter. "I've missed you too, little sister."

Releasing Nona, he said, "Let me get a good look at you." Smiling down at her, he added, "You get better looking every time I see you."

Nona laughed as she reached up to kiss his cheek. "And you can still tell the tallest tales."

She put her arm in his. "Come on, let's go see Dad. I know he's probably climbing the walls."

They talked non-stop as they went up the elevator and walked down the hall to their father's room. When they got to his room, they found that the door was closed. Riley took a deep breath as he pushed the door open. "Here we go," he said in a low voice.

Mr. James wasn't in his bed, but was sitting in the chair beside the bed looking through the newspaper. Before Riley was fully in the room, his father said as he looked at his watch, "I was under the impression that you were to arrive at three o'clock. I have now waited thirty-seven minutes past that hour."

Riley was taken aback momentarily by his father's unwelcoming words, but soon regained his composure. "Sorry, for the delay. I miscalculated the traffic patterns of those heading South out of Atlanta," he said with a smile, as he held out his hand for his father to take.

Nona stood at the door watching their exchange. She was dumbfounded by Riley's reaction to their father's chiding. In the past, his response would have been one of anger, and tempers would have escalated from there. However, this time, Riley had defused the situation by apologizing. She held her breath as she waited for her father's reply.

Instead of shaking Riley's hand, Mr. James grasped it to help him get out of his chair. "Now that you're finally here, take me home."

He walked past his son and stopped in front of Nona. "Don't just stand there. Let's go."

She put her hand on her father's shoulder as she gently said, "Daddy, you can't just walk out of the hospital. Sit back down while I find out what we need to do to get you released."

Agitated, Mr. James said, "I've already done all of that while I was needlessly waiting for the two of you to arrive."

"I believe it's hospital policy to leave by way of wheelchair," Riley said. "I'll find someone to help, and we can be on our way."

After a few delays and a heated discussion about which car he would travel home in, Mr. James was on his way home in Nona's car. Nona was glad that she was driving her father home. This gave her a chance to talk to him alone.

"Daddy, we need to talk about a few things before we get to your house," Nona said.

Mr. James had been looking out the window. He turned toward Nona, but said nothing.

Nona continued, "You do remember that the only way the doctor would release you was if someone was with you at all times, right?"

"Of course, I remember," Mr. James answered.

"Well, Daddy, that someone is Riley. He's flown all the way here from San Jose to be with you."

"What's your point, Nona?"

"My point is that you need to be nice." Nona could feel her father bristle at her suggestion. "Daddy, you weren't very nice to Riley at the hospital."

Mr. James sighed, "Nona, I need for both you and Riley to understand that I find myself in a difficult situation." In a low voice he explained, "I am not comfortable asking for, nor accepting, help from others. I find it exceptionally arduous accepting aid from a son who has never shown the slightest interest in offering his assistance before now."

Her father's words broke Nona's heart. She was well aware that he didn't like to ask others for help. He was a stubborn man who'd always prided himself on his independence.

"I'm so sorry, Daddy," Nona said, trying hard to be understanding.

He turned away to look out the window again as he said, "I'll try to be more amenable, but I'm not making any promises."

Nona was hopeful that her father might at least try.

Nona and Riley worked together to get their father settled back into his house. They both knew that one of the first things he'd want to do was go into his office alone. They understood he wouldn't want either of them to stay with him. When Mr. James shut the door to his office, both Nona and Riley sighed with relief, hoping that this meant that he was going back to his normal routine.

"Which room do you want to stay in?" Nona asked.

"I thought I'd probably stay in my old room," Riley said.

"You do remember the room you are referring to was totally redesigned several years ago," Nona laughed. "I don't think there is anything in that room that you would even recognize. Plus, it's clear upstairs at the other end of the house. I think it'd be much better if you'd stay in the room next to Dad's."

"Mom's room?" Riley asked with alarm. "I don't think I could stay there, Nona."

Riley knew that there were too many memories associated with his mother's old room. He was thinking about an alternative when an idea struck him. "What if I stayed in Miss Nadeen's old room? It's downstairs."

Nona thought about the tiny room that their housekeeper had lived in when they were children. "Do you think you'd be comfortable in that small of a space, Riley?"

"I can make it work. Plus, it's off the kitchen, which would be a bonus," he said as he patted his substantial stomach.

They both laughed.

"I'm good with it if you are."

"Great! Then, it's settled. Let me get my things out of the car."

"Do you need my help?"

"No, I've got this. I know it's been a long day for you," Riley said, as he put his arm around Nona. "Why don't you go home and just relax? I've got this with Dad."

Nona looked at her brother skeptically. "Are you sure, Riley? I can stay, you know."

"I know," Riley assured her, "but I think it's time for me to take some responsibility. You've been shouldering all of it for a long time. I've come to help."

"Thanks, Riley," Nona said gratefully, as she reached around to hug him. "It's good to have you home."

As she turned away and began to walk toward her father's office, she turned around and added, "Even though Dad's not going to admit it to you, he's glad you're home, too."

She knocked lightly on her father's office door as she opened it. "Daddy, I just wanted to let you know that I'm heading home," Nona said, as she walked over to where he was sitting in his favorite leather chair.

She kissed him on his forehead as she said, "I love you, Daddy."

Mr. James looked up at Nona. "I love you, too."

As Nona turned to leave, he added, "It's going to be okay, Nona. You know that God's watching over me."

"I know, Daddy," Nona said as she closed the door.

As Nona got into her car to leave her father's house, she prayed that her brother and father would find a way to live together peacefully for the time being. It seemed to her from the way Riley had acted at the hospital that he was willing to do that, but she wasn't so sure about her father. He'd always been so head-strong and determined that his way was the best way.

Please, Lord, let my father learn to bend.

As she turned into her driveway, she recalled her earlier conversation with Mark. With all that had been going on with her father and brother, she hadn't even thought about what he'd said until right that minute. Mark had warned her to take the threat seriously, and to take notice of her surroundings.

She took notice now. She noticed how majestic the trees that lined her driveway looked. She noticed the hydrangea bushes with their blue blooms, along with the gardenia bushes with their white blossoms swaying in the breeze on each side of the carport. She noticed the dark green of the boxwoods that framed her front porch. She noticed the lushness of the Boston ferns and the contrasting red geraniums that hung from baskets along the edges of her porch.

Wasn't she doing exactly what Mark had asked her to do? She understood Mark hadn't asked her to notice the beauty around her, but to look for danger. It occurred to her that she hadn't taken notice of her surroundings for quite a while. This beauty had been there to greet her each day, but she'd been so absorbed in her life that she hadn't noted what was right in front of her.

Right then and there, she decided that she'd much rather see what was good around her, rather than looking for what might be bad. Yet, she knew it would be foolish of her to ignore the threatening email that had been sent specifically to get her attention. She had never been foolish. She wouldn't start now.

Nona unlocked the side door and heard the soft beep of her security system warning that the door had been opened. She was grateful that Mark had advised her to have the system installed. She felt much safer with the system in place. She closed the door and punched in the code that rearmed the alarm.

It was good to be home. It'd been a long day. She looked up at the wall clock and was shocked to see that it was already twenty-five minutes past seven. Just then it hit her that she hadn't eaten a thing since breakfast. She remembered the poppy seed chicken casserole that Dixie had put in her refrigerator the other day when she'd stopped by. Dixie was always doing thoughtful things like that.

As she headed to the refrigerator to retrieve the casserole, she stopped. She had that same eerie feeling that she'd had the other night, when she felt like she was being watched. She stepped to the window over the sink. It was still light enough to see outside. She looked out and was grateful there was no one looking back at her. She didn't know what she would have done if there had been. Scream and faint, she guessed. Once again, she shook her head to clear away such a silly thought. Why would anyone be watching her?

She put the casserole in the microwave and heated it per Dixie's instructions that she'd thoughtfully taped to the outside of the dish. As she waited for it to finish cooking, she made a salad and poured herself a large glass of white wine. She was going to sit down at this table in her safe kitchen and enjoy a delicious meal, without any disturbing thoughts of being watched or someone wanting to do her harm.

Chapter Thirteen

Nona had made the decision to hand off her more time-consuming cases to Nathan. She wanted to spend as much time with Riley as she could while he was in Kerry, and trusted Nathan would handle them as well as she could, maybe even better. After all, her plans were to turn over her law practice to him within the year.

Nona was thankful that the next few days passed without incident. Riley and Mr. James had fallen into a routine that seemed to suit each of them. Riley had taken his father for each of the laboratory, brain-imaging, and mental status tests that Doctor Davis had arranged. Nona had been amazed at how her father had willingly submitted himself to each test without a fight, until today.

The final test scheduled was an MRI—Magnetic Resonance Imaging. Nona was aware of how much her father despised small spaces. He wasn't exactly claustrophobic, but the idea of being confined in a tight place made him anxious. Nona had never had an MRI, but had heard disturbing stories of not only being confined in the narrow tube, but also of being subjected to the banging noises of the magnets that were continuous. From his reaction to the news that he would be having an MRI, her father had obviously heard those same stories. He was refusing to go.

Nona was on her way to Monty's office in preparation for the pretrial divorce hearing, scheduled for early next week, when her cell phone rang.

As soon as she pressed the accept button, she heard Riley's voice filled with frustration, "You've got to get over here and talk some sense into your father."

When she heard Riley use the phrase "your father," Nona knew that Riley had reached a breaking point. "Tell me what's going on," Nona said with concern.

"He's insisting that he's through with having his body subjected to any more tests. He's refusing to go for the MRI." With a sigh, Riley added, "He's locked the door to his office and won't come out."

Nona considered her options. She could cancel her meeting with Monty and hope that he could find another time for her before the hearing, and drive back to Kerry to help Riley convince their father that he needed this test. Or, she could call the hospital lab and have them reschedule her father's MRI and make her meeting. She knew what a loving sister and good daughter should do, but wasn't sure if she wanted to be that sister or daughter today. She wanted to keep her house and Monty was the one who was going to help her do that.

Deep down, she knew she had to do what was right by her father. "I'll be there in about fifteen minutes. Riley, it's going to be all right," Nona said, hoping that she was telling him the truth.

As soon as she ended her call with Riley, she called Lily. The call went straight to voicemail. She left a message. "Hey, Lily, this is Nona. Something's come up with my father. Please call Mr. Montgomery's office to cancel my appointment for today. See if you can get me an appointment for tomorrow."

When she ended the call, she let herself into her father's house through the back door and went straight to his office. She found Riley sitting on the floor with his back against the closed office door. Nona gave him a reassuring hug as he stood.

Riley was shaking his head as he said, "He's not going to open the door."

Nona tapped lightly on the closed door. In a tender, conciliatory voice she asked, "Daddy, it's Nona. Would you open the door, please?"

After a minute, she heard a stern voice boom out from the other side of the door. "What are you doing home in the middle of the day?"

Nona looked questioningly at Riley. He shrugged his shoulders. Both Nona and Riley jumped back when the door suddenly opened. Mr. James was standing there looking down at Nona with those same disconnected, unseeing eyes that she'd witnessed the other night as he lay on the bathroom floor.

In a firm voice he said to her, "It isn't a school holiday, young lady."

At that moment, Nona knew with certainty what the results of all the tests the doctor had conducted would reveal. Looking over at Riley, she said, "He doesn't need to have an MRI today."

She reached out to her father. "It's okay, Daddy, I got permission from the principal to be home with you today."

Nona canceled her father's MRI and arranged for an appointment with Doctor Davis. By some strange luck, there had been a cancellation. Doctor Davis would be able to meet with them later this afternoon. She was ready to hear the test results, which she was sure would confirm Doctor Arnold's initial diagnosis. Once they had a diagnosis, they could work together to decide on how they were going to deal with it.

Nona had never worked well with uncertainty. She'd always wanted to know the facts, not possibilities. She was better at handling situations once she knew what she was dealing with, good or bad. When her mother's diagnosis of cancer was confirmed, she went to work finding the latest research on cancer survival, and the best medical treatment for her based on that research. Of course, she'd been devastated by the diagnosis, but knew that falling apart emotionally would not help her mother. She did the best she could to keep her alive for as long as possible. It wasn't until the very end, when all avenues for survival had been exhausted, that she'd allowed her emotions to surface.

Her father had dealt with her mother's cancer exactly the way she had. However, Riley had been consumed by his emotions from the moment he'd heard the word "cancer" associated with his mother. He couldn't deal with the fact that she might die, so he'd avoided the reality of the situation and simply stayed away. Now, Nona wondered if he'd do the same thing with their father's diagnosis. Would he find a way to escape? She hoped he'd stay this time.

Mr. James spent the rest of the day shuffling through papers on his desk and mumbling to himself. Both she and Riley tried to connect with him to bring him back to the present, but without success. Nona had been able to get him to eat a sandwich and drink some water, but he refused to step away from his desk.

When Nona told her father that it was time that they head to the doctor's office, he looked at her with confusion. Without any resistance from him, both she and Riley were able to take his hands to lead him out of his office and to the car. She buckled his seat-belt for him and closed the car door. Riley got in the back seat behind him and kept patting his father on the shoulder telling him over and over, "It's okay, Dad. It's okay." Nona didn't know if he was saying the words to comfort their father, or himself.

Nona pulled her car up in front of the doctor's office. Riley helped his father out of the car and into the waiting room while Nona parked the car. After turning off the engine, she sat completely still, enjoying the sound of silence around her. She bowed her head and said a short prayer for her father, for Riley, and for herself ending with:

Dear Lord, please give me strength to face the future.

She got out of the car ready to join her father and brother.

They didn't have to wait long before they were escorted back to Doctor Davis's private office. There were three chairs waiting for them. They had their father sit down between them as they waited. When Doctor Davis walked into the room, Riley stood to shake his hand and introduce himself. His father did the same without seeming to recognize that this was not their first meeting. The doctor smiled at Nona as he sat down.

They all made nervous small talk about the weather before Doctor Davis leaned forward with both elbows on his desk, signaling that things were about to turn serious.

Looking at Mr. James, he said, "I understand that you weren't keen to have an MRI today, Mr. Foxx."

Nona answered for her father. "I'm the one who made the decision to not proceed with the MRI today. I am hoping that you can give us a diagnosis without my father having the stress of an MRI."

He smiled knowingly at Nona. "I do believe we have put your father through enough tests."

Riley asked anxiously, "Enough to give us a diagnosis?"

Doctor Davis studied the papers on his desk before looking up at the three of them. "Yes, the tests have conclusively ruled out thyroid or B-12 deficiency. We can rule out any tumor that could be interfering with cognitive functions. With these findings, along with the high protein levels in his brain, and the results of his mental status testing, I am sorry to say that I can confirm Doctor Arnold's initial diagnosis of Alzheimer's." After his pronouncement, he sat back in his chair waiting for their reaction.

It seemed to Nona that all the air had been sucked out of the office. Even though she had been confident that this would be the verdict he would deliver today, it was hard to accept that her father would not be the man he had always been—the man she had always counted on him to be. At that very moment, her life was changed forever. She now had to accept that her dignified, strong, intelligent, beloved father would in time forget all who are dear to him—forget her, forget Riley, forget Grace, and the most devastating of all, forget himself. She pressed her lips tightly together to hold back the cry that wanted to escape.

When she'd regained control of her emotions, she looked over at Riley who had his head in his hands, and watched as his shoulders shook. It was evident that the news had crushed him. It broke her heart to see her big brother like this, but it'd been the reaction she'd anticipated.

Gathering up all her courage, Nona focused on her father. His face was blank as he stared straight ahead.

Did he understand what the doctor had just said? She wondered.

It was when she took a closer look at his face that she realized he had understood. One tear fell from his eye, rolled down his cheek and fell on his hands, which were clasped in front of him.

Nona turned away and bowed her head.

Doctor Davis allowed the family a moment to adjust to the news of the diagnosis. He'd broken this same news to more families than he could count. It was a fact in the changing world that the number of Americans living with Alzheimer's disease was growing—and growing fast. He was well aware that it was now the fifth leading cause of death among those sixty-five years old. But, it was witnessing what it did to the family as a whole that was most devastating to him.

After a few minutes, Doctor Davis began looking directly at Mr. James, "I'm prescribing some cognitive-enhancing medications that may help slow down the progress of the disease. Mr. Foxx, I cannot stress how very important it is to stay physically active. I suggest walking every day, preferably outside in the fresh air. You might even want to join a gym. The Kerry Wellness Center at Memorial General has several classes that could be beneficial. You might enjoy a water aerobics class."

He paused, allowing Mr. James time to digest the information. "It's imperative that you stay socially active as well. You need to engage in conversations with others. Don't close yourself off."

Doctor Davis looked over at Nona. Riley was still bent over with his head in his hands. "I know this is a discouraging diagnosis. You have a great many difficult decisions ahead of you, concerning the care of your father. Please know that my office is here to help in any way we can. The nurse will give you some information about Alzheimer's on your way out. I want you to understand that there are some promising developments on the horizon for treating this disease," he added, trying to sound hopeful.

Nona stood, holding out her hand to the doctor. "I appreciate your help, Doctor Davis. I'm sure we will have more questions for you as time goes by."

He took Nona's hand as he said, "I'll be glad to answer any questions you might have."

When Nona stood, it seemed to pull Riley out of his trance. He stood as well and shook the doctor's hand without adding a word. Mr. James did the same. Then the three of them walked out of the office together, as a family.

They left, armed with informational pamphlets and prescriptions for medications that would hopefully help to slow down the progress of the disease. After Riley and Nona got their father buckled into his seat for the ride home, Riley grabbed Nona up into his arms in a brotherly hug.

"What are we going to do, Nona?" he said, his voice thick with emotion.

She wasn't sure how to answer such a question. It was obvious to her that they were going to do everything they could possibly do to give their father the best life possible considering a debilitating disease. She was afraid if she said something like that to him right now, it would scare him. The last thing she wanted to do was to frighten Riley so much that he might just take the next flight out!

Hugging him back, she said, "With God's help, we're going to get through this together. Let's just take it one day at a time, Riley."

He patted her on the back before releasing her and climbing in the back seat of the car.

The ride home was a silent one until they turned down Broad Street and Mr. James spotted his favorite restaurant—*The Grill.* In a clear, coherent voice, he said, "How about eating a cheeseburger before heading home."

Both Nona and Riley smiled, knowing that their father was back with them for now.

"I've been craving one since I got back to town," Riley said with enthusiasm.

Nona couldn't find a parking place right in front of the diner, which was surprising, since it was only four in the afternoon. It was too early for the supper crowd and too late for the lunch crowd. She drove on around to a side street where she parked.

Mr. James got out of the car without any help from his son or daughter and was the first to enter the diner. He had his choice to sit at any table in the place, but sat down on a stool at the counter. Nona was surprised by his choice, but sat down beside him. Riley sat on the other side of his father. It was then that Nona realized this was where they'd always sat when he had brought them here as children, when they were out of school and went to the office with him. She and Riley had loved to spin around on the "spinning tops" as they called them. She smiled to herself just thinking about what fun she'd had as a child, spinning. She had an overwhelming urge to spin around and around on her stool now, but refrained, knowing that with her long legs she'd crack her knees on the side of the counter.

Mr. James and Riley ordered their double cheeseburgers loaded. Nona ordered the single, but they all ordered seasoned fries and fountain drinks. Their meals arrived fast and hot. The three of them talked and laughed as they recalled fond childhood memories. No one mentioned their doctor's visit or the diagnosis or the future. For now, they were all content to revel in their past together.

Chapter Fourteen

By the time they'd finished their meals and reminiscing, the supper crowd was beginning to fill up the diner. Riley paid for their meals, and they got up to leave.

"Why, Mr. James, it's been a month of Sundays since I saw you last," Arthur Billingsworth said, as he reached out his hand. "How've you been?"

Nona held her breath hoping that her father would remember Mr. Billingsworth as one of their best clients and the owner of Billingsworth Chevrolet dealership. She was preparing to step into cover for her father, when he shook the offered hand and said, "I'm doing just fine, Arthur. Thanks for asking. It's always good to see you."

Mr. James smiled and waved greetings to others he recognized as he continued walking toward the door. Nona did the same as she walked out behind him.

Nona had been thrilled that he seemed to remember so many people. She had been so afraid that his mind was gone forever. It was such a relief that she hugged her father as she said, "Daddy, I just love you so much!"

Her father returned her hug. "You were afraid I was going to blow it in there, weren't you?" Then he added with a smile, "I've still got a little of my mind left!"

Both she and Riley laughed at their father's joke, but stopped cold when they walked around the corner and saw her car. Nona put her hand to her mouth as she cried out at the sight before her. Painted along the side of her black Buick Enclave were the words she'd seen just a few days before in an email:

GOT YOUR ATTENTION NOW?

It took her a minute to notice the four flat tires and some design that she didn't recognize painted across the hood. She stood there unmoving, until she heard Riley shout out in disbelief, "What in the world? Who would do this to your car, Nona?"

It was then that Mark's words of warning came back to her. "This could be a matter of life or death."

She grabbed her father's arm pulling him back into *The Grill* as she yelled at Riley, "We need to get out of here, NOW!"

It took only a few minutes for deputies to arrive after the 911 call was placed. Nona had just gotten her father and Riley back in the diner when they pulled up. Nona recognized one of the deputies as Scott Synder, but had never seen the other one. It was all she could do to not rush outside when she saw them pull around the corner.

Riley held her back. He began to pepper her with questions. "What's going on here, Nona? Why did you need to get out us off the street so fast? What is it that you're not telling me?"

Before she could answer him, her father said, "Do you think this was done by the same person who vandalized your house?"

Nona sat down hard in one of the chairs that someone had pulled out for her. Looking at her father, she answered, "Yes, Daddy."

"'Vandalized your house'?" Riley asked disbelievingly.

"You need to sit down," she said looking at Riley, "This is going to take some time to explain."

As she waited for the deputies to come into the diner to talk to her, she told Riley about the break-in, the destruction of her bedroom, and the email. With all that had been going on lately, she hadn't even told her father about the email. Both Riley and her father listened without interrupting.

When she'd finished with her story, Riley asked, "Do you have any clue as to who is doing this to you?"

"Not a clue as to who it might be," she answered with frustration.

Riley gave her a questioning look. "Could it be Bill?"

She responded quickly, "No way, Riley!"

Before Riley could ask another question, Mark, Aaron, Nathan, and Layne walked in the door of the diner.

Layne hurried over to Nona. "We were in the middle of a family supper when Mark got the call from Scott about your car."

She held out her hand pointing to her husband and sons, "You can see that we were all concerned about you."

Nona stood, welcoming the support. "I'm sure glad y'all came," she said, as she looked at each one of them. It was pandemonium for a few minutes as the two families greeted one another. It'd been years since any of them had seen Riley.

"Let's go outside to check out the car and see what information the deputies have gathered," Mark said, interrupting their reunion.

Mark led the way, with Nona and Riley right behind him. When Nona had looked at her car the last time, she'd been frightened. Now, when she looked at it, she was angry. Whoever had done this was not going to have the satisfaction of seeing a scared her, if he or she was still watching.

Mark and Aaron talked with the deputies for a few minutes before all four of them walked over to Nona. It was Deputy Snyder who asked her questions, wanting to know what time they'd arrived, who had entered the diner, who had she talked to, what time did they leave, etc. His last question gave her pause. "Did you notice anyone suspicious around when you parked your car or entered the diner?"

Mark had told her to notice her surroundings. She had completely and totally ignored his warning. She couldn't even remember the colors of the cars around them, or if they'd passed anyone on the sidewalk, or in the street when they'd walked around to the diner. She had been oblivious to her surroundings, and she was ashamed of herself.

"I'm sorry, I couldn't even tell you if there was anyone else in the diner," she said.

Riley spoke up, "There were a couple of guys who came in a little before five who I noticed kept looking over at us. I wondered if they knew Nona, but I didn't say anything."

"Can you describe them?" Mark asked.

"They were both tall, six feet at least. One wore a baseball cap and kept it on the whole time. I remember that because it bugged me. I was raised that gentlemen take off their hats inside. The other one had longish blond hair that hung down over his ears. They were both white men around forty. If I had to guess an occupation, I would say they were tech guys of some kind."

"What makes you think they might be tech guys, Riley," Aaron asked.

"Because the one guy's hat had one of those big black spiders on it; it's the logo for a computer company."

Mark asked, "Would you recognize them if you saw them again?"

"I believe I would."

Deputy Snyder spoke up, "We've canvased the area and no one saw who did this. Of course, none of these stores have any sort of video surveillance. We don't have any leads right now, but we'll keep checking for someone who might have seen something. I've called a tow truck to come get your car, Ms. Foxx. We need to have the crime lab look at it."

"If my presence is no longer required, I believe I would like to go home," Mr. James said to Mark.

"In fact, everyone is free to leave," Mark said.

Looking over at Nathan, he added, "I'm sure Nathan would be glad to take y'all home."

Smiling, Nathan said, "I'm at your service."

"Then let me get a few things out of my car before they come to take it away," Nona said thinking of the prescriptions and pamphlets still in the car, "and I'll be ready to get home as well."

Riley went with Nona to help her get what they needed from the car. Before they'd finished, the tow truck was backing into place to take Nona's car away. At least they'd have Riley's rental until she got her car back. There was no way to know how long the crime lab would keep it, but she hoped it would only be for a day or two at the most.

Nathan helped Mr. James into the front seat of his car and was waiting for Nona and Riley to join them when Layne walked over to him. "Since Nona lives in the opposite direction of her father, I'll see that she gets home. You can take Mr. James and Riley to their house."

"That works for me," Nathan said.

As Nona and Riley walked up to Nathan's car, Nathan opened the back door for Riley. "Let me get y'all home, Mr. Riley."

"Thanks, Nathan," Riley said. He turned to Nona, "Are you coming?"

Layne answer for Nona, "I'll take her home, Riley. It'll give us a chance to talk."

"Wait a minute," Nona said to Layne, "with my car being towed away, I need to go home to get Dad's car to drive until I get mine back."

Aaron spoke up, "Nathan can take me to get your Dad's car. Then we can bring it out to your house."

Reaching over to pat Nona on the back, he added, "I think you've been through enough trouble tonight. We can take care of this for you."

"Thanks," Nona said, as she gave Aaron a hug. "You're right; I've had enough troubles to deal with for one night."

She turned and followed Layne to her car. "Did y'all drive separately?"

Layne laughed, "Almost, Mark and Aaron did ride together."

Before Nona got into Layne's car, she took one final look at her car as the tow truck was pulling it away from the scene. Shaking her head, she asked, "Who would do this, Layne, and why? I'm not a bad person, am I?"

"No!" Layne said emphatically, "But there are bad people in this world. I just hate that someone is doing this to you."

"After I told Riley about the vandalism and the email, he asked me if I thought it might be Bill," Nona said, "and I told him right away that there was no way it could be him."

Letting out a long breath before continuing, she confided, "But, Layne, a little part of me worries that it might be."

"Oh, my, gosh, Nona, you don't really believe that Bill's capable of doing something like this, do you?"

Nona didn't answer right away as she considered the events of the past few weeks. Could it be that she didn't really know the man she was married to for over forty years? Although, two years ago she never would've believed he'd leave her for another woman. But, the vandalism, the threatening email, and the spray-painted message on her car seemed like someone was tormenting her. Bill may be a cheater, but he'd never been a bully.

"No," Nona said with confidence, "I don't believe that Bill would ever do something so mean to me. There has to be someone else behind this whole thing."

"I agree that it's not Bill," Layne said as she pulled into Nona's driveway, "but have you ever considered that Amy might be the one behind this?"

Nona straightened up in her seat and looked directly at Layne. "Are you saying that you think that Amy put Bill up to doing these things to me?"

Layne pulled up next to Nona's house and turned off her car. She turned to Nona and said, "No, I'm saying that I think that Amy put someone else up to doing these things to you."

"Oh, come on, Layne, that'd be awfully convenient if we could blame this all on Amy, wouldn't it?" Nona asked skeptically. Then added as she held her hands up to show quotation marks in the air as she quotes, "Mistress Terrorizes Ex-wife."

Layne shrugged, "Well, it's just a thought, but think about it, Nona. Who else do you know who hates you as much as she does?"

Nona responded with more confidence that she was feeling. "It's not Amy, Layne."

"There's something else that I need to tell you, Layne," Nona said changing the subject. "Do you have time to come in for minute?"

Layne could tell by the seriousness of Nona's voice that it was important for her to take the time to listen to what her friend had to say. "Sure, I'm not in a hurry to get back to the house." She added with a smile, "After all, I need to give Blair and Heather enough time to get the supper dishes cleaned up before I get home."

They went in through the side door of the house, where once again Nona dealt with the security system that was quickly becoming a routine. After pouring two glasses of iced tea, she suggested that they take them out to the back deck. Layne took a seat in one of the wicker chairs while Nona sat on the swing. They sat quietly for a few minutes, simply listening to the soft night sounds as a breeze blew through the oak trees surrounding the deck.

Nona set her glass down on the table next to the swing. Without looking directly at Layne, she began talking in a low voice, "Dad was supposed to have an MRI today. It would have been his last test in the long line of tests, but, as it turned out, he didn't need that test for the doctor to give us his diagnosis today."

Layne leaned forward. "Do you mean that you found out what's been going on with your Dad today?"

Nona nodded her head. "Oh, Layne, Dad has been diagnosed with Alzheimer's." As she said those words aloud, all the worry and sadness she'd been feeling for days came pouring out in heart-rending sobs.

Layne rushed to Nona's side and simply held her, allowing Nona the chance to grieve. Layne knew that her best friend's heart was breaking, not only for her father's diagnosis, but for all the tragic events that had entered her life over these past few days. Nona was a strong woman, but there were times that even the strong needed comforting. Layne intended to be the comfort Nona needed at that moment.

When Nona's sobs subsided, the two friends sat side by side, soothed by the back and forth movement of the swing.

Nona took Layne's hand in hers. "Thanks for being here for me, Layne," Nona said in a soft voice.

"Always," Layne said as she squeezed her hand. "That's what best friends are for."

Chapter Fifteen

Nona was surprised by how well she'd slept after her breakdown with Layne. She had to admit that she honestly felt better than she had in days. Maybe it'd been a good thing to release all her pent-up emotions. Maybe she needed to do that more often.

After dressing in her new designer, navy blue suit that she'd bought on her shopping trip to Savannah, and eating a breakfast of Irish oatmeal topped with blueberries, Nona was once again on her way to meet with Monty. She'd been relieved when Lily called to let her know that she'd been able to reschedule her appointment with Mr. Montgomery for the first thing this morning. She'd been worried that his schedule would be too tight to fit her in.

Nona had to adjust to driving her father's 2003 Lincoln Continental that he'd babied since the day he'd driven it home. She parked the car, taking up two parking spaces. She got out of the car, locked it, and walked up to Monty's office. As she reached out for the handle to the office door, she was almost knocked backwards when the door was pushed open from the other side. To her surprise, there stood Monty. He was wearing a teal colored polo shirt that made his dark skin and green eyes stand out. She was struck once again by his handsome, good looks.

"Good morning to you!" he said in a cheerful voice, as he held the door for her. "So glad you could make this appointment," he added with a wink.

"Good morning to you, too," she said smiling. "Thanks for working me in this morning."

"Honey, I'll work you in any time you say," he said in a silky voice.

Nona stopped, turned around, and gave him a stern look. "If you're flirting with me, you need to stop right now." She added in a no nonsense voice, "I have enough troubles in my life without adding you to them."

In her professional life, Nona had dealt with many men who were flirtatious. Sometimes she'd even used it to her advantage, but most of the time she'd shut their insinuations of intimacy down so fast it left no doubt in their minds that she wasn't going to play.

He said with a laugh, "Sorry, I tend to do that with good-looking women."

"Well, quit it! It's not professional, and I'm here for professional reasons only."

He held up both hands as if he was surrendering. "Done!" Then, with a more serious tone, he asked, "Would you consider it 'flirting' if I offered you a cup of coffee?"

"No, I'd consider that good manners," Nona said smiling.

He poured two cups of coffee, giving one to Nona. Then he led the way to his messy office, where she once again navigated a path around the piles of papers in order to reach the chair she was pleased to find empty. She sat down in the chair as Monty sat at his desk.

"Your secretary told me that you had to cancel your appointment yesterday due to an emergency with your father. I hope you were able to handle that emergency without further complications."

She didn't want to go into her father's diagnosis with him, so she simply answered, "We were, but there have been other events that have occurred in the past few days that I need to tell you about."

Nona went on to tell him about the threatening email and the paint job that the vandal had applied to her car.

"I can't say for sure who's behind all of this," she said, "but my friend suspects the culprit just might be Bill's girlfriend."

Monty considered all that she had just told him. "But you don't." Then he asked thoughtfully, "Why not?"

"You may think that I'm naive, but I just don't think she dislikes me enough to do such awful things," Nona said.

Raising his eyebrows, he asked, "So, you think she likes you?"

"Well, I wouldn't go so far as to say that she 'likes' me," she said, "but I can't think of any reason why she should dislike me."

"So, you don't think that the fact that you were Bill's wife, whom he most likely loved for over forty years, is enough of a reason to dislike you?"

Nona hadn't thought about it in those terms. She'd believed that now that Amy had Bill she wouldn't consider Nona a threat to her relationship with Bill. Hadn't Bill made it clear that he didn't want Nona in his life anymore, but had chosen Amy?

"I would advise you to reconsider Amy as the one who's behind these acts against you."

Maybe it was time for her to consider the possibility. "I hope you're wrong, but I'll think about it."

"Now that we've settled that, let's talk about what facts we can use to make sure you keep your house."

Nona handed over the documentation that Monty had requested she bring, concerning the purchase and renovations of the house. She hoped what she'd provided would be enough to convince a judge and jury that the house should stay with her and not be awarded to Bill and Amy.

It was after eleven in the morning when Nona finished her meeting with Monty. As she drove back to Kerry, her mind was consumed with a new thought. *Could it be that Amy is the one behind the threats and vandalism?* It'd never occurred to her to even consider Amy as someone who would be capable of doing such things. Now, this notion was all she could think about. So many questions were swirling around in her brain, but she had no answers that made sense to her. She couldn't get past the question that had been her first—*Why?*

She needed to talk this out with someone she trusted. In the past, she would have gone straight to her father. In fact, when she'd left Monty's office that's where she was heading, before she remembered her father's diagnosis. It wouldn't be right to burden him with her problems when he was facing so many of his own right now.

Her second thought was to talk with Riley, but he'd made it clear that he was certain that Bill was behind the threats and vandalism. She needed to talk with someone who would listen to the facts with an open mind. She knew then who she needed to talk to. It wasn't just one person, but her three best friends. She smiled to herself as she thought about the name Mark had given the close friends—The Fearsome Foursome.

That's who she needed right now. She took note of the time and made her first call, hoping that Betty Jo would be home and not at the hospital. "Hey, Nona," she answered on the second ring. She must have had the phone right in her hand, Nona thought to herself.

"Hey, Betty Jo, please tell me that you aren't working today," Nona said.

"Okay," Betty Jo said what Nona had told her to say, "I'm not working today."

Nona laughed. "What I meant was I hope you're not working today. Are you, working, I mean?"

"Well, that depends on your definition of 'working,'" Betty Jo said, in a teasing voice.

"Okay, let me rephrase the question," Nona said. "Are you working at the hospital today?"

"No, I'm just slaving away here at home. Why?"

"Something's come up, Betty Jo, and I really need my friends," Nona explained. "How about lunch at my house in thirty minutes?"

"What's going on, Nona?" Betty Jo asked with concern.

"I'll tell you all about it at lunch."

"I'll be there in thirty."

Nona ended the call, then immediately called both Dixie and Layne hoping they weren't busy babysitting, or with some other obligation that would keep them from joining her for lunch. They were both free to come. Nona stopped by the sub shop to pick up lunch for the group. She had iced tea at home, but it was sweet tea. She hoped Betty Jo would be good with water since she had sworn off anything with sugar or sweetener.

She pulled into her drive with five minutes to spare. Gathering the bags filled with their lunch, she headed to the side door. She unlocked the door and unloaded her burden on her kitchen table. She rushed around gathering paper plates and napkins. As she reached up to get the glasses out of the cabinet, to fill with ice, she froze. It suddenly occurred to her that she hadn't heard the reassuring soft beep of her security system when she'd entered her house. She slowly turned around toward her security home base, she found herself staring at the LED green light. That meant the system was ready to be armed, but it wasn't armed.

She would have sworn that she'd armed it when she'd left the house this morning. She realized that if she in fact had armed it, it would have given off the soft beeping sound when she'd opened the door, and she would have had to enter the code to stop the beeps. She knew for a fact there had been no sound when she'd opened the door, and that she'd entered no code. With the green ready light indicating that it was ready to be armed, then that meant she hadn't armed it when she'd left the house.

How could she have been so careless as to not arm her security system when she left her house this morning? She'd believed that setting the alarm had become a habit, as automatic as locking the door. She had been distracted this morning when she left. At least she knew for sure that she'd locked the door when she left.

"Nona? Are you okay?"

It was Dixie's voice that pulled her away from her thoughts and back to the present. "Sorry," Nona said, "I'm fine, just lost in thought."

As she leaned over to hug Dixie, she saw Betty Jo coming in behind her and Layne pulling up in her car.

The Fearsome Foursome were together again.

They each chose a sandwich, chips, and a cold beverage as they settled down around the kitchen table. The prediction of a ninety percent chance of a thunderstorm kept them from eating outside on Nona's deck. They filled the next thirty minutes with eating and sharing the latest about their children and grandchildren.

Nona listened patiently as the other three talked, until she couldn't hold back her concerns any longer. She put down her half-eaten sandwich, wiped her mouth with her napkin, and cleared her throat. "All of this is very interesting, but I've asked y'all over here for lunch because I need your help with a serious matter."

Layne, Dixie, and Betty Jo stopped their eating and talking to give her their complete attention.

"What can we help you with, darlin'?" Dixie asked with concern for her friend.

"In the past two days, two people have proposed the same theory that I had never even considered, nor had I ever thought about. It never came to my mind that she could do something like this to me. To me it just doesn't make sense. Since I left Monty's office it's all that I can think about. It is literally eating away at my brain." Nona understood she was rambling, but couldn't seem to stop herself.

As she took a breath, and before she could continue, Dixie grabbed her arm tightly. "Who has done what to eat away at your brain, Nona? You're not making any sense. Give us the details—like you would when you're lawyering." She wasn't sure that her last word was even a word, but she hoped that Nona got her point.

"Sorry," Nona said, "this has just thrown me for a loop. Let me begin again in a more 'lawyering' way." Nona smiled at Dixie.

She took a long drink of her tea as she considered where to begin her story. She wasn't sure if they all had the same information, so she thought it best to start with the threatening email.

"A few days ago, I was sitting right here at my kitchen table with my laptop, checking my emails. Most of them were work related, but my attention was suddenly drawn to one with the most bizarre username of 'Got Your Attention Now' written out as if it were one long word. I almost deleted it before I figured out that it wasn't just a bunch of random letters put together." She paused as she considered what would have happened if she had deleted it. She looked around and noticed that no one was eating. They were all listening closely to her story.

"Anyway, I made the decision not to open the email. Instead, I took my laptop with the email down to Mark's office. I wanted someone who knew something about technology to have a look at it."

"And you thought that would-be Mark?" Layne interrupted.

Turning to Layne, she answered honestly, "Well, not really Mark, but I thought that someone in his office might be tech savvy enough to figure it out. And there was someone there who did. I think his name was Nate."

Layne nodded her head. "I know Nate. He's one smart guy when it comes to computers."

Nona continued. "He found out that someone had used a fake email server to set up that username, so whoever did know their way around technology."

"Did he find out what was in the message?" Betty Jo asked.

"Yes, but I can't remember the exact wording," Nona said, as she tried to recall the message. "It was full of errors that Nate thinks were done on purpose so the person sounded illiterate, but the gist of it was that if I keep ignoring this person, something bad will happen to me."

"You're kidding me!" Dixie said with total amazement in her voice.

Betty Jo added with concern, "That sounds like a serious threat, Nona."

"I hope you're taking it seriously," Layne said in a warning tone. "I, for one, am frightened for you. Especially when you add to it what happened last night with your car."

"What happened last night?" both Dixie and Betty Jo said together.

Nona put her head in her hands as she remembered the fear that gripped her heart when she saw what had been done to her car.

When Nona didn't answer right away, Layne spoke up, "I'll tell you what happened. Someone spray painted that same message as the username on both sides of her car— 'Got Your Attention Now'—along with stabbing all four tires, while she was just around the corner sitting in *The Grill,* enjoying a meal with her father and brother!"

"Oh, Nona, I'm so sorry," Dixie said, as she reached over for Nona's hand. "First your bedroom is vandalized, then you get that threatening email, and then, I just can't believe someone would do that to your car—right there in downtown Kerry!"

Betty Jo asked, "Who in the world would do such things to you?"

In a soft voice, Nona said, "That's why I needed to talk to y'all." She sighed, "I went to Bradford this morning to meet with Monty. He was the second person in less than twelve hours who brought up a possibility, one I'd never considered, of a person who might be behind these attacks."

"Amy," Betty Jo said before Nona could. "Right? I've wondered if it could be her from the day Layne called to tell me what someone had done to your bedroom."

"What made you suspect her?" Nona asked Betty Jo.

"It just seemed too much of a coincidence that all of that happened right after Bill and Amy paid you that visit to let you know they wanted the house, or should I say, that Amy wanted the house. I know Bill well enough to know that he'd never do anything like that to you, but Amy is a different story. It just makes sense to me. She took away your husband, and she wants to take away your house. It seemed obvious to both Don and me that she wants you to leave and go far, far away, Nona."

Dixie shook her head. "I have to say that I'm with you, Nona. It simply never occurred to me that Amy could be the one behind these attacks."

She paused as she considered the possibility before adding, "But now that I think about it, I can see why they suspect her. She sure has a motive to get you out of the way."

In frustration, Nona said, "That's what I just don't get. What motive could she have to want me out of the way? What have I ever done to her?"

"I don't think it's anything that you've actually 'done' to Amy," Layne said. "I think it's that she's afraid Bill still has feelings for you."

"That doesn't make any sense to me," Nona wearily. "Bill and I were married for over forty years. We have a daughter together. No matter what Amy and Bill's relationship is, common sense should tell her that Bill would have some sort of feelings for me. It's obvious that he doesn't feel love for me though, or he wouldn't be with her."

"Don't you see?" Layne said reaching out to Nona. "It's obvious to you, and to us, that Bill isn't in love with you, but it isn't obvious to Amy. That's what she thinks you've done to her. You were Bill's first love."

"Why can't she see that she's the winner? She's his last love," Nona shot back.

Layne patted Nona's hand, hoping she was getting it through to her that Amy had to be the one behind these incidents. "Amy must realize that Bill can't possibly live long enough for them to be married for forty years, and, don't forget, since Bill had things taken care of long ago, they'll never have a child together. Yet, if she can get that house away from you, instead of it being the house where Bill lived with you, it'll be where Bill lives with her."

Nona pushed away from the table, stood, and began walking around the kitchen as she considered what Layne had said. She stopped and slapped both hands down on the table. "Well, she's not going to scare me away from my own home. This will always be our home, where we were a family!"

Betty Jo looked over at Layne to see if she'd caught the words that Nona had used— "our home," "family," and the ones that really concerned her "Amy's the winner." Layne gave her a knowing look and a slight nod. They both had the same disturbing thought: *Is Nona still in love with Bill?*

As Betty Jo ran some errands in town, she couldn't get the comments that Nona had made at lunch about Bill off her mind. It seemed to her that Nona may still have deep feelings for Bill. In a way, she could understand it. After all, they'd been married for over forty years. However, after the way Bill had left her for another woman, how could Nona feel anything but hatred for him?

She knew that if Don ever did something like that to her, she'd loath him forever. She was confident that such a thing could never happen with their marriage. Don wasn't an overly affectionate man, but Betty Jo knew he cared for her. Plus, she knew he'd never go looking for someone else. It just wasn't in his personality to betray his vows.

It suddenly hit her that Nona had probably felt the same way about Bill as she did about Don. She'd known them as a couple for years. She'd never seen any warning that Bill was unhappy in his marriage and was looking for someone else. Nona had said she'd never suspected he was with another woman, and thought they would be together until death. That's the way Betty Jo felt about Don, that they'd be together until the end. She'd taken her vows before God and those witnesses at her wedding seriously. She'd always thought that Don had too.

Now, Betty Jo began to wonder if she'd missed some warning signs along the way with Don. Maybe he wasn't as content with their marriage as she believed him to be. After all, they'd gone through a rough time last year after the accident, but she'd believed that had made their marriage stronger. Yet, since his diagnosis of diabetes, she was always on him, reminding him to watch what he was eating and drinking. Maybe she'd been nagging him, and he'd grown tired of it.

She pulled up in the driveway to park her car, got out, and went straight to the garage where she knew he'd be working on the Chevy Apache that he'd almost totaled in the accident. He spent most of his free time there.

She pulled back the door and entered the garage calling his name, "Don, where are you?"

She looked around, even checking under the truck, but there was no sign of Don. She knocked on the door to the small lavatory he'd installed for convenience. No answer. Don was not in the garage.

Where else would he be?

She went in search of him in the house calling his name as she entered each room. No Don. Now, Betty Jo's concern had almost tipped over to panic. With his diabetes, he just might be in a coma somewhere or worse.

She walked out the back door and noticed the green house. Surely, on such a warm day, he wouldn't be in there. She headed that way to check. As she got closer, she heard Don whistling a soft tune. Don was an excellent whistler. She stopped and listened. She recognized the tune immediately: *We've Only Just Begun*

It was the first song they'd danced to as husband and wife as it was played at their wedding reception. She rested against the closed door remembering how happy she'd felt that day. It had felt as if they were dancing on air. She'd been so young, but had known that Don was the only man in the world for her. They had been hopelessly in love that day.

She opened the greenhouse door. When she saw his face as he looked over at her, she had no doubt that they still were.

"Hey, honey," Don said, as he handed her a bouquet of daisies. "These are for you."

Betty Jo realized, as she leaned in to kiss her loving husband, that she needed to rein in her imagination.

Chapter Sixteen

After Layne, Dixie, and Betty Jo left, Nona thought about their conversation as she cleaned the kitchen. She'd known it would help to talk things out with her friends. She was grateful for their help in making it clear to her that Amy had to be the one behind the attacks on her. Amy was desperate to get Nona out of that house and, apparently, wasn't going to stop until she'd succeeded. Nona needed to decide what she was going to do about it.

She had been so deep in thought, that when her cell phone rang, she jumped. She grabbed it up to answer without even looking at the screen to see who was calling. "Hello?"

"Hi, baby sister," Riley said. "I hadn't heard from you today, so thought I give you a call to let you know how things are going with Dad."

"Okay," Nona said hesitantly, as her body tensed, expecting the worst.

"We just got back from a walk around the block that Dad insisted we take," Riley happily reported. "And, it seems his appetite is coming back. He ate a big breakfast and lunch."

Nona let out the breath that she'd been holding. "Oh, Riley, that's such good news."

"I know it is," Riley said, "That's why I called you with it. I thought you might need some after what happened to your car."

"Well, you were right about that," Nona said.

"How about you plan on having supper with Dad and me tonight," Riley suggested. "I'll cook."

"You'll cook?" Nona said with a laugh.

"I'm a pretty good cook, if I do say so myself," Riley bragged. "As a bachelor, I've had to learn to cook in order to survive. Be here around six."

With that, he ended the call.

Nona was thankful that Riley's call had been one that brought her hope. She needed some hope in her life right now.

She looked up at the clock on the wall and noticed that it was almost two o'clock. She had work she needed to finish. She also wanted to give Monty a call to tell him that she agreed with his suspicions about Amy. She turned away from the clock and started to get up from the table when something made her want to take a closer look at the clock. She slowly got out of her chair and walked cautiously toward the clock. As she stared directly at it, she recognized that the clock hanging on her wall right now wasn't the clock that she'd bought and Bill had hung in her kitchen over five years ago.

As she gazed suspiciously up at the clock, she noticed that the hands that were pointing out the hours, minutes, and seconds were black. Her clock had gold hands. This clock had a stark white background. Her clock had a light ivory background. This clock had a solid black frame. Her clock had gold trim around a black frame. Her clock had been replaced by this one that was almost like hers, but was most definitely not her clock.

How long had this bogus clock been hanging there in front of her without her noticing it wasn't hers? Had it been this clock all along that had made her feel that something wasn't right in her kitchen? As she thought back about when she'd begun to get that strange feeling that something was "off" in the kitchen, she realized it'd started right after the break-in. Had someone replaced her clock with this impostor when they broke into her house?

Nona understood just how preposterous it was to think that someone would break into her house, completely destroy her bedroom, and then hurry down to the kitchen to take her clock off the wall and replace it with another one that was almost, but not quite, the same. Yet, someone had done just that, but for what purpose?

The clock was too high on the wall for Nona to simply reach up to take it down. She pulled a chair from the table over to the wall, stood on it, and reached up to take down the clock that had been set up as a decoy. As she lifted it from the nail that was holding it up on the wall, she almost dropped it. It was heavier than she'd expected, much heavier. She wondered what could make a kitchen clock so heavy? She held tightly to it as she stepped down off the chair and carefully placed the clock on the table.

As she inspected the front of it, she could understand why she hadn't noticed that it was a different clock. It was so much like the one she had bought, with only slight differences. She turned it over to examine the back. The first thing she noticed were six screws that secured a hard-black plastic cover to the clock. Her kitchen clock hadn't had any cover, just a wheel for changing time that was attached to a box that held the mechanism for keeping time and a place for the battery.

Nona was curious as to what the plastic cover was covering up. She went to the kitchen junk drawer in search of a screw driver. She rummaged through the drawer moving aside playing cards, pens, pencils, random screws, paper clips, notebooks, etc.—no screw driver. She was on her way out to what had been Bill's workshop before he cleared it out, hoping that he'd left behind at least one screw driver, when a thought stopped her.

Someone took the time to put that clock up on my wall because it was important to them that it be on my kitchen wall.

That was the answer to why it was there. This clock held something that was important to someone, somewhere, for some reason. If she did get it open, would she know what to do with what she found? She needed to get someone over here to check it out; someone who would know what to do with what they found inside. It was time to call for professional help.

She carefully picked up the clock from the table, returned to the chair, stood on it, and replaced the clock on the wall. Then she took the chair back to the table, picked up her cell phone, and walked out the back door to the deck. She'd call Mark, but not in front of the clock.

Nona sat down in the swing as she pressed the quick call button for Mark. She put the phone to her ear, trying to decide how she was going to explain this situation with the clock so it'd make sense. It was going to be tough since even she couldn't make sense out of it. The call went to voicemail. She decided not to leave a message. Hopefully, he'd see that she'd called and return her call. If not, she'd call back later.

She wasn't sure what to do in the meantime. She had a few hours before she was to be at her father's house for Riley's special supper. She needed to do something to occupy her mind, or she'd sit here thinking about that crazy clock. She remembered that she had plenty to do at the office that would keep her busy for hours. She went back inside her house, got her purse and keys, and made sure that she set the alarm on the security system. She glanced up at the clock before closing the door and observed that the clock looked out on that door.

Lily seemed surprised to see Nona. "I thought you weren't coming in today," Lily said. "Nathan told me what happened to your car. Are you okay? I've been worried about you."

"I'm fine, Lily," Nona said reassuringly. "I came in to get some work done. I feel like I'm so far behind."

"You don't need to worry about the office, Nona," Lily said. "Nathan's handled everything."

Nona looked up at Lily from the mail she was thumbing through. "That's good to know." She set the mail down on her desk. "Would you please ask him to come in here?"

"Aaron's in there with him right now," Lily said. "I'm not sure why he's here, but they've been in there together for a while, with the door closed."

"Aaron's with him?" Nona asked without really expecting Lily to answer.

She paused for a moment. She'd decided on the drive over to the office that she was going to talk to Nathan about the clock. It was a stroke of luck that Aaron was with him. It'd be even better to have Aaron as part of the discussion. "Would you please ask both Aaron and Nathan to come to my office?"

"Yes, ma'am."

Nona had just settled in behind her desk when Nathan tapped on her open door. "You wanted to see us?"

"Even me?" Aaron said peeking around Nathan.

"Yes, even you. Come on in," Nona said to the brothers, as she stood to greet them.

"I have the feeling that I've just been called into the principal's office," Aaron said looking around.

"It's nothing like that. I promise," Nona said, as she directed them to the two chairs in front of her desk.

Nona sat back down behind her desk. "Something has happened at the house that has me concerned. It worked out in my favor that you are here with Nathan, Aaron. I tried to call your dad, but he didn't answer."

Both Nathan and Aaron leaned forward with concern. "What's happened?" Aaron asked.

Nona cleared her throat and told her bizarre story about someone switching clocks in her kitchen.

When she'd finished, Nathan and Aaron looked at one another in disbelief. Nathan spoke first. "Let me see if I've got this right. You're telling us that you believe that someone broke into your house in order to take your kitchen clock, replace it with one that looks almost like it, hoping that you wouldn't notice the switch."

"I know how crazy it all sounds, but the clock that's hanging in my kitchen right this minute is not my clock," Nona said shaking her head. "I even took it off the wall to check it out. It has a back on it that is secured with six screws. I know for a fact that my clock did not have a back on it. And that clock was so heavy I almost dropped it."

Aaron had sat quietly listening to Nona's story about the clock and considering motives that someone would have for replacing the clock in Nona's kitchen. He could only come up with one. He was ready to share his theory. "I think I might know why someone would swap your clock with theirs."

Both Nona and Nathan stared at him waiting for him to continue.

"To watch you," Aaron said with certainty.

"Watch me?" Nona asked, not understanding how a clock could be used to watch her.

"Yes, think about it for a minute," Aaron said. "The clock is heavy because it has a camera in it that's recording every move you make in that kitchen."

"A camera?" both Nona and Nathan asked skeptically.

"I saw something like this when I was working with Georgia State Patrol in Savannah, in a store that was a front for dealing drugs." Aaron explained, "The camera was pointed at the door of the store and recorded everyone who walked in or out. There was someone in another room watching all of it on their computer, in real time. It was all done through a wireless network."

He paused before adding, "Guess where the camera was hidden?"

"A clock," Nathan answered.

"Nope," Aaron said with a chuckle, "but it was in a small cannon that was on the shelf above the counter, pointing directly at the door."

"Oh, Aaron," Nathan said in frustration.

"My point, dear brother," Aaron said, looking pointedly at Nathan, "is that with the technology available today, a wireless recording device can be so small that one can be placed inside almost any object, even a clock."

Nona shuddered at the probability that someone could have been spying on her. She couldn't deny that she'd had an eerie feeling several times when she'd walked into the kitchen. She'd dismissed it as a post break-in over reaction. Now, it seemed she may have been right about her feelings of being watched.

"Your mother, Dixie, and Betty Jo are convinced that Amy is behind all of this—the break-in, the threatening email, the message on my car. I'm beginning to think they're right. Amy has made it clear that she wants me out of my house."

She turned to Aaron and asked, "Can you think of any reason why Amy would want to go to the trouble of putting up a clock with a camera to spy on me?"

"She wanted to watch what you were doing in the house," Aaron said. "Or, it could be that she simply wanted to know when you got home and when you left home."

Aaron got up out of his chair heading for the door. "No matter what the reason, we need to let Dad know about this latest development, and that you suspect Amy might be behind it."

As Aaron was walking out the door, Nona called out to him. "Thanks so much for your help. It was lucky for me that you were here today."

It suddenly struck Nona that Aaron rarely stopped by the office and when he did, it was usually to talk to Nona, not Nathan. Aaron was almost out the door when she asked him, "By the way, would you mind telling me why you were here today?"

Aaron gave her a broad smile that lit up his face and with a wink said, "To ask my big brother to be my Best Man." He turned and walked out of the door, leaving Nona open-mouthed, staring after him.

Shocked, Nona looked to Nathan for an explanation.

"Believe it or not, Aaron's asked Jenny to marry him."

"Jenny? Mark's nurse from the hospital?" Nona asked.

"That's the one," Nathan replied with a smile. "He's been seeing her since Dad got out. Mom didn't tell you?"

"She mentioned that they were dating, but never said anything about Aaron getting serious about her."

"Well, I guess they're serious," Nathan teased.

"I'm happy for Aaron, but it's just such a shock. I know that Layne's always worried that he'd never settle down."

"I guess he just hadn't met the right woman until Jenny."

"I'm glad Jenny's the one!"

Chapter Seventeen

It only took Mark a few minutes to decide what he needed to do after Aaron told him about the clock in Nona's kitchen. He'd called Nona to meet him at her house so he could get that clock. Nate needed to check it out as quickly as he could. When Aaron told him about his theory that someone had replaced Nona's clock in order to spy on her, it'd instantly filled Mark with anger. Whoever was doing this had moved to a new low. And he wasn't going to stop until he'd apprehended that person.

Nona pulled in right behind Mark's sheriff's car. She had her house key in her hand as she got out of her car. "Mark, I'm going to let y'all in, but then I need to hurry on over to Daddy's house. Riley's cooking for us this evening, and I don't want to be late for that first-time-ever event," Nona went up the steps and opened the side door that led into the kitchen.

Nona froze as she entered. She was once again met with silence. Absent was the soft beep of her security system warning that the door had been opened, waiting for her to enter her code. There was absolutely no doubt in her mind whatsoever that she had set the alarm when she'd left earlier.

"What is it, Nona?" Mark asked.

"Mark, someone has been in my house," Nona said in a frightened voice reaching out for Mark. "I know for a fact that I set the security system before I left this afternoon, but now it's not on."

"Are you sure, Nona?" Mark asked in a low voice.

"Positive!"

"Listen to me carefully and do exactly what I say," Mark said as he helped her back down the steps. "Get in your car and lock the doors. Do not get out of that car!" Looking her straight in the eyes, he added, "Do you understand?"

"Yes," Nona said, as she hurried to her car.

Mark looked at Aaron, who was taking out his gun. "Let's check this out," he said, as he took out his own gun.

Aaron nodded and followed his father through the door. As a team, they went through the house, clearing one room at time. When they got to Nona's bedroom, they found the door closed. Aaron cautiously pushed the door open allowing his father to enter first. After searching the room, they both sighed with relief at finding the room undisturbed.

As they walked back down the steps, Aaron said to his father, "Do you think that she might have been mistaken about setting the security system before she left?"

"That's a possibility, but she was adamant about having armed it before she left the house," Mark said. "I think something else is going on here, Aaron, and we're going to find out who it is."

Aaron had gone out to retrieve a relieved Nona from her car while Mark put on gloves to take down the bogus clock from the wall. He had just placed the clock face down on the kitchen counter to exam it.

"I hope you brought a screwdriver, Mark, because you won't find one here," Nona said. "I looked everywhere for one."

Mark pulled out a knife from his pocket. "I'm pretty sure that I can get the back off with my dependable Swiss Army knife."

Both Nona and Aaron stood nearer to Mark, trying to get a closer look at what secrets that clock held. When Mark pulled off the black plastic that covered the back of the clock, they gasped. It was evident that this was no ordinary clock.

"I'm not exactly sure what I'm looking at," Mark said, "but I do know that this is not your typical kitchen clock. I need to get this to our tech department to let them have a look at it."

"Well, one thing is for sure," Aaron said to Nona. "Whoever put this clock to spy on you now knows that it's no longer where they placed it. I think that makes for a dangerous situation for you. You definitely do not need to stay here until we figure out who put this clock here."

Nona thought about this for a minute, then let out a long, frustrated breath. "I don't like the idea of whoever this is thinking that they have scared me away from my own house." Nona said looking to Aaron, "But I do think you're right, Aaron. I'll pack a bag and spend at least tonight with Daddy and Riley."

"I think that's the smart thing to do, Nona," Mark said.

Then to Aaron he instructed, "Go out to my car to get an evidence bag so I can put this clock in there while Nona goes upstairs to pack her bag."

Before leaving to go to her bedroom to pack, Nona asked, "Y'all won't leave without me, will you?"

Mark smiled at her. "No, we will all be leaving together."

After packing her overnight bag, Nona joined Mark and Aaron in the kitchen, where they'd finished putting the clock into the evidence bag. They made sure they'd set the security system and locked the door before leaving together. Nona checked the time on her cell phone and was relieved to see that she was going to make it just in time for Riley's supper.

While she was packing she'd made the decision not to share with her father and brother anything about the suspicious clock. Until she knew something for certain, there was no need to worry them. They had enough to deal with for now. However, she did need to come up with an excuse for why she needed to spend tonight, with the possibility of several nights, with them. She thought about making up a story about the water pipes bursting or a tree falling on the house, but she hated telling lies, especially to her father.

As she drove down the driveway and parked behind the house by the back door, she'd decided the best thing to do was to tell them a half-truth. She was staying there because she was afraid to be home by herself. With all that had been going on in her life, she was confident they would open their welcoming arms to her.

The familiar aroma of fresh baked bread welcomed her as she entered the kitchen. "James Riley Foxx, did you make Mom's homemade bread?" Nona called out. The one thing their mother made on a regular basis when they were growing up was a yeast bread made from scratch. Most Southern mothers made biscuits, but their mother wasn't like most. The smell brought back pleasant memories of a time that was long gone.

"I most certainly did," Riley said, as he walked over to wrap her up in a big hug. Tears came to her eyes as she realized just how much she'd missed her big brother. The one thing she needed from him at that moment was his hug, making her feel loved and safe.

As she returned his embrace, she said, "Oh, Riley, I've missed you so much."

"I've miss you, too," Riley said as he released her, giving her a quick kiss on the top of her head. "I decided this was a special night so we needed something extraordinary to go along with the exquisite meal I've fixed for us. I thought Mom's bread would be just the right touch."

"I'm sure you're right about that," Nona said looking around. "Where's your father?"

"He's in the living room sipping on his daily glass of bourbon."

"I didn't think he was supposed to be drinking, what with all of the meds he's taking," Nona said concerned.

Riley said with a smirk. "Why don't you be the one to tell him that, baby sister?"

"I will," Nona said with determination, as she headed to the living room to confront her father.

Mr. James was sitting in his favorite chair with his eyes closed and a big smile on his face as he listened to one of his favorite recordings, *Chattanooga Choo Choo* by Glenn Miller. Nona was hit by another nostalgic memory of her father and mother dancing to those big band tunes. She and Riley had often joined them. She'd loved listening to that music as a child growing up in this household, but hadn't listened to big band music in years. She hadn't realized that her father still did.

She made the decision right then that if it made him happy to have an occasional bourbon, she wasn't going to stop him. She wanted him to have as many happy moments as he could for as long as he could.

"Hi, Daddy," Nona said, as she walked over to give him a kiss on the cheek. "Looks like you're having a good time."

"I am," he said, as he reached out to take her hand. "May I have this dance?"

Nona laughed, "Oh, Daddy, I'm not sure I even remember how."

Her father stood up and took her in his arms. "As long as I remember, all you need to do is follow."

Nona was aware that there are precious few moments in life when you recognize when a true blessing is coming down from God. At that very moment in her life, as she and her father danced around the living room, she knew this was one of those moments. She could almost hear God whispering, "This is for you, Nona."

Mark and Aaron went straight back to the Sheriff's Department after leaving Nona's house. On the way there, Mark had called Nate to ask him to wait for them. He didn't want to waste any time in finding out all he could about the clock that had shown up mysteriously on Nona's wall. His gut told him this clock also had something to do with the glitch in the unarmed security system.

Nate met them at the front door where they handed the clock over to him. He put on his white gloves so he wouldn't transfer his fingerprints to the clock. Then he carefully removed it from the evidence bag. After examining it for only a few minutes, he looked up at Mark and asked, "This clock was in someone's kitchen?"

"Yes, it was hanging on the kitchen wall."

"Well, someone was using this clock to spy on that person," Nate announced.

Aaron said, "We figured that, Nate, but what can you tell us about this clock?"

"It's basically a self-powered spy camera. Not the most expensive one, but not the cheapest either," Nate said, as he examined the clock.

"It's a fully-functional wall clock with a one-piece camera and a digital video recorder, DVR," Nate began explaining. "How long was it up on the wall?"

Mark answered, "About two weeks. Why?"

"It has a high powered rechargeable battery that would probably last about thirty days," Nate answered. "So, who ever put it there wouldn't have had to go in to change it out."

Mark and Aaron watched closely as Nate began to remove parts from the clock.

Nate continued with his explanation, "This camera unit seems to have an internal human body thermal detector. It would turn the camera on to record when it detected the heat from a human body that was within about twenty feet of the camera. These units usually turn off about three minutes after no heat from a body is detected."

"So, you're saying that when a person walked into the kitchen, this camera would turn on and when they left, it would turn off?" Aaron asked.

"Yep," Nate said, "it would record the whole time the person was there in the kitchen or within twenty feet of the camera, but what's different about this one from the regular spy camera is that it doesn't use a memory card to store the recording, but, you see this part here," Nate said, as he pointed to what seemed to be a small black box, "this is a wireless device that sends the camera images straight to a computer where someone could watch it in real time or record it to watch later."

Both Mark and Aaron stared at the part Nate was pointing out. "That would mean that someone might have been watching Nona as if they were sitting right there in the room with her," Mark said finding all this hard to believe.

Looking over at Nate he asked, "Nate, with the device, could someone listen to what was being said in the room?"

"Yes."

"Can you find out where this information was being sent, what computer was 'watching'?" Aaron asked.

"I can try," Nate said, "but it's going to take some time."

Mark patted him on the shoulder. "Nate, I need this information as soon as possible."

"Let me see what I can do."

"Thanks," Mark said.

Chapter Eighteen

Nona spent the weekend at her father's house. It turned out to be one of the best times she'd had in a long time. She even found the time to read and relax, without thinking about Amy, her impending divorce, or her father's illness. Riley had been true to his word about learning to cook. He'd cooked every meal. Nona had offered to help, but he seemed to enjoy his time in the kitchen. Neither her father nor brother had questioned her reason for wanting to stay there. They'd both seemed glad for her company.

Nona left the house early Monday morning, before either one of them had come out of their rooms. She'd told them the night before that she'd be leaving early. She wanted to stop by her office before meeting Monty at the Kerry County Courthouse for her pretrial divorce hearing. She found, to her amazement, that she was looking forward to seeing Monty. Now that she'd gotten used to his arrogant ways, she'd begun to find them amusing.

Nona had fussed over her appearance before leaving her bedroom. She wanted to look like a woman that any sane man would never leave. She'd finally decided on the cobalt blue suit that brought out the attractiveness of her short gray hair. She was even wearing heels, which she only wore on rare occasions.

When she walked into her office, Nathan greeted her with a low whistle. "Wow! Don't you look nice."

Nona smiled at the compliment. "Thanks, I'm headed to the court house to meet with the judge about the divorce. Since Amy and Bill are going to be there, I wanted to look my best."

Lily came from around the corner. "Well, you nailed it."

Nona blushed at the attention. Maybe she'd gone too far from her normal look. "Is it too much?" she asked Lily.

"Not at all," Lily said with a smile. "It's just right for the occasion."

Nona hurried into her office to pick up the papers Monty had asked her to bring. "Pray for me," she called as she left.

Monty was waiting for her in the lobby of the courthouse, pacing back and forth. The smile that usually lit up his handsome face was missing. "Where have you been?" he asked sounding annoyed.

"Good morning, to you, too," Nona said with a bit of sarcasm in her voice. Then quickly answered his question. "Remember I told you I'd stop by the office on my way over here to get those papers you said we might need."

"Oh, right," Monty said, "I forgot about that. It's just that I was worried about you, with all the threats and stuff that have been coming at you lately. I was concerned, okay?" he asked, looking intently at her.

"Okay," Nona said, as she touched his shoulder reassuringly, "but I'm fine, Monty. No need to worry about me."

Reaching out and taking her hand in his, he said with sincerity, "But, I do worry about you, Nona." He gave her hand a squeeze.

Monty's gesture caught Nona off guard. With all she had going on in her life at this moment, she was sure she couldn't handle anything personal from Michael Montgomery. She thought she'd made it clear that she was only interested in him professionally—nothing personal.

Offering Monty a brief smile, Nona said patting his hand, "You don't need to worry about me, just worry about helping me keep my house." She handed him the papers she'd retrieved from her office. Then she turned and walked down the hall toward Judge Hammond's chambers for the pretrial divorce hearing. After a moment, Monty followed after her.

When Nona walked into the judge's outer office, she was surprised to see both Bill and Amy, along with their attorney, Mandy Jackson, there ahead of her. Bill had rarely been on time for anything in his whole life, let alone early. This was the first time that Nona had seen Amy since she'd become suspicious of her being the one behind the vandalism and the threats to her safety. Instead of following her strong desire to smack Amy in the face, she slapped a smile on her face and said with good ol' Southern hospitality, "How nice to see y'all."

Bill stood and answered nervously, "Good to see you as well, Nona." He waited for Nona to sit before he sat down.

Nona took a seat next to Mandy saying, "Hey, Mandy. How are you doing?" Nona had known Mandy professionally since she'd opened her law office in Kerry. She was several years younger than Nona and often came to her for advice.

Mandy shook her hand warmly. "I'm doing well, thanks for asking. You're looking mighty fine this morning, Nona."

"Why, thank you, Mandy."

Nona could feel the anger radiating off Amy. After hearing the friendly exchange between Mandy and Nona, she purposefully turned away, sighing loudly.

Monty walked in and took a seat across from Nona without saying a word to anyone.

Judge Hammond's secretary asked if anyone wanted coffee or water. All declined her offer. "It'll be a few minutes before the judge can see you," she informed them.

After waiting fifteen minutes, Judge Hammond opened the door to her chambers. "Sorry to keep y'all waiting," she said, as she walked into the office where they were all sitting and took a seat beside Monty. "I know this wasn't what you had planned, but after going over all of the papers that each side has presented to the court, I've decided that I will only be meeting with the lawyers today."

Looking at Mandy and Monty, she said as she turned to leave, "Please join me in my chambers."

Nona was stunned. She hadn't expected this turn of events. She stood up to protest, but when she looked at Monty, it was clear that he thought voicing her objection now would be a bad idea. Nona was well aware they needed Judge Hammond on their side. She reminded herself that the more cooperative they were the better chance of having a positive outcome in her favor. She smiled and sat back down.

"Just a minute," Amy said, as she stood and stomped over to the judge. By her reaction, it was obvious that Amy wasn't about to let this go forward without voicing her opinion of Judge Hammond's decision.

"Amy, it's okay," Bill said, trying to calm her down.

"I have every right to be in that hearing today. Who do you think you are?"

Pointing at Nona she shouted, "I wouldn't put it past her to have paid you off to rule in her favor, so she can keep that house away from me!"

Everyone turned to stare at Amy in disbelief. They were stunned by her outburst, but it was Judge Hammond who spoke. "I'll tell you who I am," she said in a low, controlled voice as she walked back to stand in front of Amy. "I am the one who has the authority to have you arrested for making such an accusation against my integrity as a judge."

When she was confident that Amy understood her message, she turned and walked into her chambers, followed by Mandy and Monty. The secretary followed, closing the door behind her.

Staring straight ahead, Nona couldn't seem to move. She was beyond offended by Amy's claim that she might have "paid off" the judge. In all her years as a lawyer, no one had ever made such a charge against her. It was Bill rushing to Amy that pulled Nona out of her trance.

Bill grabbed both of Amy's arms. "Why would you accuse Nona of such a thing?" he asked outraged.

"Because that's the kind of person your soon-to-be-ex-wife is," Amy answered without shame.

Bill stared at Amy as if he was seeing her for the first time. After a moment, he released her arms, allowing them to fall to her side. Shaking his head in disbelief, he left Judge Hammond's office without looking back.

Amy watched him leave, then, turning her attention back to Nona, she spit out, "Can't you see what you're doing to Bill? You're slowly killing him. You need to give up and leave Kerry, and you need to do it soon!"

The look on Amy's face was one of pure hatred. There was no doubt it was Nona she hated. Nona had never before been the target of such hatred. She wasn't quite sure what she should do. Her instincts urged her to fight back—hurl that hatred right back at Amy to hurt her like she'd been hurt. As Nona felt Amy's hatred pouring out of her and aimed directly at her, a strange thing happened. All her anger toward Amy evaporated as a calm feeling came over her. She was suddenly filled with sympathy for Amy.

Nona understood what a terrible burden it had to be to carry in your heart such hatred toward another person. That hatred had to eat away at Amy's life every minute of every day, until there was no room left for love. Nona could feel only sadness as she looked into Amy's eyes burning with such loathing toward her.

Nona reached out her hand toward her. Amy jerked her hand back. Nona continued to hold out her hand as she said gently, with tears in her eyes, "I'm so sorry for you, Amy."

"You don't need to feel sorry for me, Nona Foxx!" Amy erupted with the full force of her fury. "You're the one who's going to be sorry!"

Something deep down inside of Nona told her to keep silent. She turned away from Amy. She stepped into the hall, hoping Amy wouldn't follow. She hurriedly walked down the hall to the front doors. She thought she heard someone call her name, but she didn't look back. Her only focus was to get out of the courthouse and as far away from Amy as she could.

When she got outside, it took her eyes a few seconds to adjust to the bright sunshine. She quickly walked down the courthouse steps and out to her father's car. She unlocked the car and got in. When she closed the car door, all she could hear was the beating of her heart and the sound of her own breathing.

She could no longer hold back her tears. Nona put her head against the steering wheel, trying to regain control of her emotions. Something had happened in that room with Amy, which she'd never experienced before, and she didn't know if she was ready to accept it. There was no doubt in Nona's mind that Amy was the one behind the vandalism and the threats that she'd suffered through these past few weeks. She should be feeling nothing but disgust at the sight of Amy. Yet, that was not at all what she was feeling.

She suddenly sat up, dried her tears, and knew without a doubt what she had to do. She needed to talk to the person she'd always run to for help since she was a little girl. Nona started the car, backed out of her parking place, and turned the car toward her father's house.

Monty hadn't anticipated that move by Judge Hammond. He'd been through many pretrial divorce hearings in his career, but had rarely met with the judge without his client in attendance. The look on Mandy's face told him that she hadn't expected this either. As the door closed behind them, he caught a glimpse of the shock on Nona's face. He wondered if she was shocked by not being allowed to come with him or by Amy's reaction. He imagined it was a combination of both. He hated leaving her out there with Bill and Amy, but had no choice. Now, he needed to turn his attention on Judge Hammond.

As Judge Hammond took her seat behind her desk, she said, "Mrs. Jackson, I hope that is not the type of behavior that we will be seeing from your client in my courtroom."

"No, Your Honor," Mandy said respectfully.

"Good to know," Judge Hammond said, "Now, let's get down to the business at hand. I have a full day ahead, as I'm sure you both do as well. I have reviewed the documents that were sent to my office relevant to this case," the judge said, as she opened a folder before her. "I have questions I would like to have answered to clarify some issues.

"The first question is for you, Mr. Montgomery. Why is it that your client is not asking for the monetary compensation for which she is entitled? From the financial records filed by Mr. Harris, that could be a substantial amount."

"Ms. Foxx does not want nor need money from Mr. Harris. My client is asking the court to grant her full ownership of her home and the surrounding property," Monty said, looking directly at the judge.

"I have no doubt that you know this request is highly unusual," Judge Hammond directed her remark back to him.

He was aware how unusual Nona's request was. The standard was equitable division of assets, with the assets being both monetary and physical. Nona had made it clear to him each time they met or talked that she did not want Bill's money. She wanted Monty to do everything he could to secure the house and property for her. Period.

"Yes, Your Honor, I am aware, but this is a firm directive given to me by my client."

Judge Hammond smiled at his comment. "I am aware of the many 'firm directives' Ms. Foxx makes of the court." Many of Nona's cases had been brought to her court. Nona's reputation labeled her headstrong and determined to win her cases.

"What do you say to Ms. Foxx's directive, Mrs. Jackson?" Judge Hammond asked.

"As you know, from the documents we have filed with the court, Mr. Harris is asking for an equitable division of the assets that they acquired while married. However, he is not willing to allow her to take the home that had been in his family prior to their marriage."

"Oh, come on, Mandy," Monty interrupted, "Mr. Harris didn't give an ant's behind about that property until his mistress decided she wanted to live there. He has no right to pull the 'family home' card. We can prove that he wanted to tear down that house rather than restore it. He didn't care about the family connection then."

"Oh, come on, yourself!" Mandy countered. "She has no right to take that property from my client. No sane judge would ever award it to her alone."

"Excuse me, Mrs. Jackson," Judge Hammond interjected. "Are you questioning my sanity?"

Mandy looked down at the floor to answer, "No, Your Honor, I take back that comment. It was out of line."

"Yes, it most certainly was," Monty agreed.

The judge turned on Monty. "I most certainly do not need your help in handling this matter, Mr. Montgomery."

Then addressing both lawyers, Judge Hammond said, "At this time, I am open to hearing further arguments concerning Ms. Foxx retaining her home and property. I would like to put this on the court calendar for two weeks from Thursday. Will that date work for both parties?"

"It works for me, Your Honor," Monty quickly said after checking his calendar.

Mandy said, "For me as well, Your Honor."

"Good," Judge Hammond said as she stood, indicating that the meeting was over.

Monty walked out of the judge's office expecting to find Nona waiting for him. The office was empty. Monty walked out disappointed.

Mark had been out of the office most of the morning. There'd been a fatal accident less than a quarter of a mile from where his own accident had happened almost a year ago. As he drove away from this accident, he said a quick prayer of thanks that his had not been fatal. He was grateful to be alive.

When Mark returned to his office, he had a note from Nate telling him that he had more information about the infamous clock. He hoped that Nate had been able to find out where the video from the clock had landed. He quickly dialed Nate's office.

"Sheriff Weaver, I have a lead on where the video was streaming. I don't know the computer yet, but I do know the server that handled the traffic," Nate said excitedly.

"That's good news, Nate," Mark said. "How long do you think it will take to find out what computer has the video?"

"Well, if I can get the server to talk to me, it should tell me where that computer is housed."

Servers talking to computers didn't make much sense to Mark, but it sounded like Nate was getting close to discovering who put that clock in Nona's house. "Keep working on it, Nate, and let me know what you find out. Thanks!"

As Mark hung up his phone, he sat down at his desk. He didn't know how he felt about Nate finding out whose computer the video feed was downloading to. Layne had told him how the Fearsome Foursome had concluded that Amy was the one behind the vandalism and threats. They were convinced that Amy wanted that house so badly that she would do almost anything to get it from Nona.

Bill had told him that he'd offered to build Amy a new house with anything in it she wanted. Amy said she didn't want a new house. She wanted Nona's house. It seemed that she was so desperate for that house that she was willing to do just about anything to get it. Mark wondered if Bill had a clue what Amy was doing. He knew Bill, one of his oldest friends, well enough to know that he wouldn't approve of Amy's actions.

Mark knew that he was jumping to conclusions based on hunches and not on facts. He needed to wait for the facts before confronting Amy or telling Bill that Amy was a suspect in this case. He'd wait to hear from Nate. Mark turned his attention to the paperwork that had piled up on his desk waiting for him to complete.

Chapter Nineteen

For the entire drive back to her father's house, Nona prayed for her father to be "himself" today. She hadn't seen that empty look in his eyes for days, and hoped it wasn't there today. She held onto the hope that with the help of the medicine and exercise, she and Riley could keep the effects of Alzheimer's on her father at bay. She wanted more than anything for his Alzheimer's to be stopped dead in its tracks, and for the disease to never again take the father she'd always known away from her.

Nona pulled her father's car in behind the house. She checked herself in the rear-view mirror. She didn't want her father or Riley to know that she'd been crying. That would bring on too many questions she wasn't willing to answer at this time. Her eyes weren't red and there were no tear tracks going down her face, so they shouldn't suspect.

As she opened the back door that led into the kitchen, she could hear Riley muttering to himself. She put on a smile as she entered the kitchen.

"So, now you're talking to yourself?" Nona asked playfully.

Riley stood up and turned toward her. "They say that talking to yourself is okay. It's when you answer yourself that you need to worry," Riley countered cheerfully. "Well, don't you look nice today," he said, when he finally looked up.

"Thanks!" Nona said, as she gave her brother a peck on the cheek. "What're you up to, now?"

"Dad said something about how he loved it when we had waffles and ice cream, so I thought I'd make homemade waffles for dessert. I've been searching this blasted kitchen for an hour looking for the waffle iron that Miss Nadeen would use to make us those Belgium waffles. Do you know where in the world it would be?" Riley asked, as he opened another cabinet door.

"Not a clue," Nona answered, leaving Riley to continue his search.

"Well, aren't you a big help," Riley called after her as he slammed the cabinet door shut.

Nona went to her room to change into jeans, t-shirt, and her comfy slippers. She couldn't wait to get out of her high-heels. They were killing her feet. As she hung up what was now her favorite suit—since everyone had told her how good she looked in it—she thought about all her nice clothes that had been ruined in the attack on her bedroom. It was still hard for Nona to believe that Amy would want to wreak such havoc on her. She knew it was unlikely that Amy had physically destroyed her bedroom, but it was almost certain she was the force behind it.

As Nona thought about Amy, she remembered the look on her face as she spewed those words of hatred at Nona. When she thought back on the scene, she hadn't expected to feel such sadness. She hoped her father would help her understand why she was feeling this way.

Nona found her father where she'd hoped she'd find him, his office. He was sitting behind his big wooden desk furiously writing on a yellow legal pad with his favorite fountain pen. As Nona looked at his head bent over the pad, she noted that at his age, he still had wisps of gray hair covering his head. Most men his age were bald, but not her dad. For some reason, this made her feel happy for him as a strange thought came into her head: *At least Dad hasn't lost all his hair.*

He hadn't noticed her standing outside his door, so she tapped lightly on the door. For a moment, she feared what she might see in his eyes. When he looked up, she saw the connected, intelligent eyes of her father. A smile spread across his face when he saw her standing there.

"Nona, come in," he said, as he set his pen down and moved the pad he'd been writing on to the side.

"Hi, Daddy," she said, as she closed the door and sat down in the familiar worn leather chair facing his desk. "Can we talk?"

She wondered how many times over the years she'd said those words to her father. Hundreds? Thousands?

"What is it?" he said, putting his hands together as he leaned forward across his desk giving her his attention. "You seem troubled."

Nona told him what had happened at the courthouse, with the judge only allowing the lawyers into her chambers.

"That's not unusual," he said. "That can't be what has you upset."

She took a moment gathering her thoughts. "It wasn't that, it was the ugly scene that followed," Nona softly said shaking her head.

"With Bill?"

"No, it was Amy, Daddy." She'd promised herself she wouldn't cry, but knew she'd broken her promise as a tear rolled down her cheek.

Trying to keep emotion out of her voice, she told him about the accusations Amy had made concerning Nona bribing Judge Hammond and the threats she'd made to her if she didn't leave Kerry. She went on to confess that the true reason for staying at his house was that someone had placed a spy clock with a camera in her kitchen. She ended by sharing her belief that Amy had engineered the vandalism and threats.

Mr. James shook his head in disbelief as he listened to Nona. When she'd finished, he reached his hand across the desk and asked, "Why would you withhold the information about that clock and your suspicion that Amy was behind everything?"

"Because, Daddy, I don't think I was ready to accept it or admit it even to myself," Nona said.

"When Amy confronted me with such hatred at the courthouse, I didn't react in my usual way, by striking back," Nona said, placing her hand on her father's. "When I looked into Amy's eyes, which were filled with such loathing for me, true hatred, instead of hitting her back with my hatred and my rage for how she wrecked my life, I was overwhelmed with a deep sadness for her." In a hushed voice, she added, "I didn't feel anger, Daddy, only sympathy for her, and I don't understand why. She's hurt me in so many ways, not just by taking away my husband. I should be furious with her, not feeling sorry for her."

Mr. James patted his daughter's hand before withdrawing it and leaned back in his chair. He turned his chair around, away from Nona, looking out the window at the grass where there had once been his wife's flower garden. He missed seeing the bright colors of the blooming plants. He wondered if he'd ever told his wife how much he enjoyed looking out on the bright colors of her flowers.

Nona sat quietly waiting for her father. It had always been his habit to look out of the window to digest what he'd just heard, and to contemplate the advice he would offer his daughter. After several minutes, he turned his chair back around.

"Nona, there are things we expect, and accept, will happen in the course of our lives. We expect that our children will outlive us. We accept that we will one day pass from this world. We don't question the natural order of life," he paused for a moment before continuing.

"Then there are things you never thought would be a part of your life journey. Things like Alzheimer's or cancer or divorce. These are the things that you must make a conscious effort to accept or refuse. If you refuse them, then you will find yourself in a battle with them, you'll be angry because of them. If you take the refusal course of action, you will be the one left battered and bruised from the fight. I'm not saying you give in to these things, but if you accept that these things have now become an unexpected part of your life, then you can handle them on your terms, not theirs."

Mr. James once again took Nona's hand in his. "It is most important for you to remember that the only way you can faithfully accept these unexpected and unwanted life experiences is with God by your side. He is our hope and strength when we face these life challenges."

Nona looked questioningly at her father. "I hear what you're saying, Daddy, but I'm not quite sure what that has to do with my situation with Amy."

"It has everything to do with your situation with Amy," Mr. James explained. "When you didn't react to Amy's words of hatred with your anger, you were showing her your grace. What she's done to you, to your life, calls for severe consequences, but instead of giving her what she deserved, you showed grace. That's what we are called by God to do, just as He has done and continues to do for us."

Seeing that Nona still did not understand, Mr. James got up from behind his desk and went to her side. "Don't you see that God was right there with you today, Nona, helping you accept this unexpected life event with grace. God's grace is the reason that you didn't react with the anger Amy deserves."

Nona considered her father's words. She was aware that in the many situations when she'd reacted to life's challenges in ways she knew were wrong, God had shown her grace by forgiving and continuing to love her. Nona was pretty sure she wasn't at the point where she could love Amy, but she could show her grace by forgiving her—even when she didn't deserve it. She stood up and wrapped her arms around her father's neck. "Oh, Daddy, what a perfect explanation. I love you so very much!"

They remained in their loving embrace until they heard Riley call out from the kitchen, "I found the waffle iron. Who's up for some waffles and ice cream?"

Nona wiped away a tear as she and her father smiled at one another and called back to Riley, "Me!"

Bill had been completely caught off guard by Amy's outburst in Judge Hammond's office. He was well aware that Amy detested Nona, but he hadn't expected her to make such outlandish accusations about Nona. He was so angry with her for what she'd said to the judge, that he couldn't handle being in the same room with her. He was afraid of what he might do to her. When he left the office, he walked the halls of the courthouse, hoping it would calm him down. He was heading back to talk to Amy when he caught sight of Nona leaving. Bill considered hurrying to catch up with Nona, but decided against that move. He was embarrassed by Amy's absurd accusations about Nona. He wasn't sure what he would say to her about the whole situation. Instead, he headed back to Judge Hammond's office.

When Bill opened the door to the office, he didn't see Amy right away, but he heard her. She was in a chair in the corner of the room sobbing. He rushed over to her. Had Nona hurt Amy in some way?

"What's going on, Amy? Did Nona do something to you?" Bill asked tenderly, as he sat down next to her.

At first, Amy was crying too hard to answer. He held her as he waited patiently. When she'd finally regained her composure enough to speak, she began to explain her version of what happened after he left the office. "That woman is a horrible person, Bill. I don't know how you stayed married to her for all those years," she said in a halting voice.

Bill asked, "What happened, Amy? What did she do to you?"

"She told me she was sorry for me," Amy blurted out, as she began to cry even harder than before.

From the way that Amy was crying, Bill had suspected that Nona had called her an ugly name or put her down, as Bill had witnessed Nona do to others on numerous occasions. He wasn't quite sure why Amy was crying over Nona feeling "sorry" for Amy. To Bill, it didn't seem like such a bad thing. He wasn't quite sure how he should comfort her.

He took her hands in his, and softly said, "I'm so sorry that Nona said that to you."

Amy turned and buried her head in his chest. "She wanted to hurt me, Bill. That's why she said it."

Bill didn't say anything else; he just held her, hoping her tears would soon end.

The door to Judge Hammond's chambers opened. Bill watched as Nona's lawyer walked past them and out the door. Mandy sat down in the empty seat next to Bill.

Still trying to comfort Amy, Bill asked, "How did it go in there?"

"Not as well as I'd hoped, Bill," Mandy answered honestly. "I have to tell you that what Amy said to the judge didn't help our case any."

Bill shook his head, but didn't respond. He knew from the look on the judge's face that she had found Amy's comment inappropriate.

Mandy continued, "I really don't know how she's going to rule about the house. There's a distinct possibility she might award it all to Nona."

This got Amy's attention. She sat up, wiping away her tears as she looked over at Mandy. "That house rightfully belongs to me and Bill. Nona doesn't deserve that house. Your job is to take it from her. That's what we're paying you for," Amy said bitterly.

Amy's hostility surprised Mandy, "That's what I'll work to do, but in the end, it will all be up to the judge."

"Come on, Amy. If we don't get that house, we can build a brand-new one made just for you," Bill said hopefully to Amy, as he tenderly pushed her hair away from her face.

Looking directly at Bill, Amy said determinedly, "I don't want a new house. I want that house."

"Hopefully, that's what will happen, honey," Bill said, as he wondered why she was so determined to live in that old house when she could have a brand new one.

After eating her fill of Belgium waffles topped with vanilla ice cream with Riley and her father, Nona left the house, explaining that she needed to go to the office to take care of a few things. After talking to her father about the situation with Amy, she needed some time to think about what she was going to do next. She was still puzzled by the absence of animosity she was feeling toward Amy. Was her father right about God being with her and the whole thing about grace? She believed that God was always with her, but she hadn't had many experiences where she'd felt Him truly change her heart toward someone. It was a lot to consider.

After driving around for an hour, reliving the drama with Amy and her talk with her father, Nona had come to a life changing decision. She needed to talk to Layne about the decision she'd made because of all that had happened. She hoped that she'd find Layne at home, with time to talk. With the garage door closed and no cars in the driveway, she couldn't tell if Layne was home or not. She decided to check it out as she got out of her car. She knocked several times and was turning to leave when the door suddenly opened. She was caught off guard when she saw Jenny standing there, looking so cute with her hair pulled up in a ponytail. Even though she knew Jenny would soon be part of Layne's family, she hadn't expected her to answer Layne's door.

"Hi there, it's Nona isn't it?" Jenny asked politely.

"Yes, it is."

"Come on in," Jenny said with a smile, as she stood back to allow Nona to enter. "Layne will be down in a minute. We've been in the attic checking out a few things."

Nona followed her through the living room to the back of the house. "Can I get you something to drink?" Jenny asked.

It was obvious to Nona that Jenny must have been spending a great deal of time at Layne's house, to feel comfortable enough to offer her a drink. "I'd love a glass of iced tea, if there's some made."

"Sure," Jenny said, as she walked to the refrigerator.

"Hey, Nona," Layne said, coming up behind her. "To what do we owe the honor of your presence?"

"I'm sorry. Have I interrupted something?" Nona answered, suddenly feeling like she had intruded on their afternoon.

"Not at all. We were up in the attic scouting out my wedding dress. You've heard that Aaron and Jenny are getting married, right?"

"I have," Nona said. Turning to Jenny, she said, "Congratulations and best wishes!"

"Thanks," Jenny said excitedly, "I'm hoping that I can get married in the same wedding dress Layne got married in."

Nona looked at Jenny skeptically as she took the glass of tea Jenny had fixed for her.

"I know that I'm shorter than Layne, but Dixie thinks she can alter the dress so it'll fit perfectly."

"I'm sure it will be beautiful on you," Nona said.

Jenny looked at her watch. "Oh, I have to go. My shift starts in thirty minutes. Good to see you, Nona."

"How are you getting to work? I didn't see any cars in the driveway," Nona asked.

"I told her to park in the garage, since it looked like rain," Layne explained.

Jenny rushed over to Layne to give her a kiss on the cheek as she hurried out the door.

"She's like a tiny whirlwind," Nona said.

Layne smiled. "Yes, a Yankee one at that."

"That's going to take some getting used to," Nona said smiling back.

"Let's sit down in the family room," Layne said, as she poured herself a glass of tea.

When the two had gotten comfortable, Layne asked, "What's up? I can tell that something's on your mind."

"You know me too well," Nona said, as she began to tell Layne the story, starting with the scene Amy made at the courthouse. She described as best she could the look of hatred on Amy's face.

"Layne, I've never felt so much hate coming from one person, aimed right at me!" Nona paused, "but as I looked at the loathing Amy bore for me, burning in her eyes, I was filled with such sadness for her. You know me better than anyone, and you know that my usual reaction would be to strike back."

Layne nodded her head. "Now, that's the Nona I know so well."

"I don't know what it was exactly that I wanted to do, but she looked so miserable that I just couldn't find the strength to retaliate. I truly felt her pain and anguish. My heart was breaking for her, Layne." As Nona recalled the scene, she felt those same emotions coming back to her.

"Nona, you were showing Amy grace." As she broke out in a grin, she added, "And we all know that grace is not the norm for you, especially in your profession as a lawyer."

"Oh, my gosh!" Nona said with disbelief. "You're using the exact same word that Daddy did."

"What word, 'lawyer'?"

"Grace!"

Layne chuckled. "Well, isn't it grace when Amy deserved to be smacked upside the head and you didn't?"

Nona thought about this for a minute. "Well, Layne, if you find it hard to believe that I showed Amy grace, then what I'm about to tell you next is really going to throw you for a loop."

Nona cleared her throat. "This thought has been in my head since my encounter with Amy and my talk with Daddy." She pushed away her urge to cry as she looked over at Layne. "I'm thinking about just letting Amy and Bill have my house."

Layne stared at Nona with amazement. Had she heard her correctly? She'd never known Nona to give up a fight—ever. She was speechless.

From the look on Layne's face, Nona realized that her announcement may have sent her into shock. She needed to explain what had brought her to this decision. "With all Amy has been willing to do to get me out of my house, topped off by what she said in Judge Hammond's office, I finally understood that the house means much more to Amy than it does to me."

Layne wasn't convinced. "Nona, you love that house. That's your home."

"You're right about that," Nona agreed, "but I've been thinking that maybe I've been loving that house for the wrong reasons."

Nona stood up and began pacing back and forth, trying to put her thoughts into words that would help Layne understand how she was feeling about the house. "After losing Bill to another woman, and then losing Grace to that same woman, I began to think of the house as the place where I still had both of them with me. We made so many memories when we were sharing our lives in that house. I think I even embellished some of those memories to make me feel better about our life there as a family, that we were happier there than we really were. I was holding on to Bill and Grace through that house."

Layne nodded as she began to understand.

"After facing these facts, I believe I'm ready to move on to a place where I can make new memories, instead of clinging to the past through that house," Nona said with confidence.

"Maybe you are," Layne said, offering support to Nona's decision.

Nona sighed deeply. She was tired of the drama of this day and wanted to break the tension of this drama.

"How about another glass of tea?" Layne offered.

"Thanks; that would really hit the spot."

As Nona was walking back to her car to head back to her father's house, her cell phone rang. She took it out of her back pocket and checked the screen to see who was calling. It was Monty. She answered anxiously, "Hey, Monty, how'd it go with the judge?"

"I think it went well," Monty answered without hesitation. "I'll tell you one thing, Amy's verbal assault helped us out. The judge was none too pleased with that."

"That was nothing compared to what she hit me with after y'all went into the judge's chambers," Nona said.

"Oh, did she ask if she could be your best friend?" Monty said sarcastically.

"Sure, she did," Nona responded with a laugh, "or something very close to that!"

"I'm not exactly sure what happened with you two after we left, but I can tell you what happened in Judge Hammond's chambers," Monty said. "I think there is a good chance that she's going to find in your favor for keeping your house."

"Interesting," Nona said unenthusiastically.

"It's more than just 'interesting,' Nona, it's good news for our side," Monty said, confused by her response. "I thought you'd be happy to hear this news."

Monty waited for Nona to say something more, but there was only silence on her end of the conversation. "Is everything all right, Nona?"

"Monty, I need to tell you something that you may be less than thrilled about," Nona began. "I've changed my mind about wanting to keep the house," she blurted out.

"What?" Monty cried into the phone. "Nona, you've told me over and over that all you wanted was the house. You were adamant that it was to be my one and only objective."

"I understand that you're shocked about this change of course," Nona said, "I'm in shock about my decision as well, but I believe that it's the right one for me. When I had you go after Bill for the house, I was being sentimental, not thinking about what I really wanted."

Her declaration was met by silence. Nona gave Monty some time to adjust to her news.

In a much calmer voice, Monty asked, "What is it you want out of this divorce, Nona?"

Nona answered without hesitation. "I want a fair settlement," then added, "for both myself and Bill."

Resigning himself to Nona's new directive, Monty said, "Okay, then we need to scrap everything and start over."

"I agree," Nona said.

"Can you be in my office tomorrow morning, first thing?" Monty asked.

"Yes, first thing," Nona agreed before ending the call.

Chapter Twenty

It had been another long day for Mark. He was heading home when he was called by dispatch asking for his location. "I'm on highway 41 heading home," he responded.

Dispatch came back with, "Nate has some important information that he believes you'll be very interested in, Sheriff."

Mark hoped that meant Nate had found the location of who had been watching Nona through the spy clock. "Tell him I'm turning around and heading back. I'll meet him in his office," Mark replied.

Mark was back at the Sheriff's Department and walking into Nate's office in less than ten minutes. "What have you found out, Nate?"

"I think you're going to be pleased with what I've learned about where that video feed was being sent," Nate said, as he handed Mark a two page print out.

As Mark read through the pages, Nate explained what he was looking at. "I was able to trace the Internet Protocol, or IP address, from the wireless router that was in Mrs. Foxx's house. It's hard to believe they used her router, anyway, that IP address was sent out by an Internet service provider, or ISP, in Savannah."

Nate said with pride, "Once I contacted the network administrator of that ISP, the network administrator was able to trace that IP address to a computer that is housed at the address listed at the bottom of the second page."

Mark looked up from the pages to Nate. "You mean that this is the address of where that video feed was being sent?" Mark hadn't expected that they could get an address. It seemed too easy.

"Yes, sir," Nate said with a smile. "That's the beauty, or the problem, of technology—depending on which side you're on."

"Good work, Nate," Mark said patting him on the back. "Now, all we need is a warrant to search for this computer at that address."

"I don't think you'll have a problem getting the warrant, but there might be a problem with finding the right computer, Sheriff," Nate said. "That address is a warehouse over in the industrial park."

"Why is that a problem?" Mark asked.

"Well, sir, it's a computer warehouse!"

"You're kidding, right?" Mark asked.

"No, sir," Nate said, "but most of the computers housed there will still be in boxes. It's just that if they've set up a network there with a proxy server, then that could create a problem locating the exact computer where the feed is going."

Mark shook his head in frustration, wondering why he was always getting hit with complications. He wanted a day of everything just going smoothly, without any glitches. He knew all too well that those days were few and far between.

"We can start with getting the search warrant and go from there," Mark said, as he walked out of Nate's office looking at his watch. One good thing was that it was only three in the afternoon, which meant he'd be able to find a judge to sign the warrant without any problems. One bad thing was knowing that he was looking at a long night ahead.

Nona's phone rang almost the second she'd ended her call with Monty. It was Riley. "Hey..." Nona said into the phone, but Riley broke in before she could say another word.

"Nona, I can't find Dad," Riley said in a panic.

"Calm down, Riley," Nona said, trying to keep her voice even, "have you looked everywhere in the house?"

"Of course, I have," Riley snapped back at Nona. "I've searched the house, the yard, the garden, but he's nowhere to be found."

Nona was only about two blocks away from the house. "Hang on, Riley, I'm almost home. Don't worry, we'll find him," Nona said, hoping what she was saying was true. She'd heard reports over the news where a person with Alzheimer's had gotten disoriented and couldn't find their way home. Sometimes they weren't found for days, or never at all. She prayed that wasn't the case with her father.

Riley was standing in the driveway when Nona pulled in. She could see the terror on his face. He rushed to her side of the car even before it had come to a complete stop. He pulled at the handle on the door to open it. Nona stepped out into her brother's arms.

Riley held onto Nona. "Oh, Nona, I'm a terrible son. I wasn't paying attention. I got distracted and now he's gone."

Nona released Riley. "He's not gone," she said, trying to keep her composure. "Tell me exactly what happened, Riley."

Running his fingers through his hair, a nervous habit of his since he was a boy, Riley said, "Dad came into the kitchen and said he wanted to go for a walk. I had just pulled everything out of the cabinets so I could put the kitchen in order."

Looking up at Nona he added, "You know how it was, so disorganized. I couldn't find anything in those cabinets."

"I know it was a mess." Nona shook her head, agreeing with him.

"So, then what happened?" she asked, encouraging him to continue with the part about her father.

"Dad said he wanted to go for a walk. I told him that I couldn't leave right then, with everything in such a disarray, but it would take me about an hour to get it all put up. I said we could go for a walk then. He seemed okay with that and walked out of the kitchen. I thought he'd probably go to his office and piddle around for an hour. But when I went to his office to get him for our walk, he wasn't there. I called for him and searched the whole house."

Riley paused, as he relived that moment when he'd realized his father was missing. Nona could see the tears running down his cheeks.

"I looked outside, calling his name over and over, but he never answered," Riley said. "Why didn't I just stop what I was doing and go for a walk with him?"

"Riley, we're going to find him," Nona said shaking his shoulders. "Have you checked with the neighbors to see if they saw him leave the house or the yard?"

"No, I'd just finished checking the garden when I called you."

"Let's check the neighborhood before we start to panic," Nona said.

The two separated, knocking on their neighbor's doors as they went down the street. When they met back at the house, no one had seen their father leave the house or walking around in the neighborhood. She knew the route her father took when he went for a walk, but he was nowhere along that route. She wanted to scream out, "Daddy, where are you?" loud enough that he would hear her no matter where he was.

Nona knew she needed to keep a clear head and not give in to the fear that was beginning to grip her heart. She prayed a quick prayer, asking for God to help them find her father and to give her strength to get through this.

With renewed determination, she turned to Riley. "It's time to call for help, Riley. We need more people to help us search, and we need them now. We only have a few hours before it'll be dark. I'm calling Mark."

"Looks like we already have some help, Nona," Riley said pointing to the front lawn where people from their neighborhood were gathering, offering their support and assistance.

Mark had just gotten his search warrant, when his phone rang. He was surprised to see that the call was from Nona.

As soon as he answered, Nona blurted out, "Mark, Dad's missing. He went for a walk by himself about an hour ago and he's not back. I'm afraid something has happened to him, Mark!"

"I'm on my way," Mark said, as he ended the call.

He immediately hit the quick call button for Aaron as he was rushing out the door. "Aaron, get to Mr. James's house as fast as you can. He's missing," he said urgently.

When he got in his patrol car, he called Layne. "Layne, you need to get over to Mr. James's house. He went for a walk about an hour ago and hasn't been seen since. I know that Nona will want you there with her."

"Oh, no, Mark," Layne said, "that's terrible. I'll get over there as fast as I can."

Aaron had begun organizing volunteers into search parties as soon as he'd gotten on scene, sending them out across the county along with a deputy leading each group. Within the hour, there were over one hundred people, besides the deputies, out looking for Mr. James. He was a well-liked and respected man in the community, and people wanted to help in any way they could. Nona wanted to join the search, but Aaron had convinced her that someone needed to stay at the house, just in case her father called or found his way home. Kerry wasn't a big town, but it was big enough that it was going to take hours for a thorough search.

As soon as Betty Jo, Don, Dixie, and Alex, along with their children, heard about the search for Mr. James, they were there to help.

Since Don had once been the Game Warden for the county, he knew the nooks and crannies where others might not know to look. Alex, Nathan, Jason, Zeke, and Josh went with him to search those areas. Dixie did what she did best by cooking, so if the search went past supper time, she'd have a hot meal for everyone. Betty Jo was answering the house phone, and keeping track of the names of all of those who had joined the search. Layne was staying close to Nona, offering her support and trying to keep her calm and hopeful.

"I just can't believe this is happening, Layne," Nona said distressed. "I keep telling myself that everything is going to be all right, and Daddy is going to be home soon, but I'm starting to wonder..."

"Don't you dare do that," Layne interrupted. "You can't give up hope."

"Oh, Layne, I've been praying and praying for Daddy to be found safe, but I'm so worried that hope feels far away right now."

"Nona Jane Foxx, if you give up hope, how will that help your father?"

Nona looked at Layne with pleading eyes. "Oh, Layne, what will I do if..."

"Nona, I know that you have had one heck of a tough day even before this happened with your father," Layne said taking Nona's hand, "but we aren't promised a life without tough days. It's all about how we choose to react to things and what we decide to focus on. When we focus on the negative, we get negative. And, when we focus on the positive, we reap positivity. You need to quit thinking about the bad things that can happen to your dad and think of the positive. Just look at all the people who have stopped what they were doing and are out there looking for your dad, because they have hope they will find him."

Nona reached over to hug Layne. "You are so right, Layne. I choose to be hopeful that we will find my Dad."

Mark had delayed carrying out the search warrant for the computer at the computer warehouse. That could wait until after Mr. James was found. He was driving around town in his patrol car, checking the places he knew that Mr. James frequented. No one had seen him recently, but promised if they did see him, they'd hold onto him and call the Sheriff's Office. How was it that Mr. James had been able to walk around town without being noticed?

He'd alerted the hospital to be on the lookout for the possibility of someone bringing in a confused elderly man. The radio station had put a bulletin out about a missing elderly man with Alzheimer's. It seemed the whole town was looking for Mr. James. Mark was confident he'd be found, but concerned about what shape he'd be in when he was finally found.

What worried Mark at present was that the sun was going down. The search would be ten times harder if they had to look for Mr. James in the dark. He pulled over to the side of the road to consider what place Mr. James might go if he was confused or if he was living in the past. Nathan and Lily had gone to the Foxx and Foxx office to check to see if he'd gone there. They'd even searched the attic and basement where old records were stored, but hadn't seen any signs he'd even been there. Mark checked in with Aaron on the progress of the search parties. So far, there were no signs as to where Mr. James had been, or where he might be heading.

He pulled his car back out onto the road. A thought came to him as to where Mr. James might have gone on a typical afternoon when he was practicing law—the Kerry County Courthouse. He'd driven by it several times, but hadn't stopped to search the premises. It was worth a shot. As he pulled up to the courthouse, it occurred to him that it was after six and the courthouse would be closed now, but when Mr. James took his walk it would have been open for business. He reached in his glove compartment for the keys to the courthouse. With keys in hand, he raced up the front steps and opened the door.

"Mr. James," Mark called out loudly, "it's Sheriff Weaver." His voice echoed on the walls of the front lobby. He hoped for a reply, but his words were met with a deafening silence.

Mark headed down the hall toward the County Clerk's Office to see if Mr. James might be down that way, before calling Aaron for help in searching the courthouse. He called out once more, "Mr. James, it's Sheriff Weaver. Are you here?"

No answer came. He had just reached into his back pocket to pull out his cell phone when he heard a faint sound. He wasn't sure where it came from. Mark took out his flashlight, turned it on, and began searching the dark hall.

He called out, "Mr. James, where are you?" He stood completely still, holding his breath, alert for any sound.

He let out his breath when he heard his name. "Sheriff Weaver?" The voice was weak, but clear.

Mark shined his flashlight down the shadowy corridor to his right. "Mr. James, I'm here. Can you tell me where you are?"

The beam of Mark's light passed over a figure hunched in an office doorway, looking forlorn and disheveled. He'd found Mr. James.

After calling Aaron to let him know where he'd found Mr. James, Mark sat down next to Mr. James, who was half-way sitting and half-way lying.

"Mr. James, you're going to be okay," Mark said reassuringly, as he helped him up into a more comfortable sitting position. He saw that his shoes were covered with mud and his pants had been ripped just above his knee. At first Mark thought his face and hands were splattered with blood, but upon closer examination he was relieved to find that they were splotches of dirt. He could find no apparent signs of injury, but he'd told Aaron to send an ambulance just in case. It was Mr. James's eyes, which carried a haunted emptiness, that most troubled Mark.

Mr. James looked around with a forlorn look on his face, and said to Mark, "I seem to have been abandoned in this cathedral."

"Mr. James, I promise you that no one has 'abandoned' you. Nona and Riley are on their way, and until they get here I'm going to stay right here with you," Mark said as he held him closer.

Mark was relieved when he heard the sound of sirens, at first faintly, but then louder as they came closer. He heard the clanging of the courthouse doors as they opened, and then the sounds of urgent footsteps echoing down the hall as others raced toward them. He saw Nona and Layne as they turned the corner rushing toward them.

Nona was the first to reach her father. "Oh, Daddy," was all she could say before she was overcome with sobs of relief. With tears streaming down her face, she knelt next to her father and tenderly caressed his face in her hands.

Mark stood up and turned away, recognizing it as a private moment between father and daughter. "Let's give them a moment," Mark said to the paramedics, as he reached out for Layne's hand.

"Oh, Mark, I was so afraid that Mr. James might not be found alive," Layne said, as she held onto Mark's hand. "What made you think of looking for him in the courthouse?"

Mark thought about this for a minute. He really wasn't sure what had made him check out the courthouse. "It seemed to me that it might just be the place Mr. James would go. I'm just glad I did."

"Daddy, you scared us all to death. I was so worried about you," Nona said hugging her father. "Don't ever do that again."

"If you tell me what it is that I've done, young lady, I'll make every effort to not repeat the deed," Mr. James said, seemingly confused.

When Nona sat back to look at her father, she recognized that look in his eyes. The father who had given her such great advice this afternoon was not the same man who was sitting on the floor of the courthouse. This father didn't seem to know that he was even talking to his own daughter. She leaned in to hold him tighter.

Layne leaned down next to Nona. "Nona, it's time to let the paramedics take your father to the hospital where he can be checked out."

Nona nodded her head, releasing her father. She held onto Layne as she watched the paramedics put her father on a stretcher to carry him to the hospital. The three of them followed the paramedics out of the courthouse.

"Where's Riley?" Mark asked, just now noticing that Riley was not there.

"He stayed back at the house," Nona answered defensively. "He didn't think he could handle seeing Daddy right now."

Mark found his absence strange, but didn't say anything. It was obvious it had upset Nona that he'd chosen not to come with her.

Chapter Twenty-One

T he doctors decided to keep Mr. James in the hospital for the night. It was indeed amazing that he had walked almost five miles, using the back roads from his house to the courthouse, without sustaining any major injuries. He had a few scratches. At some point, he must have fallen, but the fall had only resulted in a large bruise on his knee. Everyone said he was a lucky man.

Nona was overwhelmed by the community support her family had received. When Layne had taken her home after she'd made sure that her father was resting comfortably, she found that many of the people who had volunteered to search were waiting around to find out how her father was doing. She recognized their caring as a true blessing from God and was grateful to each and every one of them.

Dixie and Betty Jo waited until she got home as well. They wanted to make sure that Nona was okay and had everything she needed. When Nona asked where Riley was, Dixie told her that he'd gone to his room right after she'd left with Layne. No one had seen him since. Nona suspected that Riley hadn't gone with her to the courthouse because he couldn't face his father. She knew that he was blaming himself for his father's disappearance.

After everyone had gone home, Nona began to go through her father's house turning off the lights and locking the doors. When she turned off the lights in the kitchen, she could see a light shine from under Riley door. Taking a chance that he was still awake, she lightly tapped on his door.

"Riley, it's Nona," she said softly, "I thought you'd want to know Dad's spending the night in the hospital."

Nona waited a few minutes for a response. Deciding that he must be asleep, she turned to go up to her bedroom. She'd talk to him in the morning. She'd just reached the door to the dining room when she heard the creak of her brother's bedroom door opening.

"Nona?" Riley called out in a soft voice.

"Yes," she answered.

"Can we talk?"

"Of course, we can," Nona said as she turned toward her brother. "How about a cup of tea?"

"That sounds good me," Riley said.

"I'll meet you in the kitchen in ten, but first let me get out of these clothes and wash my face," Nona said. She went quickly to her bedroom, where she changed into her pajamas, washed what makeup was left off her face, and brushed her hair. She stepped into her slippers and made her way back down to the kitchen. Nona had filled the copper tea kettle with water and put it on the stove to heat up before Riley came into the kitchen. He stood in the doorway with his arms crossed for several minutes before she noticed him. When she caught sight of her big brother standing in the doorway of the kitchen in the same robe he'd worn when he was in high school, she smiled up at him. That robe had probably been hanging in his closet since he'd left for college years ago.

"How's Dad doing?" Riley asked.

It was apparent Riley had been crying. His thick glasses magnified his red-rimmed eyes. He'd never meant for anything bad to happen to his father, but she could tell that he was blaming himself for all that had happened. Her heart went out to him.

"Dad's going to be fine," she said reassuring him. "Just a few scratches and bruises, but nothing serious. They're going to keep an eye on him overnight just to be safe."

Nona turned away from Riley to the whistling tea kettle that was demanding her attention. "Go ahead and sit down over there," she said, pointing to the small breakfast table in the corner of the kitchen. "I'll get this tea fixed, then we'll talk."

Instead of getting down the china tea cups like she had done for her father, she pulled two mugs out of the cabinet, dropped in an Earl Gray tea bag, then filled each cup with hot water. Nona carefully carried them over to the table where Riley was sitting, then went back for the sugar and cream she knew he liked to put in his tea.

Nona sat down across from Riley and blew over her cup, cooling down her tea. Riley sat unmoving, with his head down. "Riley, you have got to stop blaming yourself," she said, more sternly than she'd intended.

Then in a gentler voice, she added, "Alzheimer's made Dad walk out of this house and got him lost. We're just going to have to watch him more closely so nothing like this happens again."

Riley raised his head to look at his sister. In a low voice that Nona had to lean closer to hear, he said, "Nona, I think we need to put Dad someplace where they know how to take care of Alzheimer's patients."

Nona pushed her chair back, irritated that he would suggest such a thing. "Dad's not an 'Alzheimer's patient,' Riley, and we're not putting him 'someplace'!" She took a sip of her tea in an effort to calm herself.

"I cannot believe that you'd even suggest such a thing," Nona said, glaring at Riley.

"Then what are we going to do, Nona?" Riley asked, scowling back at her, "Lock him up in his room so he can't escape?"

"Riley, if you stayed here in Kerry, the two of us together could take care of him right here in this house."

"You expect me to stay here?"

"I've had a long, trying day, Riley," Nona said, as she ran her hand through her hair in frustration, "And I don't think this is the right time to be having this conversation with you. I have an appointment early in the morning, and I'm going to bed."

Nona got up from the table, emptied her tea cup into the sink, and walked out of the kitchen, leaving Riley sitting at the table staring after her.

Mark realized he was starving when he got home and decided to fix himself a couple of ham sandwiches while he waited for Layne. He wasn't sure how long she would stay with Nona after taking her home, but guessed it wouldn't be long, since Nona had to be exhausted from the day she'd had.

As he sat on the stool at the kitchen island, eating his sandwiches, he thought about the troubling day he'd had. He'd thought that the wreck first thing that morning would be the worst part of his day, but ending the day with finding Mr. James like that may have been worse. It was tough to see such an intelligent, dignified man so confused and broken. Alzheimer's was a terrible disease. He hoped that it wouldn't be one that ever touched his family.

As Mark was cleaning up the mess he'd made in the kitchen, he heard Layne pull her car into the garage. He was relieved that she was home safe and sound. She came into the kitchen, hung up her keys on the peg, and went straight into Mark's open arms.

"Oh, Mark," Layne said into his shoulder, "I was so scared that no one would find Mr. James. Thank God you thought to look in the courthouse." She held him tighter.

Mark kissed her on top of the head. "I have no doubt that it was God who put the thought in my head to look in the courthouse, Layne."

She patted him on the back. "I'm just glad that's over," Layne said as she stepped back out of Mark's arms, "and that he's okay."

"What was the deal with Riley?" Mark asked. "Why didn't he come with Nona to see his father?"

Layne shook her head. "I have no idea, but it's the strangest thing to me. Dixie said that when he got back to the house, he just went to his room, closed the door, and didn't come out."

"Well, Riley's always been a little bit to the left of normal," Mark said with a grin.

Layne gave him a friendly hit him on the arm. "That's not nice."

Mark grabbed his arm where she'd just hit it. "But you do know it's true, right?"

Layne smiled, but didn't answer.

"I'm beat," Mark said with a yawn. "I'm ready to hit the sack."

Together they walked out of the kitchen and up the stairs to their bedroom turning off the lights along the way. They had just gotten to their bedroom door when Mark's cell phone rang. Layne looked at Mark with concern. They both knew that if he was getting a call at this late hour something was wrong somewhere in Kerry County.

Once Mark had checked the screen to see who was calling, he quickly answered. "Aaron, what is it?"

"Dad, the patrol car that was assigned to keep a watch on Nona's house just called in. They've picked up on some activity at the house, Dad. I'm on my over there, but I thought you 'd want to know," Aaron said.

Without hesitation, Mark said, "I'm on my way."

He turned to Layne explaining, "Looks like someone is at Nona's house. I'll call you when I know something." He leaned over and gave her a kiss.

"Please be careful, Mark," Layne called after him as he ran down the stairs and out the door.

Layne had never gotten used to these late-night calls that took Mark away into the night. She said a quick prayer for his and Aaron's safety, and went back down the stairs. She knew there was no way she'd be able to get to sleep now. She briefly thought about calling Nona, but decided that was a bad idea. Until they knew something, there was no need to cause her more worry.

Aaron had just pulled up to his apartment when he'd heard the call to dispatch about Nona's house. He'd immediately backed his car up and let dispatch know that he was on his way to the scene. He then called his father, knowing he'd want to know right away. Aaron pulled in behind the two patrol cars that were parked at the end of Nona's driveway.

Deputy Branson had been the one who called it in, saying he'd observed what appeared to be a beam from a flashlight inside the house. He'd watched as the beam moved from room to room as if searching for something, but for the past ten minutes seemed to have stopped in the kitchen. Aaron could see the light and was curious as to how someone had gotten inside the house without triggering the alarm.

Just as the three deputies were deciding the best way to approach the house, Mark pulled up. He got out of his car and walked toward the group.

"Sheriff Weaver, we were just deciding how to approach the house," Aaron said. When on official duty, Aaron preferred to call his father "Sheriff" rather than the too familiar "Dad."

"Do we know how many there are in or out of the house?" Mark asked.

"No, sir," Deputy Branson answered, "but there appears to be only one beam of light in the house. We're not sure if there is anyone else inside or outside."

After thinking it over for a minute, Mark offered a plan. "Let's check the perimeter to see if there are others."

With guns drawn, the four of them carefully worked in a grid pattern securing the area outside of Nona's house. They found no one lurking around outside. However, they did find an electric golf cart parked near the side door leading to the kitchen, but there were no other vehicles in sight. Both Mark and Aaron verified that Nona didn't own a golf cart.

It appeared as if the person who had broken into Nona's house had driven a golf cart right up to her house and entered through the side door. After taking a closer look at the side door, it was obvious from the lack of damage to the door that whoever was in there had opened the door with a key and entered the code disarming Nona's security system.

Mark motioned for Aaron to cover the front door and the second deputy to cover the back door that led to the deck, in case the perpetrator tried to exit out of another door. Deputy Branson and he would enter through the side door. When Mark was sure he'd given the others enough time to get to their posts, he nodded at Deputy Branson, who opened the door as Mark rushed in with his flashlight on and his gun drawn.

Sitting at the table before them was a man surrounded by wires and cables, with a flashlight propped up to shine its light over the paraphernalia spread out before him. It took a few seconds for the man to register that he'd been caught in the act. He slowly turned around. With his gun still drawn, Mark reached over and turned on the overhead light.

The man covered his eyes with his hands to protect them from the sudden bright light. "What are you trying to do, blind me?" the man sitting at the table protested.

As Mark came around the table, still pointing his gun at the man, he realized he knew him—Max Freeman. Max was still dressed in his Palmer Computer Warehouse uniform, with his name embroidered over the pocket. He was wearing a baseball cap with a tech logo just like the one Riley had identified as what one of men at *The Grill* was wearing the night Nona's car was vandalized.

"Max," Mark said as he holstered his gun, "what in the world are you doing here?"

Max gave a defeated shrug. "Doing my job, Sheriff Weaver, a man's got to make a living somehow," he said, resigned to the fact that he'd been caught in a criminal act.

Looking over at Deputy Branson, Mark said, "Cuff him and read him his rights."

By the time the deputy had given Max the order to stand and put his hands behind his back, Aaron was at the door. He glanced around, taking in the scene before him.

"Ah, Max, what have you gotten yourself into?" Aaron said, shaking his head. He and Max had been buddies from first grade through their junior year in high school. He knew that Max was on the wrong track back then, but never thought it would lead to a time when he'd have to arrest him.

Max looked up at Aaron. "Guess I got myself caught this time, bro," Max said with regret.

Pointing to the wires and cables spread out on the table, he asked, "What is all of this stuff anyway?"

"Surveillance," Max answered, "you know, observation."

"You wanted to observe Nona Foxx?" Aaron asked, finding it hard to believe that Max was interested in Nona enough to watch her.

"No, man," Max said with a smirk, "not me. Someone else was interested in what she was doing."

Mark said to Aaron, "Okay, enough of this. Let's get him printed and booked before we continue with the questioning."

Aaron stepped aside, allowing Deputy Branson to escort Max to his patrol car.

Mark turned his attention to Aaron and the other deputy. "You two process this evidence," Marks said nodding toward the table. "Then make a thorough search of the house."

Max had been processed, and was waiting in one of the interrogation rooms when Aaron entered. Mark decided to watch the interrogation for now. He believed that Max would talk more freely with only Aaron present, given the history they shared. Aaron was holding two cups of coffee. As he handed one cup over to Max, he asked, "Who is it that hired you to watch Nona Foxx?"

Max took a sip of his coffee, then smiled. "So, you want to get right to it, then?"

"It's late and you declined having a lawyer present, so why not?" Aaron asked, without smiling.

Max leaned forward, more serious now that he could see that Aaron wasn't playing. "Can't we work out some sort of deal here, Aaron, for old times' sake?"

Aaron tipped his chair back so it rested on only the back two legs, while sipping his coffee. He looked over his cup, as he said casually, "I'm not in the 'deal' business, Max. I'm in the 'tell me what you know before I get angry' business."

When Max didn't answer, in one swift move Aaron put down his coffee cup and set all four legs of his chair on the floor. "Maybe we need to start with a simpler question." Leaning in he asked, "How about you tell me how you got in the house tonight without setting off the security system? Seems like that would take someone who's very smart to pull off."

Aaron could see by the look on Max's face that his flattery was working. He had his attention now.

"The easy part was getting a duplicate key made for the door," Max began explaining, "The hard part was getting the security code. That took me a few days."

Aaron acted impressed. "You say getting the key was 'easy,' but it seems to me that it would take some skill to do."

"Not when someone leaves their keys out on their desk all day, even when they go to lunch with a friend," Max said with a grin.

"Are you telling me that you were able to get into Mrs. Foxx's office, get the key, make a copy, and then get it back to the office without anyone noticing you?" Aaron asked.

"Not me, man, but someone else."

"Is it the same person who hired you to watch her?" Aaron probed.

Max went on, as if Aaron hadn't asked the question. "It was when she installed that security system that gave us the biggest problem, but when I saw that the device I put in her house was pointing right at the security system pad, I knew if I kept watching her enter that code time after time, I'd eventually get it," he added with pride, "and I did!"

"I have to say, I'm impressed, Max," Aaron said. "So, if you were the one who put the 'device,' which I'm assuming is the kitchen clock, in the house," he paused as if he was thinking about this, "then you're the one who broke in to begin with and destroyed her bedroom."

Max quickly looked away as he answered, "I didn't say that."

"You said that you watched her put in the code from the 'device' you put in."

Max turned to Aaron with anger and warned, "Quit putting words in my mouth."

The door suddenly opened and Mark walked in. "I've had enough of this dancing around, Max."

Mark slammed his fist down on the table near Max. "Tell us now who hired you to vandalize and terrorize Nona Foxx, and I promise you that I will help you work out a deal with the district attorney."

"Come on, Max," Aaron urged, "you were caught in the act tonight. This is your best chance."

Max was silent for a minute considering his options. Having made his decision, he looked up at Mark to confess the name of the person who'd hired him.

Chapter Twenty-Two

Max was taken away to a cell after his confession. Mark would talk to District Attorney Menard sometime in the next two days, as promised, to help Max get a deal. Mark and Aaron were beyond exhausted. They made the decision that it was too late to bring in the person Max had just declared as the instigator of all that had been done to Nona and her property.

Mark walked in the door of his house around two in the morning to find Layne sleeping on the couch. Since his accident, it had become her habit to wait up for him when he was called out late at night. This time she must have given in to her fatigue. As he looked down at her sleeping so peacefully, he was overwhelmed with the love he felt for her. He'd heard other people talk about how love faded away after years of being with the same person, but his love for Layne had only grown stronger with each passing year. He knew with every fiber of his being that it'd been her strength and deep faith that had pulled him through his coma, and back to life. He'd forever be grateful to her.

Mark decided not to wake her, but instead pulled the afghan that her mother had knitted from the back of the chair to cover her. Mark knew that he wasn't just doing this for Layne, but also for himself. Layne would have questions for him. She'd want him to tell her everything that had transpired since the minute he'd walked out of the door. He was too tired to talk and wasn't ready to share his night with her. He kissed her on her forehead and went up the stairs, where he fell into bed. Before falling asleep, he set his alarm for five-thirty. It'd be best if he were out the door before Layne woke up.

Mark was up, dressed, and in his car before six. He knew that the task before him would be a difficult one, but it was one that he had no choice but to carry out. He was the sheriff, so this duty fell on his shoulders. He headed to the *Dream Bean Coffee Shop* for coffee and a bite of breakfast, believing that it was too early in the morning for any type of unpleasant confrontation.

Mark bought a newspaper on his way in, with the intention of reading it through as he ate his breakfast alone, something he rarely took the time to do. He purposefully chose a table in the back corner, hoping he wouldn't be noticed or disturbed. He'd placed his order and had just picked up his paper when he heard a familiar, yet unexpected, voice.

"Want some company?" Bill said.

Mark put down his paper and stared at the last person he'd expected he would see this morning. He said the only thing he could say in this situation, "Sure."

Putting his paper to the side, Mark said to Bill, "What brings an old retired guy like you out this early in the morning?"

"Coffee," Bill answered flatly, "a good cup of coffee for a change. I can't seem to get that at home and knew I'd get one here."

Bill smiled up at the waitress as she filled his cup to the brim. He ordered the Sunrise Breakfast then turned his attention back to Mark.

"What are you doing here? I thought Layne got up every morning to fix you a home cooked breakfast," Bill teased, knowing that Layne rarely was up before Mark left for work.

Mark laughed, "Don't I wish."

The two made small talk about the weather and shared some local gossip as they waited for their breakfast. Mark was about to bring up the subject that had been on his mind since he'd looked up to see Bill standing at his table, when their waitress brought their orders to the table. They ate their breakfast in a comfortable silence.

Mark had put the last piece of his toast in his mouth and picked up his cup. As he sipped his coffee, he studied the man across from him who had been his friend since they were boys together. They'd made it through many tough times together, and Mark didn't like the idea that he was handing him another one that was going to change his life from this moment forward.

Gathering his courage, Mark put down his coffee cup, and looked over at his friend. "Bill, I've got something to tell you," he began with a serious tone, "and I'd appreciate it if you'd let me finish before you say anything."

Bill stopped eating to give his full attention to Mark. It seemed to Bill, at that moment, they were the only two people in the room. "Sounds serious. What is it, Mark?"

"You know all the trouble that Nona's had these past few weeks with someone breaking into the house and destroying her bedroom and almost everything in it."

Bill nodded his head.

Mark continued, "What you might not know is that she got an email that basically threatened her safety and even her life. Then right after that, someone spray painted the message 'Got your attention now' in silver paint on that beautiful black car of hers while she and her dad and Riley were eating supper at *The Grill*, right down town." Mark shook his head, still finding all this hard to believe.

"I felt that the threats and vandalism warranted extra patrolling of Nona's house and last night, we got lucky. We caught a man inside Nona's house working to set up a surveillance system in order to watch her!"

Bill had tried not to interrupt Mark, but when he heard that they had caught someone, he couldn't keep quiet any longer. "That's great news, Mark. Was he responsible for all of it? Did he confess?"

"Yes, he confessed that he was responsible for carrying out the vandalism and the threats, but Bill," Mark said, leaning in closer to Bill so that what he was about to tell Bill couldn't be overheard by those around them, "this is the part that's going to be hard for you to hear."

Bill looked at Mark skeptically. "How can catching the guy who was doing all of those terrible things to Nona be hard on me?"

"Because, as part of his confession, he gave us the name of the person who hired him to do all of those 'terrible' things to Nona." Mark paused looking directly at Bill, "Bill, it was Amy."

Bill was caught by surprise. "My Amy?" he asked incredulously.

"Your Amy,' Mark confirmed.

Leaning over the table, Bill put his head in his hands and shook his head back and forth. "It just can't be Amy. It can't be."

"Bill, according to his confession, Amy wanted that house, and it seems that she was willing to do whatever it would take to get Nona to leave her house, even if it meant..." Mark didn't finish that thought, but Max had admitted he feared that Amy might ask him to end Nona's life.

Bill looked up in desperation at Mark. "You don't believe him, do you, Mark? You have to know that there's no way that Amy would do these things to Nona."

"I am sorry, Bill, but I do believe him. Everything he told us has checked out," Mark said in earnest, as he watched Bill's world fall apart. "After breakfast, my plan is to go to your place to arrest Amy."

"Can I get y'all anything else?" the waitress asked, interrupting their conversation. She cleared away their dirty dishes and poured each of them another cup of coffee, giving Bill the time he needed to come to a decision.

"Mark, let me tell Amy about her being named in a confession. I need to see her reaction. Would you let me do this for old times' sake?" Bill begged.

Mark thought about what Bill was asking. He knew his friend wouldn't do anything that would be against the law, like help her get away before Mark could arrest her.

"Okay, Bill, I'll let you tell her, but you need to do it this morning," Mark said.

"I have one more favor to ask of you, Mark. Would you let her turn herself in rather than going to the house to arrest her?"

Mark knew his answer to this question right away. "Of course."

Nona was up and out of the house before daybreak. She wanted to be out of the house before Riley came out of his bedroom. She was sure she couldn't handle his negative attitude this morning. As she turned the key starting her father's big car she made a mental note to call the Sheriff's Department to see when her car would be released. She'd already called Sampson's Body Repair to let them know she'd need a paint job as soon as she got her car back. Chuck Sampson had been one of her first clients. She was confident that Chuck would do an excellent job restoring her car.

Nona picked up two bacon, egg, and cheese biscuits from a fast food drive through. She knew that, like her, Monty was a person who liked to get to his office early. She pulled into the almost empty parking lot outside of Monty's office at ten minutes after six. There was one car already parked. She recognized it as Monty's tiny sports car. As she walked by it, she shook her head, amazed that someone who was well over six feet tall could fit comfortably in such a car, and wondered why they would want to.

She found the door to his office was locked. At first, she knocked gently, but when no one came, she pounded with her fist. She stood back tapping her toe as she waited impatiently. After a few minutes, the door opened and Monty stepped out. "Well, someone really wants to come in," he said teasingly.

"I thought I was going to have to huff and puff to get the door opened," Nona said grinning up at him. "Let me in," she said holding up the fast food bag, "I come bearing breakfast,"

Monty bowed deeply letting her pass by him. "Then you are most welcome to enter, my lady."

Nona laughed. "I'm hoping you have coffee to go along with these biscuits."

Monty closed the door behind them and went around Nona to lead her down the hall to a small room filled with the aroma of coffee. She set the bag on the table in the corner and took out the two wrapped biscuits. Monty handed her a Styrofoam cup of coffee as she handed him a biscuit.

As they sat there making small talk as they enjoyed their breakfast, Nona realized that somewhere along the way, something happened that she'd never dreamed would happen. She'd begun to like Monty. As she glanced up at him, half-way listening to a story he was telling about his daughter, she couldn't deny that he was one strikingly good-looking man, with his thick gray hair and deep green eyes, and he dressed well. What she'd first perceived as arrogance in him, she was now finding charming.

When she looked down at what she was wearing, it occurred to her that she'd chosen her outfit specifically for Monty. A disconcerting thought entered her mind at that moment. Could she possibly be falling for Monty? She almost choked on her biscuit.

She swallowed hard, took a sip of coffee, and cleared her throat to speak. "Monty, we need to get down to the business of my divorce. I've got a long day ahead."

"Me, too," Monty agreed, as he jumped up from the table pitching his trash into the waste basket like the star basketball player he'd once been. He started out the door, then turned to Nona, seeming surprised to see her still sitting there. "Well, are you coming?" he asked.

Nona hurriedly gathered her things and followed him as he walked to his private office. The mess didn't even faze her this time. She simply stepped around it, recalling the pathway to her seat.

Monty folded his hands together as he leaned forward and asked with sincere concern, "Nona, are you one hundred percent sure that you want to do this thing of surrendering your house to the other woman?"

Without a moment's hesitation, Nona answered with confidence, "One hundred and ten percent sure."

He leaned back and slapped his hands on the desk. "Okay, let's do this."

For the next hour and a half, they thoroughly examined Bill's finances and holdings that had been handed over in discovery. Then they went through Nona's finances and holdings. Nona was amazed at how much the two of them had amassed in over forty years of marriage. After much persuasion, Monty finally convinced Nona not to just hand over her house to Bill and Amy, but to have them buy her half of the house. Nona didn't want anything financial from Bill such as alimony. They would ask that the stocks and bonds that they jointly owned be sold and divided between them. The stocks and bonds that they individually owned would remain with the owner.

"That all works for me," Nona said, relieved that they were coming to the end of this meeting. She was ready to put this behind her and move on with her life. "Now, you can send this over to Mandy so she and Bill can look it over. Then, hopefully, they'll agree and all can move forward with the divorce."

"I wish you would reconsider taking financial compensation from Bill, Nona," Monty urged.

"I know you do, Monty, but this is what I want."

"Then, it's what I want for you," Monty said giving her a smile. "I'll start the ball rolling today."

Nona stood up and held out her hand to Monty. "I appreciate all of your help and understanding, Monty," she said honestly.

Monty took her hand in his. "In all honesty, it has been my great pleasure, Nona."

They stood for a moment still holding hands smiling at one another. Monty started to say something, but a knock on the door stopped him.

His secretary opened the door. "Mr. Redmond is here for his appointment, Mr. Montgomery."

Monty squeezed Nona's hand as he released it. "Thanks, Betty," he said as he sat back down at his desk, "you can send him in. Ms. Foxx was just leaving."

"I'll see you out, Ms. Foxx," Betty said, holding the door open for Nona.

Nona turned around on unsteady legs and followed Betty out of Monty's office.

Nona went straight to the hospital after her meeting with Monty. She was anxious to see how her father was doing this morning. As soon as she walked in his room, she could tell it was the father she knew, sitting up and giving orders to those around him.

When Mr. James saw Nona standing at his door, he said, "Nona, tell these good-hearted nightingales to quit fussing over me, and hand over my clothes so I can exit these premises."

Nona was relieved to hear her father's complaining. She went over to him and kissed his cheek. "Daddy, you can't go home until the doctor releases you," she said, as she straightened up his pillow. "Anyway, your clothes aren't here. I took them home last night, so you'll have to wait for Riley to bring some to you."

"Good grief!" Mr. James shouted in frustration.

"That's just the way it is, Daddy, so you might as well accept it."

Nona was curious as to what her father remembered from last night. However, she knew she needed to be careful with the way she brought up the events of last night so as to not agitate him if he didn't remember anything.

"How's your knee feeling this morning?" Nona asked casually, as she refilled his water glass.

"It hurts like the dickens," Mr. James answered, as he reached down to rub his knee.

With concern, Nona said, "Let me take a look."

Mr. James pulled back the sheet to expose his knee, which had turned nasty shades of purple and black.

Nona sucked in air through her teeth as she gingerly touched it. "It's good that the x-ray they took last night didn't show any bones broken," Nona said, as she examined her father's knee. "You're lucky you didn't do any permanent damage to it when you fell."

Mr. James gave his daughter an uncertain look as he asked, "When I fell?"

Nona kept her tone even as she answered, "You know, when you took your walk last night."

It was obvious by the look on his face, that he had no recollection of taking a walk or anything that happened on that walk. It was also apparent he was finding this lapse in his memory upsetting.

Nona took his hand, and keeping her voice as soothing as she could, she began to fill in the missing parts of his memory for him.

"Daddy, you had an incident last night that we can totally blame on your Alzheimer's."

She noticed his body tense, but she continued with her explanation, "You went for a walk by yourself yesterday afternoon and lost your way. You must have fallen somewhere along your way to the courthouse. That's what caused the bruising on your knee, along with various scratches and bumps."

Nona promised herself she wouldn't cry, but it was taking all her strength and determination to not break that promise. The look of bewilderment on her father's face broke her heart. She waited for any questions he might have. When he didn't say anything, she took a deep breath and continued, "We're going to have to make some changes around the house so that something like this doesn't happen again."

Her father looked up at her questioningly.

"Daddy, I know this has upset you, but I need for you to remember what we talked about yesterday." Lovingly patting his hand, she reminded him. "We talked about the choices we have in life when we're faced with the unexpected—refuse or accept."

Mr. James nodded his head as he remembered their conversation. "If you accept the unexpected, then you can handle it on your terms," he said, holding tightly to Nona's hand.

"That's right," she said smiling down at him, "and we're going to accept Alzheimer's, but on our terms."

He smiled back at her as he recalled what he'd told her was most important. "We need to remember that our hope and strength comes from God when we face life's challenges. We need God by our side."

"We're going to hold onto the knowledge that with God on our side, we can get through anything," Nona said to her father, who'd always been there for her helping her through life's battles, hoping that now she could help him with this life battle.

"We're not going to allow Alzheimer's to make us feel hopeless, Daddy." With her voice filled with emotion, she added, "We're going to put our trust in God. He will see us through this."

"She's right, Dad."

Nona and Mr. James turned to see Riley standing just inside his father's hospital room. He'd entered so quietly neither one had heard him come in. Riley had been there to hear most of their conversation.

He went to his father's bedside, leaning close, he said, "I need to hold on to the hope that you will forgive me, Dad. I should have gone for a walk with you when you asked."

Mr. James reached out to embrace his son, something he'd rarely done in his lifetime. They remained like that for several minutes before he spoke with feeling, "There's nothing to forgive, Riley, nothing at all."

Watching the scene before her, Nona broke her promise. She allowed her tears to roll down her cheeks.

Chapter Twenty-Three

Amy began to dance around her bedroom after being awakened by a call from Mandy, Bill's divorce attorney. Mandy had given her the most unbelievable news, and Amy couldn't wait to share it with Bill. When Mandy had first told her that Nona wasn't going to fight for the house, she thought it was some kind of sick joke, or an evil trick that Nona was playing on her, but Mandy had convinced her that it was all true.

Amy had dreamed of living in Nona's house even before she'd met Bill. It was one of those old Southern homes that radiated character and charm. She just knew from the start that she could be a special person living in a house like that. When Nona had dug her heels in and refused to leave, Amy realized she'd have to take some drastic measures in order to blast her out. She'd met Max Freeman at the gym where she worked. It was obvious that Max liked her, but she was already involved with Bill. Needless to say, that hadn't stopped her from using his attraction to her to get him to do a few favors for her. When she'd added a monetary incentive, Max had agreed to do what he could to get Nona out of that house. She was beyond thrilled that their plan had worked. She wondered how quickly Nona would get out, so that she and Bill could move in.

Amy was getting out of the shower when she heard the garage door open and close. That meant that Bill was home. She excitedly pulled on her clothes and put her long blond hair into a pony tail. She hurried out of the bedroom, excited to share her good news about the house with him. When Bill turned to look at her as she rounded the corner of their living room, she could see that he was terribly upset about something. His face was a mixture of anger and disappointment.

Amy went to embrace him, but he turned away from her. "What is it, Bill? What's happened?" she asked with concern.

Bill held his arms down by his side, restraining them from grabbing Amy to shake some sense into her. "Sit down, Amy," Bill said, trying to stay calm.

Amy gave Bill a worried look as she took a seat on their love seat. She looked up at him apprehensively, and waited for him to tell her what had upset him. She thought about telling him her good news first, but from the serious tone in his voice, decided her news could wait.

Bill began to pace back and forth in front of her, running his hand through his hair, hoping the right words would come to him.

"Amy, I just had breakfast with Sheriff Weaver," Bill said still pacing, "and he gave me some disturbing news that I need for you to either confirm or deny."

"Okay," Amy said apprehensively.

Bill stopped his pacing to stand directly in front of Amy so he could look her in the eye. "Did you hire someone to scare Nona out of her house?"

Bill saw the truth flicker in Amy's eyes for one brief second, but soon the truth was clouded over with the creation of lies.

Amy started to speak, but Bill held up his hand stopping her. "Amy, what you say to me next will determine our future," Bill warned, "so think carefully before you speak."

Amy lowered her head. When she finally looked up at him, he could see anguish on her face and sorrow in her eyes. Her voice was so soft that Bill had to lean closer in order to hear her. "I just wanted that house so badly, Bill. I deserved that house. I was certain that when Nona understood just how vulnerable she was after Max broke-in and destroyed her bedroom, she'd move out. But, when she didn't, we decided that threatening her would scare her off for sure. Then, that didn't work, and we had to keep coming up with more things to frighten her so she'd get out!" Amy was almost shouting when she finished.

As Amy told her story, Bill listened carefully. He heard her voice filled with anger and confusion, but not once did he hear remorse. It would seem that Amy didn't feel any guilt for the things that she and Max had done to Nona. She only regretted that all they had done hadn't worked to make Nona leave.

Looking up at Bill through her tears, she begged of Bill, "Why didn't she just give up and move out then? Why'd she wait until now?"

"Now?" Bill asked.

With a hint of a smile, Amy wiped away her tears. Amy shared with Bill the news she'd wanted to give him the moment he walked in the door. "Mandy called this morning to tell us that Nona isn't going to fight for the house any longer. It's ours, Bill!"

Bill shook his head. "Oh, Amy, you don't even understand what you've done to yourself—to us," he said sympathetically. "You're never going to live in that house after what you've done to Nona."

Bill could tell by the look on Amy's face that she didn't understand what he was trying to tell her. "Amy, Max Freeman was caught last night in Nona's house, and he confessed to everything he'd done," Bill explained reaching out to Amy, "and he named you as the instigator who'd paid him to do it."

Amy fell into Bill's arms, sobbing. Even after all that Amy had done, Bill's heart broke for this woman he'd once believed he loved and would spend the rest of his life with. He continued to hold her until her crying subsided.

Bill knew that what he needed to say to Amy was going to be hard for her to hear, but the time had come for her to face the consequences of her actions. Still holding Amy, Bill broke the silence. "Amy, I know that this next part is going to be hard for you, but you need to face reality."

Amy pulled back from his embrace and looked apprehensively at Bill, waiting for him to continue.

"What you did to Nona was against the law," Bill said sympathetically, "and there are consequences that you now have to pay. Mark said that he will allow you to turn yourself in, rather than him coming out here to arrest you. It will look better to the judge if you surrender, Amy."

"What do you mean, Bill! Are you telling me that Mark wants to arrest me?" Amy's words along with the shock on her face were almost more than Bill could handle. Had Amy in fact believed there wouldn't be a penalty to pay for what she'd done to Nona?

Bill stepped back looking at Amy in disbelief. "What did you think was going to happen, Amy? Did you think that Mark would just let you walk away from what you did? You broke the law, and he's sworn to uphold the law."

Amy sat down, putting her head in her hands. She remained like that for several minutes as the reality of the situation hit her. Finally, she looked up at Bill with pleading eyes. "Will you go with me?"

"Of course, I will," Bill answered tenderly.

Mr. James was released from the hospital later that afternoon, after Dr. Davis had completed a thorough exam. He reiterated that they were lucky that their father had sustained only minor injuries. Nona and Riley understood the incident with their father's disappearance could have been worse. He urged them to secure full time care for their father— either at his home, or by placing him in a facility that specialized in the care of those suffering from Alzheimer's.

The first thing Mr. James did after getting back home was go to his office. Nona was sure he was tired of being watched and probed. He wanted to be alone in his own space. When her father closed the door to his office, it was his signal that he didn't want to be disturbed, and would probably be in there for the remainder of the afternoon.

After changing into jeans and a t-shirt, Nona went in search of Riley. They had some unsettled issues that needed to be discussed. She found him sitting on the floor in the front living room, surrounded by old photo albums that had been stored on the book shelves on each side of the fireplace. Their father had been the family photographer, but it was their mother who had developed the film, then lovingly placed each photo in an album organized by date.

When Nona walked into the room, Riley smiled up at her. "Have you looked at these lately? They're a hoot," Riley said, as he moved an album over, making room for Nona to sit next to him.

Nona sat down next to Riley and picked up an album labeled "1963." She opened it to the first page and laughed as she quickly covered up a picture. "No way am I going to let you look at this one," Nona said giggling.

Riley reached over and pried her hand away from the picture. "Oh, my goodness! I remember you looking just like that. In fact, I think I'll take this one out and have it framed," he said teasing her.

Nona shook her head as they both looked over the picture. "What made me ever think I looked good with a perm? My mouth full of metal just sets it all off, don't you think?"

"No doubt," Riley said, as he lovingly pulled on his sister's straight, short hair.

They sat on the floor for hours, talking as they passed the albums back and forth while precious memories came flooding back to them from their childhood. Finally, Nona closed the album she had just looked through and turned to Riley.

"Some great family times we all had together, wouldn't you say, big brother," Nona asked, with a serious tone.

"They sure were, little sister," Riley agreed, as he continued to turn the pages of an album.

Putting her hand on his album, Nona said, "Great family times don't have to be over, Riley."

Riley closed the album and looked over at his sister. "I know, Nona."

Nona brought up the topic that they'd been avoiding. "There are still memories we can make, Riley, if you stay here in Kerry with Dad and me for the remainder of time Dad has left," she said, believing that if they stayed together as a family they could get through anything.

Riley lowered his head, looking away from Nona's hopeful face. "I know what you're hoping I'll say, Nona." He raised his head, allowing his eyes to meet hers. "Remember when Mom was so sick and weak with cancer, and everyone was sure she was near the end? Well, Dad called me, begging me to come home to be with her. Nona, I got on a plane ready to fly home to be with Mom, but I just couldn't go through with it. I got off that plane and didn't come home, because I didn't want to see my mother sick like that. I wanted to remember her as she'd been, not as she was then."

Tears were streaming down Riley's face. He went on without wiping them away. "I can't stay here and watch the father I have always known fade away. I don't have the kind of strength that you've always had, Nona. I know you like to think of me as a strong person, but I've never been that strong person you and Dad needed me to be, but I've learned to accept who I am. Can you?"

"Oh, Riley," Nona said, as she reached out for him, "I hoped that this time you would choose to be strong for me and for Dad."

"I wish I could, Nona," Riley said, with his voice filled with regret, "but it's just not in me. Please try to understand."

Nona sat on the floor of the front living room across from the brother she loved, surrounded by the memories of a past life they'd shared, and wept for her brother, her father, and herself.

A few minutes before noon, Amelina May Patten walked into the Kerry County Sheriff's Department along with Bill and their lawyer, Mandy Jackson, to turn herself in. Mark was relieved. He hadn't been sure Bill would be able to convince Amy to surrender, but had hoped that he could avoid having to arrest Amy at her home.

Once Amy had been booked, Mark made two important phone calls.

Nona answered on the second ring. "Hey, Mark, hope you got some sleep last night, after all you did to find Dad," Nona said.

"Turns out that finding your Dad wasn't the end of my night time adventure," Mark said.

"Something else happened after you found Dad?"

Mark thought about all that had happened since he'd left her father at the courthouse, but decided that for now, he only needed to give her the information she'd be most interested in. "Do you remember Max Freeman?"

"Sure," Nona said, confused as to why Mark had called her about one of her former clients, "I represented him a couple of times for minor things. Why?"

"Max was the one who broke in, destroyed your bedroom, sent the emails, put the clock up, and painted your car," Mark said.

"Max, not Amy?" Nona asked.

"Max was the one who did it all, but it was Amy who hired him," Mark clarified. "Max made a full confession after we caught him in your house last night,"

There was silence at the other end of the call as it took Nona a minute to process it all.

Mark continued, "Amy just turned herself in a little while ago. Nona, it's over. We got them!"

"Oh, Mark, that's unbelievable!" Nona said excitedly. "I can't believe it's over."

"Well, it is, Nona. You can rest easy now, because we have both in custody."

"Thank you, Mark, for all of your hard work and diligence in solving this case." Nona said sincerely. "I don't know how I'll ever repay you."

Mark laughed, "You don't have to, Nona. That's the job."

He ended the call with a big smile on his face. It was time to make his second most important call. The call went to voicemail. He left a message. "Layne, call Nona. She's got some good news to tell you."

Chapter Twenty-Four

Since Riley had fixed supper, Nona volunteered to clean up. She was putting the last of the dirty dishes from supper in the dishwasher when she heard the front door bell ring. She couldn't imagine who would be stopping by this late in the evening without calling first. She knew that both Riley and her father were in the front of the house, surely one of them would answer the bell.

She turned back to the dirty dishes and was deep in thought when she felt a tap on her shoulder. She jumped at the touch. Expecting it to be her brother, she whipped around ready to give Riley a piece of her mind for scaring her half to death. But it wasn't Riley behind her, and she was even more frightened at seeing who it was.

"Bill!" she said in surprise.

"Sorry, I didn't mean to scare you," Bill quickly apologized, "I told Riley I needed to talk to you alone, so he told me where you were. I called your name first to get your attention, but when you didn't turn around I just thought..." His voice trailed off.

"Well, you thought wrong," Nona said angrily, as she snatched the dish towel from the counter to dry her wet hands. "Why are you here, Bill?"

"I have something that I need to tell you, Nona," Bill said. "Can we sit down and talk for a minute, please?"

"If it's about Amy being the one behind the vandalism and all, I already know about it," Nona said coldly, "Mark told me."

Bill tried again. "Please, sit down with me."

All that Nona wanted from Bill at that moment was for him to leave her alone. She didn't want to hear any of his excuses for Amy's actions. She was done with the both of them, and wanted to put the whole thing behind her so she could get on with her life. She was about to tell Bill all of this, in no uncertain terms, but when she looked in his eyes she saw something she hadn't seen in a very long time—compassion. She decided it wouldn't hurt to take a few minutes to listen to what he had to say, this one last time.

"Okay, Bill," Nona said cautiously, "I'll listen to you this one time. Let's go out back." She opened the back door and led the way out to the chairs that had been set up where her mother's rose garden had once been.

With the setting sun, the evening was cooling down from the sultry temperatures of the afternoon. Nona stood for a moment, breathing in the sweet fragrance of the Confederate Jasmine that grew along the side of the gardening shed. She took her seat and looked over at Bill as he sat in the chair next to hers. She smiled to herself, remembering the many times they had sat just like this enjoying a warm Southern evening together. Her smile left her as she remembered that they were not together now.

"What is it that you need to tell me, Bill?" Nona asked, emphasizing the word "need" while bracing herself for the barrage of excuses he would throw at her in Amy's defense.

Bill remained silent for a few minutes. Nona waited. When he finally did speak, Nona could hear a deep sorrow in his voice that she'd never heard in all their years of marriage.

"I need to tell you how sorry I am that I didn't turn out to be the man you needed me to be, Nona. I'm sorry I betrayed your trust and our love."

To say that Nona was shocked by Bill's declaration would be an understatement. These were the words that another man might say to his soon-to-be-ex-wife, not words that an arrogant, self-centered man who wanted others to believe he never made mistakes would ever say. Nona was—as Layne would say—flabbergasted.

Bill waited for Nona's response, but hearing none, he continued, "I have no right to ask you for your forgiveness, but I hope you will. That's what I'm clinging to now, Nona. Hope that you can forgive. Hope that you will trust me. Hope that we can be friends."

Bill paused as he took a deep breath, "Most of all, Nona, I hope that you can love me again."

Bill sat for a minute, hoping Nona would say something. When she didn't, he stood up and walked out of the back yard, down the driveway, got in his car, and drove away.

Nona sat there in the back yard for a very long time, thinking about all Bill had said and wondering if she had heard everything correctly. She wished she could do an instant replay to confirm what she thought he said.

I hope that you can love me again.

Nona wondered how he could, after all he'd put her through, even hope for such a thing, and why was it that those words made her heart beat a little faster?

Chapter Twenty-Five

After Riley made it clear he would be returning to San Jose, Nona made the decision to move in with her father. With all that had happened with her own home, she wasn't interested in staying there any longer. Bill had no interest in living there, after all that had happened with Amy. They made the decision to sell it and split the profit.

When Nona approached her father about moving in with him, he hadn't been too keen on the idea. He didn't want someone living there to "watch" him. However, when Nona explained to him the reasons for her reluctance to return to her own house, and he would be helping her out, he was more than happy to help by offering his home to her. Nona was still in the process of moving out of her house and settling into her childhood home. She hadn't decided if she was going to store her furniture, especially the antiques, or sell everything. She'd called Grace several times to see if she wanted anything from the house, but each time it went to voicemail. Grace still wouldn't take her calls. Nona wasn't sure what was going on with her daughter, but decided to leave her alone for now.

Nona had dreaded this day. Riley was leaving Kerry to return to his life in San Jose, California. She'd tried to prepare herself, but was finding it hard to watch him leave.

"I don't know what I'll do without you here with me, Riley," Nona said, as she hugged her brother.

Riley hugged her back, knowing she didn't really need him there to help her. She could handle everything by herself. "You know I wouldn't be much help to you if I stayed, Nona. I'd just be in the way."

Still holding onto his embrace, Nona said, "You would never be in my way, Riley."

She pulled away to look him full in the face. "I wish you would reconsider," Nona begged him once more.

"Nona, don't make this any harder than it is," Riley said, breaking away. He kissed the top of her head as he turned to get into his rental car. "I'll be back before you know it."

Riley had made it clear he couldn't stay, but he promised he would come back to stay for a few days at a time. Nona would just have to be satisfied that he made the commitment to come back every few months. She clung to her father's advice about accepting life changes, and with God's help she was finding acceptance in her heart for Riley's decision.

She waved as Riley drove down the driveway and turned left toward the highway that would take him to the airport. She was proud of herself that she hadn't cried. She turned to walk back in the house. It was a beautiful morning, maybe she and her father could take a walk before the Georgia temperatures began to rise. As she went in the back door, she heard the front door bell ring. She wondered who it could be. She hadn't seen anyone pull up in front of the house.

Her father was closing the front door as she walked into the living room. "Who was at the door, Daddy?" she asked casually.

When her father turned toward her, she could see he was holding an exquisitely cut crystal vase that held one tiny red rose bud. Curious, Nona took the vase from him. "It was Abe Johnson's boy, who works for that new florist in town."

Looking curiously at the single rose bud as she took the vase from him, he added, "And I don't think it is for me."

"I can't imagine who would be sending me a single red rose bud in such an elegant vase," Nona said puzzled.

Her father pulled off the card that was tied to the vase with a red ribbon. "Maybe this card will give you some direction on that," her father said, as he handed her the card.

Nona put the vase down on the end table and pulled the card from its envelope. She read it silently.

Here's hoping! Love, B

Nona's knees buckled. She quickly sat down on the chair behind her. That "B" was how Bill had always signed the notes and cards he'd given her over the years.

"Who's it from?" her father asked.

"Bill." she answered, still finding it hard to believe that Bill had sent her flowers.

"Hmm," her father asked, "what's he hoping for?"

Nona hadn't read the card out loud, so why was her father mentioning hope? Confused, she looked up at her father. "What makes you think he's 'hoping' for something, Daddy?"

Mr. James looked at her amused. "Because, my darling daughter, a red rose bud symbolizes hope."

Chapter Twenty-Six

Nona could hear the sound of her footsteps echoing through the empty house. She was making one last sweep through each room to make sure that the movers hadn't left anything behind. It appeared they'd gotten it all. She was having her furniture stored for now, since there was no room in her father's house for her things. She had moved her bedroom suite into her father's house. Even though it was the house in which she had lived as a child, it hadn't been her home for many years. She needed something familiar to make it feel like it was her home once again.

She stepped out onto the back deck. She was glad she'd made the decision to leave the swing. This swing belonged on this deck, looking out on this view. She sat down on the swing and began to swing back and forth. She was going to miss this deck, this swing, and this view. She wondered how many hours she'd spent just like this, swinging and watching the wonders that surrounded her house. She'd enjoyed watching the birds most of all. Even though she'd filled the bird feeder just yesterday afternoon, she noticed that it was almost empty. She'd remind the Petersons, the new occupants, that they needed to keep it filled for the birds who'd become depended on it.

Layne had asked Nona if she was sad to leave this house that had been her home for almost thirty-seven years. She wasn't quite sure how to answer her. She had loved this house from the first time Bill showed it to her, even though it was close to falling in around them. Nona had realized right away that what this house needed was some tender loving care, and that's what she'd given to it. She was proud of the time and effort she'd put into restoring this old house to its former glory. Yet, after the events of the past few months she'd come to realize that it was time to leave this house behind for a new family to love and cherish. It wasn't the house that Nona was sad to leave. She was sad to leave behind the life she'd once lived there, but she was also looking forward to the life that was ahead of her.

Nona couldn't have imagined her life would take such twists and turns in only a few short months. One of the biggest twists was that she was going to be taking care of her father for as long as she could. She knew it wasn't going to be easy, but there was no way she was going to walk away from this challenge. It was another life lesson in acceptance and grace for both her father and her. Together, they could make it, with God's help.

Nona smiled, thinking of the way things had turned around in these past months. When Bill left her for Amy, she'd made peace with the fact that she'd be alone for the rest of her life. However, it seemed that may not have been God's plan. If Bill hadn't filed for divorce, Michael Montgomery, Monty, might never have come into her life. Nona smiled, thinking of how she could hardly tolerate Monty's arrogant behavior when she'd first met him, and now, she was wondering if she might be falling in love with the man.

The biggest turn in her life was Bill. She never in a million years would have imagined that Bill would want to come back to her, or that she would ever consider taking him back. Yet, that's what appeared to be happening. Bill seemed determined to make amends for the awful things he and Amy had done to her. He sent her a single red rose bud weekly, with a message about hope with each one. Nona still wasn't ready to put the past behind her, but who knew what the future might hold.

Nona got up from the swing and looked around her backyard one last time. She would be late for her *Skinny Dippers'* meeting if she didn't hurry. She walked back into the house, closing the door behind her. She picked up her purse from the kitchen counter as she took one final look at the house that she had once been certain would be her forever home. She turned away and walked out of the door for the last time.

Nona rushed up the back stairs of *The Dream Bean Coffee Shop* hoping she hadn't missed the weigh-in portion of *The Skinny Dippers* meeting. She was pretty sure that she had lost at least two pounds since her last weight check. When she flung back the door to the meeting room, she saw that everyone was seated and Francine, the new leader of their group, was giving one of her motivational you-can-do-it talks. Nona caught the door just as it was ready to slam against the wall. As silently as she could, she tiptoed over to the chair beside Layne that she always managed to save for Nona every time she was running late.

"Sorry, I got held up at the house," Nona whispered to Layne.

"You haven't missed much," Layne assured her, rolling her eyes indicating that the speech Francine was giving was far from motivational.

Dixie leaned forward to whisper in Nona's ear. "Watching paint dry might be more motivational than listening to Francine."

"Come on, y'all," Betty Jo scolded, "give her a chance."

They heard a loud "Shh," as one lady from the front row turned around to give them a dirty look.

It all began with Layne's soft chuckle. When Nona looked over at Layne and their eyes met, she couldn't help but join her. The chuckle leapt back until Dixie and Betty Jo were caught up in it. What had begun with Layne's soft chuckle spread throughout the group until the room was filled with laughter. Nona swore she even heard Sharon, the proper prude in the group, snort. It was several minutes before Francine gave up on her talk and ended the meeting.

When Layne regained control of herself, she went to Francine to apologize for what she'd started. Francine graciously accepted her apology and assigned her the job of motivational speaker for their next meeting. When Nona, Dixie, and Betty Jo heard this, the laughter started all over again and didn't stop until they were seated in their usual spots at their usual table.

"That may have been one the best meetings this year," Betty Jo said, with a grin on her face. "I think I might have lost a pound or two just from laughing so hard."

"I agree with Betty Jo," Dixie said, wiping a laughter tear from her face.

Layne looked across the table to Nona. "You said you got held up at the house? I thought you were all moved out."

"I just wanted to check to make sure the movers had gotten everything out before I turned over the keys," Nona explained. "What held me up, though, was when I decided to sit down on the swing on the back deck."

Layne nodded her head with understanding. "You got caught up in some memories, didn't you?"

Nona looked at Layne as she answered. "I did." With a sigh she added, "And thinking about the future, or rather the uncertainty of it."

"How is your father?" Dixie asked as she turned toward Nona.

"He's truly doing well," Nona smiled over at Dixie. "The medicine and the exercise are doing their job. He still gets confused and a little uncertain of where he is sometimes, but we're working through those tough times. I have even convinced him to join the Kerry Senior Citizens Association, the KSCA."

"I don't think I've ever heard of that group. What is it they do?" Betty Jo asked.

"It's a group that gets together twice a month to discuss issues concerning the elderly. They do some mentoring and social projects, but mostly it's a way for Dad to interact and socialize with his peers," Nona said.

Nona smiled as she thought about her Dad's reaction when she'd suggested he join the group. "At first Dad called them a bunch of 'old geezers,' but I think he's beginning to realize that he might just be an 'old geezer' himself."

"I'm so glad it's all working out, Nona," Betty Jo said sincerely. "Don and I have worried about you and all you've gone through these past few months."

"Thanks, Betty Jo, I appreciate that."

"Here we are, ladies." They all looked up as Alice, their waitress, placed their orders down on the table.

After Alice had finished serving, and had refreshed their cups of coffee and tea, Nona, Betty Jo, and Layne looked to Dixie to bless the food as they bowed their heads.

"Thank you, Lord, for the blessings that you have given us and continue to shower upon us. Bless this food to the nourishment of our bodies, and our bodies to Thy service. Amen."

The table was quiet for minutes as they each enjoyed their food. Dixie finally broke the silence. "I heard that Amy's leaving town."

Nona looked up from her muffin. This was new information to her. "Left town? I thought she was on probation for the next five years. How can she leave?"

Amy had confessed to her part in hiring Max to vandalize and threaten Nona. She'd verified the confession Max had made to District Attorney Menard. Mandy, Amy's attorney had worked out a plea bargain with the DA which Judge Hammond signed off on. Amy was sentenced to pay a hefty fine, serve five years' probation, and complete 100 hours of community service, but no jail time. Amy had spent only seven days in jail before finally being bailed out by her brother, who'd been out of the country when she'd turned herself in. Nona had been surprised that Bill hadn't put up her bail, but a little part of her was glad he hadn't.

"I don't know," Dixie said, "that's just what I heard."

Nona looked over at Layne who hadn't looked up when Dixie made the announcement. "You know something about this, don't you?"

Layne raised her head to focus on her friends. "I don't know if I'm supposed to talk about it or not, but Mark never said specifically not to say anything about it," Layne said cautiously.

"Come on, Layne, tell us," Betty Jo said, as she leaned in closer.

Layne took a long sip of coffee before beginning her story. "As you know, Amy was fined quite a bit of money that she has to pay the Court. She can't find a job anywhere in Kerry, no one will hire her after all she's done. However, she did find a job working in a gym over in Boatwright, Georgia. I think she has an aunt who lives there. Anyway, the judge has given her permission to leave Kerry to serve her sentence out in Boatwright. Mark's understanding is that she left last Saturday."

Nona looked at Layne with disbelief. "You're telling me that she's gone, Layne, for sure?"

"That's what I'm telling you, Nona," Layne smiled at her friend.

Nona sat back as the realization that Amy had moved away from Kerry hit her. It was such a relief to know she wouldn't cross paths with Amy when she went to the grocery store or anywhere in Kerry. Amy was out of her life—and Bill's.

Nona wanted to shout out for joy, but instead said with a broad smile on her face, "God is good!"

"Yes, He is indeed!"

About the Author

Carol Cannon's dream of becoming an author began when she was in fifth grade with the encouragement of her teacher and father. When she retired after thirty years of teaching, she decided it was time to pursue that dream. She released her first book in the Kerry Series, *Forgiveness. Peace* and *Joy* will follow *Hope* to complete the series..

Carol grew up on a farm near the small town of New Market, Indiana with two sisters and three brothers. She left the farm to attend Manchester College where she met and fell in love with her husband, David. They married and had three wonderful children who have blessed them seven precious grandchildren.

Carol has loved living in the Hawkinsville, Georgia, area for the past forty years with her husband in the log-home that, along with their children, built from the ground up. She thanks God every day for her many blessings of family and friends.

www.ingramcontent.com/pod-product-compliance
Lightning Source LLC
Chambersburg PA
CBHW061229210726
48293CB00003B/714